P9-DTU-589

"I always had a weakness for a woman with a guilty conscience."

"Oh!" Tess spun around. Her horse spooked and stepped sideways.

In the shadows below the cliff Adam slouched in the saddle of his black mare. His smile gleamed like the Cheshire cat's. "What brings you over my way?"

"I'm just out for my afternoon ride," she said casually, leaning down to pat his bloodhound. "And what are *you* doing up here? Lose a cow?"

"I'm looking for rustlers, trespassers—or anybody who speaks English instead of Dog. You know there's a toll for using this trail, don't you?"

Her heartbeat fluttered in her throat. How did Adam do this to her with just a look? "Th-there is?"

"Yep. You have to come to my cabin and let me make supper for you. And you have to say something besides 'woof' while I cook it."

"I...don't know if that's such a...good idea."

"Goodness never even crossed my mind," he assured her huskily. "Still, that's the forfeit and it's got to be paid."

This was crazy. At best, Adam Dubois would complicate her life, which was complicated enough already.

And at worst?

His grin was wicked. Welcoming. She wondered how he'd kiss.

Dear Reader,

Well, here you have it, the sixth book in my series about the imaginary town of Trueheart, Colorado, and its surrounding ranches. You may remember Tess Tankersly from *The Wildcatter*. Last time we looked in on her, she was a mischievous twelve-year-old. A passionate bird-watcher and horse lover, Tess was barely starting to discover that most fascinating beast of all—man.

Thirteen years later (as time is measured in Trueheart), Tess is ready to meet her own alpha male. Not that she's precisely looking, you understand. Tess has a couple of woebegone lynx on her hands—and one short summer in the high country to help these endearingly big-footed cats learn to survive in the wild. But can Tess survive the attentions of a mysterious, maddening cowboy named Adam Dubois?

You might also recall Adam from *True Heart*. He was the line camp cowboy whom rancher Tripp McGraw saw as dangerous competition in his courtship of Kaley Cotter. Now Adam's back, and it turns out he's much more than a smiling Cajun cowboy. He's a moonlighting detective, with a mystery to solve and an elusive woman to chase.

So there are hearts for the capture and the game is afoot. Hope you enjoy it!

Peggy Nicholson

More Than a Cowboy
Peggy Nicholson

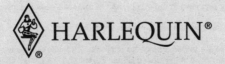

TORONTO • NEW YORK • LONDON
AMSTERDAM • PARIS • SYDNEY • HAMBURG
STOCKHOLM • ATHENS • TOKYO • MILAN • MADRID
PRAGUE • WARSAW • BUDAPEST • AUCKLAND

If you purchased this book without a cover you should be aware
that this book is stolen property. It was reported as "unsold and
destroyed" to the publisher, and neither the author nor the
publisher has received any payment for this "stripped book."

ISBN 0-373-71217-0

MORE THAN A COWBOY

Copyright © 2004 by Peggy Nicholson.

All rights reserved. Except for use in any review, the reproduction or
utilization of this work in whole or in part in any form by any electronic,
mechanical or other means, now known or hereafter invented, including
xerography, photocopying and recording, or in any information storage
or retrieval system, is forbidden without the written permission of the
publisher, Harlequin Enterprises Limited, 225 Duncan Mill Road,
Don Mills, Ontario, Canada M3B 3K9.

All characters in this book have no existence outside the imagination of
the author and have no relation whatsoever to anyone bearing the same
name or names. They are not even distantly inspired by any individual
known or unknown to the author, and all incidents are pure invention.

This edition published by arrangement with Harlequin Books S.A.

® and TM are trademarks of the publisher. Trademarks indicated with
® are registered in the United States Patent and Trademark Office, the
Canadian Trade Marks Office and in other countries.

www.eHarlequin.com

Printed in U.S.A.

This one's for Amy Mower the cat-lady
and her surly half-pint lynx

Don't miss any of our special offers. Write to us at the
following address for information on our newest releases.

Harlequin Reader Service
U.S.: 3010 Walden Ave., P.O. Box 1325, Buffalo, NY 14269
Canadian: P.O. Box 609, Fort Erie, Ont. L2A 5X3

CHAPTER ONE

"OH, SWEETIE! Oh, baby! Oh, you poor thing!" Tess Tankersly crouched before the pen and laced her fingers through the metal mesh. "How could they *do* this to you?"

The furry shape huddled at the far end of the cage didn't open its eyes. Lying in a filthy nest of shredded newspaper, the big cat looked dead at first glance. Its ribs and shoulder blades and hipbones stood out starkly below the matted pelt.

Was it even breathing? Tess drew her nails along the mesh—and was rewarded with the faintest quiver of one black-tasseled ear. "You don't belong in there," she crooned to the animal. "Locked away from the sunshine. No snow to run through. No trees to climb. This isn't right! Not right at all."

She sat back on her heels and looked up at the hand-lettered sign wired to the top of the home-built cage.

Danger! Look, but don't touch!
Canadian Lynx. Killer of the North Country!

"Yeah, right. Bunny rabbits, beware." Tess leaned forward again to peer through the wire.

A free spirit of the forest and mountains imprisoned

in a box so small it could barely turn around! Tess doubted the lynx could have stood upright in there.

But was it even well enough to stand? Tess had grown up on a ranch. She knew a sick animal when she saw one—the harsh coat, the hunched misery.

She had never been able to bear cruelty to animals. Hated to see wild things caged. Normally you couldn't have dragged her to a roadside petting zoo, for fear of sights just like this. But one of her pickup's tires had gone flat a few miles back toward Albuquerque. Although she'd changed to her spare, with two hundred miles to go between her and home, and a forecast of a late-spring snowstorm for this evening, she'd thought it wiser to stop and have the flat repaired at the first gas station she came to.

Killing time till the mechanic could get to her job, she'd made the mistake of following the signs that beckoned from across the two-lane country highway. Hazeltine's World-Famous Petting Zoo promised

Adorable, Exotic Animals!
Thrilling Beasts and Hideous Reptiles!
Hug the Llamas and Hold the Rabbits!

There wasn't a child in all of New Mexico who would've allowed his hapless parents to drive past that sign without stopping. And even at twenty-five, Tess still had a child's delight in animals. Growing up far from the nearest town, she'd had more friends with four legs than two. So she'd paid her dollar admission and entered the dimly lit, dingy concrete-block building that housed Hazeltine's zoo.

And past the not-so-huggable llamas—llamas bored

enough to spit—then the pen of black-and-white goats who begged for treats and nibbled at the hem of her jacket... Beyond three cages of resigned rabbits and a cracked aquarium housing a surly bull snake mislabeled as a Deadly Diamondback Rattlesnake! she'd come at last to this...this outrage.

She gazed around, angry words leaping to her lips as the proprietor shuffled up behind her. "This cage is too small. And your lynx, Mr. Hazeltine, just look at him! He's sick."

"She. Ol' Zelda's just taking a catnap, missy. She don't get lively till sunset."

"No, sir, I'm sure she's ill. See how her eyes are running? And her nose? And clearly she hasn't been eating. I'm a wildlife biologist, and believe me, you've got a sick animal here. She needs a vet."

Bristles rasped as he rubbed his weathered jaw. "Well, maybe she has a cold. She'll get over it, same way we all do. Sniffle and wait."

Or she wouldn't. Maybe Zelda had no reason to live, if this smelly box was all life offered. She hadn't been made for this. "Do you even have a license to keep wild animals?"

"Hey, *hey,* if you're going to start ragging on me, maybe you should take your money back and get on outta here. I do the best I can. And Zelda there'd be a lady's coat if it wasn't for me. Bought her off a fur farm up in South Dakota last year. She's got nothin' to complain about. Only one complainin' is you."

Tess stood, wove her fingers together and clenched them till they ached. Temper. She had a hot one at the best of times, and when she saw things like this— She swallowed a swift retort. Probably Hazeltine *was* doing the best he could. But whether he was or not, the point here was to save all that ragged, desperate beauty before it slipped away.

That was the whole point of her life, trying to save the creatures that ought to be saved.

"I'm sorry. I'm glad you took her away from a fur farm. How anybody could—"

But that was another wonder, for another day. How much money would she have left after paying for the tire? Eighty dollars? Maybe ninety and change? Somehow Tess didn't think Hazeltine's World-Famous Petting Zoo accepted credit cards, and it must be miles to the nearest ATM. The cat needed hope and help now—right now. She thrust a hand into her coat pocket and gripped her wallet. "Considering that she's sick and she needs a vet, would you sell her to me? I'm headed up past Santa Fe. I'm sure I could find a doctor there to look at her."

Hazeltine scratched his jaw again, and his squinty little eyes slid away over the surrounding pens. "Hadn't rightly thought 'bout lettin' her go. Zelda's the star attraction, you know. Kids like to be scared of something."

"You've still got that magnificent rattler," Tess wheedled. "And truly, I don't think you'll have Zelda much longer without a doctor. And vet bills for an exotic cat can't be cheap."

He grunted wry agreement and bent to look down into the cage. Blew out a disgusted breath and straightened. "Reckon I could take two hundred for her. Cash."

"I…could do that." The mechanic across the road had admired the elaborate stainless-steel rack system on the back of her pickup, a gift from her father at Christmas. Surely she could cut some sort of deal, if she offered it to him cheap? "I'll take her! Umm, please."

Hazeltine's smile shifted from wary to *gotcha*. "Then there's the cage. Lotta work and material went into buildin' that cage. You wanna buy that, too?"

THE NEW ORLEANS Police Department health plan didn't allow for private hospital rooms. As soon as they'd determined that Detective Adam Dubois meant to go on living, they'd moved him from the blessed isolation of Intensive Care down to a double room on a post-surgical ward.

If Adam hadn't been sworn to uphold the law, protecting and serving civilians everywhere, no matter how undeserving, he'd have thrown his roommate out their fourth-floor window. Him and his television that yammered from lights-on till lights-off beyond the curtain that Adam had insisted on drawing. Him with his nonstop snoring that sounded like a chainsaw with water in the gas tank—*Gasp, wheeze, rumble, snort-rumble-grumble!*

Adam gave himself one more day of this nonsense, then he was out of here, even if he had to crawl.

Clutching a pillow over his face with his good arm, teeth gritted and muscles tensed, he didn't hear his visitor arrive. When a finger tapped his wrist, Adam jolted half-upright, then swore at the pain. "*Crap!* How many times do I have to tell you not to wake me?"

But when he dragged the pillow down, he wasn't glaring up at Nurse Thibodaux, with her sexy smiles and her offers of backrubs. Or Nurse Curry with her prune mouth and her ready syringes. "*Gabe!* What are *you*—?"

But the answer was obvious. Adam and his cousin had always been close, as close as two grown men could be who lived a thousand miles and a world apart. If Gabe was the one who'd been shot, nothing would've kept Adam from his bedside. "Who told you?"

"Hospital contacted me—or contacted my answering machine. Sorry I couldn't make it sooner. I was up in the San Juans, snow-tracking lynx. Didn't get the message for almost a week."

Right, he'd listed Gabe Monahan as his next of kin on the insurance forms. There was nobody closer, legally or emotionally. Still. "You didn't need to…" His voice had roughened and his eyes stung. Damn! His emotions had been up and down, all over the map, since the shoot-out. He swallowed audibly and swung his head toward the curtain, while tactful Gabe busied himself with pulling up a chair and settling in.

"Sure, but it was a good excuse for a break," he said, his words discounting the worry in his eyes as he looked Adam over, then studied all the damnable devices he was hooked up to—monitors, IV lines and worse gizmos. "Figured I'd drop by and pay my respects, then chow down on crawfish at Mam' Louisa's before heading back to snow country." He leaned closer and scowled at Adam's chest. "They've sure got you gift-wrapped. What's below all the bandages?"

By now Adam had learned better than to shrug. "Coupla busted ribs." He'd taken a few kicks there, before he'd rolled far enough away to draw his gun. "Cracked collarbone—bullet clipped it." The same bullet that had collapsed his right lung.

"Nurse at the desk said you almost bled out, that was why all the intensive care. Took 'bout five quarts to top you up, she said?"

Adam shifted irritably. His life was his own to control. And information about it was strictly his to dispense or withhold, and generally he withheld. But let a pack of bossy women start giving a man sponge baths, and next thing you knew, they'd figure he was theirs to gossip about. "I wasn't counting. Took a hit in my thigh, that was the bad one. Grazed an artery."

"Ouch!" Gabe winced in sympathy.

"Oh, could've been worse. I must've straddled that bullet. Two inches higher and an inch right, and I'd be singing the lonesome blues, falsetto."

"You always had the devil's own luck."

Which was a ludicrous statement, on the face of it. Adam was the cousin who'd lost his alcoholic father to a car wreck when he was twelve, then lost his mother a year later when she collapsed under the burden of grief and double shifts as a barmaid, trying to support them. Gabe was the cousin who'd grown up surrounded by a large and loving family on a southwest Colorado ranch. He'd been nurtured by a stay-at-home mom during the same years that Adam had passed through a grim series of foster homes, skipping school to run with the toughest street gang in the city.

Adam's luck had turned around when his mother's brother—Gabe's father—had discovered his whereabouts and his situation. From age fifteen to eighteen, he'd lived with Gabe's family, learned to cowboy, and re-learned what it was to be loved by good, caring people. Another year and it would've been too late. He'd seen enough lost kids in his job to know how close he himself had come to the edge. So, yes, he supposed he did have his share of luck. "At least at poker," he admitted wryly.

"And women."

Short-term scoring, sure, he did all right, but the long-term win? His one time at bat—with Alice—he'd struck out big time. Swung for the bleachers and fallen flat on his face.

He started to shrug, then caught himself. "What can I say? Women are crazy for badges. And uniforms. Can't tell you how I hated giving mine up when I moved into Homicide. Was a real heartbreaker trade-off."

"Yeah, I can see you're hurting." The cousins grinned at each other till embarrassment set in, and Gabe glanced down. He plucked at the sheet hem. "So…when do they let you out of here?"

"I'm leaving tomorrow."

"That's not what the nurse—"

"Tomorrow, or I start tossing TVs." He hooked a thumb toward the racket beyond the curtain.

"Ah." Gabe nodded understanding. "Okay, but after that? I suppose they'll be giving you some recuperation time?"

"More than I'll want." Being a homicide detective wasn't simply a job, it was a calling. Maybe if he'd had a woman or a family to distract him—but then, how could a good cop allow himself to be distracted?

The cases were endless and they were fascinating, and they tended to eat a man up. You might stagger home wired yet exhausted, night after night, but your job counted for something. You felt it made a difference.

Feeling like that, you didn't tend to set it aside at the end of your shift, or switch your focus to the things that mattered to civilians. Because what hobby could be half as meaningful? What sport could give a man the same rush as going eyeball-to-eyeball with a gunman? What woman could compete with the adrenaline high of a righteous arrest?

Which was why so many detectives lived wistfully single in spite of themselves.

"That's what I figured. So I was wondering…" Gabe still fingered the sheet. "Maybe once you're back on your feet, you'd consider helping me out?"

Adam cocked his head. Gabe, the golden boy, needed his help? Gabe, who'd always had his ducks in a row, be they feminine, academic or professional. "Sure, but with what?"

"You know I've been working on the lynx reintroduction project? For four years now."

"Big spotted cats, with goofy clown feet and Mr. Spock ears," Adam remembered. "Bringing 'em back to Colorado." Gabe had explained his mission with enthusiasm several Christmases back, when the project was just getting off the ground. He was a conservation biologist for the Colorado Division of Wildlife, DOW for short. A few years ago, the DOW had concluded that lynx had become an exceedingly endangered species in Colorado—there were maybe two left in the state, as far as anyone knew—and it was time to save the critters from extinction.

In spite of the howls of protest from the cattlemen and sheepmen and skiers, they'd imported a hundred or more of the big cats from Canada and Alaska. Then they'd freed them in the San Juan Mountains, the wildest, roughest region of the southern Rockies, hoping they'd go forth and multiply. "You brought in the fleabags at a thousand a pop, I think you told me. So?"

Gabe turned up his hands and showed them empty. "So then…where are they?"

CHAPTER TWO

"WILL SHE LIVE?" Standing across the exam table from the veterinarian, Tess cupped one of Zelda's outsize paws between both her hands.

Dr. Liza Waltz glanced up from the sedated lynx, then down again at the thermometer she held. Her sandy brows drew together. "I don't know yet. Three degrees above normal." She set the thermometer briskly aside and returned with a stethoscope.

Tess stroked silky gray, black and buff-brindled fur and watched anxiously as the examination proceeded. Waltz was supposed to be the best vet for exotic cats in Santa Fe. After each of four phone calls to local vets had brought up the woman's name, Tess had driven straight to her office. The vet had interrupted a scheduled appointment to walk out to Tess's pickup. She'd peered into the cage in the truck bed, which Tess had covered with a tarp against the wind, sworn under her breath, then run back for sedatives and a noose pole to control the cat.

Zelda had been too weak to fight the injection. Within minutes Waltz had her on the table, and now Tess bit her bottom lip as she waited for a verdict.

The vet muttered something to herself and removed the stethoscope from her ears. "Not good," she allowed, fixing Tess with accusing gray eyes. "How long has she been this way?"

"I don't know." Tess explained how she'd acquired the lynx, and from whom. "Hazeltine mentioned there'd been a second lynx, a male, who shared Zelda's cage."

"Two in a cage that size!"

"Exactly. He bought them from the same fur farm last year. I asked him what had happened to the male, and he hemmed and hawed, then told me he'd sold him a few days ago to somebody who needed a barn cat. But frankly, I think he was lying. My guess is the male died, and it suddenly occurred to Hazeltine that I might back out on the deal if I thought Zelda was that sick. So he spun me a feel-good story instead."

Waltz growled something under her breath as she switched her attention to the cat's belly. Her gaze grew distant while her fingers gently kneaded and squeezed.

"Checking for pregnancy?"

"Right, although she'd have to be four or five weeks along for me to feel kittens. Or for an ultrasound to show them. Is there any chance she could have been bred in the past week or two?"

Tess turned up her palms. "I suppose anything's possible. But given the size of their cage, and that the male was removed recently, and that he may have been ill—"

"Seems unlikely," the vet agreed. "Malnourished as she is, it'd be a miracle if she could conceive, even if she were bred. So…" She patted the lynx's shoulder, then turned to a refrigerator in the corner. She stood, considering vials for a moment, then chose one and reached for a syringe. "I'll have to culture her saliva to be sure, but we're going to assume it's not simply viral pneumonia— that by now she's got bacterial complications. We'll see if a bolus of antibiotics can knock it back while I'm waiting for the results.

"Meanwhile she's dehydrated and underfed, so I'll run an IV line. Give her saline and glucose for now. Tubal feeding by tomorrow if she isn't eating." Her left hand probed delicately across a gaunt gray haunch, then she set the needle, injected its contents and glanced up at Tess. "If I can save her, this isn't going to be a cheap fix. She's badly run down."

Tess grimaced in agreement. And there was no way she could go to her father for help on this one. Ben Tankersly might have more money than God, but like most cattlemen, he wasn't fond of predators. He'd tell her the only good lynx was a dead one, and he had his own stuffed specimen in his office to underline the point.

But Tess had worked each summer through college, and socked every spare penny away. Like both her older sisters, she'd learned early that if she didn't want to dance to her domineering father's tunes, she had to pay her own piper. "I can handle it."

Waltz pried open the lynx's jaws and bent close to study her curving fangs. Gently she lifted the gums aside to reveal the back teeth. "All intact. That's something, anyway. So what did you pay for her, if you don't mind my asking?"

"Two hundred dollars."

"Pretty steep for a half-dead cat."

"Now ask me what he wanted for the cage," Tess suggested, straight-faced, then added as the vet raised an inquiring eyebrow. "*Five* hundred."

As they burst out laughing, she realized that here was somebody who might become a friend. They clearly shared the same passion for animals. Though the vet was inches shorter than Tess's slender five-foot-seven, she had a combative bounce and an intensity that made her seem much larger. Tess suspected she couldn't have picked a better ally to help her save this cat.

"Slick," Liza Waltz agreed, when she could speak.

"Very slick. I was tempted to say, 'keep your crummy ol' cage,' but then I took another look at Zelda's fashion accessories." Tess pressed a thumb gently against the center pad of the cat's forepaw. Saber-sharp claws flexed into view, then retracted as she released the pressure. "And I thought…mmm…well, yeah. Maybe I *don't* want her riding in my cab, till we've gotten to know one another better."

"I should probably tell you this after you've paid my bill, not before, but…even if I can save her, if you're thinking you've bought yourself a thirty-pound lap cat, you'd better think again. Lynx make rotten pets."

"No, she's a wild animal. I understand that."

But Waltz had already launched into a passionate lecture that she'd obviously made before. "If I had a dollar for every bozo who thought he wanted a lion or a tiger or an ocelot for a pet! I mean, sure, it's a wonderful fantasy—I wanted a cheetah when I was ten. But reality's quite another thing. For instance, this kitty…" She paused to smooth her hand across the lynx's soft tawny and cream-colored belly. "Once she gets her strength back, she'll be able to clear twenty-four feet in a single bound. Now picture that in your living room.

"And will she scratch the furniture? Oh, baby—we're talking shreds! Ribbons! She'll go through a couch a week if you give her the run of your place.

"And as for spraying…male or female, spayed or unspayed, exotic felines mark their territory—*and* you—

and everything else they can find to anoint. And we're talking buckets."

"*Euuuw!* No, I'm not up for that."

"But I can't tell you how many people are—till they try to live with a wild cat. Then once they do figure it out, they come crying to me or the zoo or the pound or a big cat sanctuary, because although they love their pet, they just can't keep it. So naturally, they want to find a loving, happy home. But…"

"But?" Tess fingered a black-tasseled ear. Yes, she could see how someone could fall in love with the idea of owning a lynx.

"But since people just keep on buying and trying, seventy or eighty of these animals come up for adoption each year in this country. Every last zoo is full to overflowing— they don't need another lynx. The big cat sanctuaries are desperate for operating funds and cage space. They can't afford to take on more pets-gone-bad. If the pound dares to place a lynx, then it just comes bouncing back again, once the new family gives up. So…" The vet shrugged, turned away, washed her hands at the sink.

"So?" Tess wondered.

"So when the owners run out of options, they dump the animal in some forest and try to tell themselves a cat that's lived all its life in a cage or indoors will learn how to hunt before it starves. Or if they're responsible, they put the poor beast down. Or suddenly the wife is wearing a fancy coat and a sheepish grin. But any way you cut it, there's no happy ending. Which brings me to you."

Tess jumped as the vet swung to aim an accusing finger at her.

"Assuming she lives, what do you mean to do with her?"

"I…haven't thought it out, very far. This wasn't something I planned. Zelda just happened."

"Start thinking."

"Well…I live on a ranch north of Trueheart, Colorado. At least, that's where I'll be living this summer, while I finish writing my dissertation. I suppose I figured I could free her there, maybe, and set up a feeding station outside. And hope that eventually she learns to hunt."

Though she'd have to do this secretly. The cattlemen of Colorado were up in arms about the recent reintroduction of lynx to the San Juan Mountains. Tess's father had been one of the main financiers of the lawsuits that had tried and failed to block the Division of Wildlife from bringing the animals back to the state. And when Ben Tankersly drew a line in the sand, his ranch manager and all his cowboys stepped up and toed it, if they valued their jobs. So Zelda would find no welcome at Suntop.

"Well, Problem One. If you're talking about one of those suburban excuses for a ranch—a ten-acre ranchette—forget it. Lynx are territorial, but they need a range of five to a hundred square miles. You've got a female, so figure on the smaller side of that, but all the same. Have you got that kind of room?"

"More than enough." Suntop was larger than Ted Turner's ranch, larger than Forbes's. Back in the 1890s, Tess's great-great-grandfather had carved his vast spread out of the foothills of the San Juans, and Tankerslys had guarded it jealously ever since. Now Ben ruled there, king of his own small kingdom.

"I live at Suntop," Tess admitted. When pressed to say anything at all, she generally put it like that. Strangers tended to assume she worked on the ranch rather than that she was a member of the family. She hated the way people looked at her when they learned she was a Tankersly. As if they were calculating her worth to the penny. And once they started adding it up, she was too proud to explain that she might be land rich, but she was cash poor. And likely would always remain so, if she wanted to live life her way.

So it was best just to disclaim or downplay all connection with Suntop, whenever possible.

"Suntop!" Liza Waltz let out a long, low whistle. "Yeah, that should be room enough, but here's Problem Two. Lynx hunt at six thousand to nine thousand feet. Is the ranch that high?"

"Not the home range," Tess admitted. "But the summer grazing, up in the high country, borders on that kind of elevation. Then north of that is all national forest, the San Juans, hundreds and hundreds of square miles of wilderness, going up and up."

"That would do. That's not far from the area the Division of Wildlife chose for its lynx restoration program. Which brings me to another point." The vet paused for a minute while she set up an IV bag on a pole, then taped Zelda's left forepaw to an immobilization board. "You're sure Hazeltine purchased her from a fur farm?"

"Yes. I insisted he give me all her papers, and they prove it."

Liza grunted as she inserted the needle in a vein, nodded in satisfaction, then hooked up the tubing. "I'll need to check those. The reason I ask is, if by any chance Hazeltine lied—if he trapped himself one of the Colorado DOW's lynx—we've got to hand her over. They're protected by the Endangered Species Act, state and federal, and believe me, we don't want to mess with those guys!"

"No, but I'm certain her papers are in order."

"I'll have to call that fur farm to confirm it, because the DOW's imported one hundred twenty-nine lynx into Colorado over the past four years, and do you know how many of them are left?"

"I haven't really followed it lately. I know the program hasn't gone as well as they'd hoped."

Liza snorted. "The numbers have dwindled down to forty-seven cats, which can still be tracked by their radio collars. If Zelda isn't one of the missing lynx, then where the heck are they?"

BY THE TIME Gabe returned with their take-out supper, Adam had managed to gimp his way to the picnic table on the screen porch. The evening breeze was mild for April, but not cool enough to dry the sweat he'd broken getting on his feet. He wiped a wrist across his forehead and called, "I'm out here," when Gabe came through the kitchen door bearing grease-spattered brown paper bags.

"Geez, I turn my back for ten minutes and you're out of bed!"

"Barbecue ribs and clean sheets are an ugly mix. Besides which, I was bored." When Adam had insisted on signing himself out against his doctor's advice, Gabe had decided to extend his visit and see him settled at home. But three days of devoted nursing and nagging was getting on both men's nerves. It was just as well Gabe was headed back to Colorado tomorrow.

Adam sighed at the thought. "Wish *I* was headed west. Spring skiing, instead of swatting mosquitoes."

"Then come with me," Gabe suggested, as he tossed napkins and a bottle opener on the table. He ducked back into Adam's pocket kitchen for plates and silverware.

"Plenty of room at the home ranch, and you know Mom would love to pamper you. Since the twins went off to college, she's got too much time on her hands. She's been wallpapering everything but the border collies, and bugging Dad to take tango lessons. A mission to whip you back into shape is just what she needs."

Adam grinned, shook his head and, popping a cap off a *Negra Modelo* beer, handed it over. "Thanks, but no thanks. Connie's overwhelming enough when a man can run, but right now, while I'm feeble… First thing your mother would do, is start matchmaking."

Gabe clinked his bottle against Adam's in a rueful salute. "Too true. She couldn't believe, when I called them yesterday, that you don't have a steady girlfriend to take over once I'm gone." His voice rose an octave and turned fretful. "A pussycat like Adam? Are those Louisiana women all blind and crazy?"

"Plenty of foxes in these woods, but they're all marriage-minded, even the ones who swear they aren't. So me, I'm taking a much-deserved sabbatical. Sleep this month, chase women later." Adam took another swallow of beer. "Unless you still want help with your missing lynx problem?" Gabe hadn't said a word about it after his first visit to the hospital.

His cousin's brows drew together above a sticky red curve of sparerib. He set the bone aside to wipe sauce off his mouth. "I'm thinking maybe I was a bit hasty, suggesting that. Seems like you're going to need a long, relaxing recuperation, and we're racing the clock here."

"They're disappearing that fast?"

"Roughly four a month since January."

They gnawed for a while in meditative silence till Adam said, "You sure you've got a problem? I mean, one of outside interference. You had more than average snow-fall this year, didn't you? So maybe they froze to death. Or they couldn't find game in all that snow. You'll find their bodies come snowmelt."

Gabe shook his shaggy blond head. "They're all wearing radio collars, which transmit to both satellites and planes, when we do flyovers. And each collar has a kill switch. If the animal stops moving for four hours or more, the collar sends out a death signal. Then we try to get somebody out there *pronto,* because sometimes not moving means the lynx is injured or trapped and we could help it.

"But of the cats that have vanished since January, all of their collars simply stopped sending. No live signal, no dead signal. Just…silence."

Adam reached for the salt shaker. Reached an inch too far—a burst of sizzling fire streaked across his chest. He paused, blinking, then drew his hand back. Sat, testing each breath for a minute, then said casually, "Would you pick up the signal if the cat was down in a canyon, or holed up in a cave?"

Gabe lifted the shaker, used it, then set it down six inches closer to Adam. "You wouldn't. The signal's strictly line of sight. But when he came out, the satellite should pick him up again."

"Well, maybe there was a cat convention at some point, in a cave. A St. Paddy's Day blow-out or a Valentine howl-along? And an avalanche wiped out the whole tribe at once?"

Gabe grinned. "'Fraid not. Lynx are notoriously anti-social. They hunt and live alone. In mating season, March through early April, they keep company for maybe a week, but that's it."

"Except for mamas with kittens, I suppose."

"Right, but since we haven't had a single female deliver a litter in four years of hoping and waiting and praying, that isn't an issue, either."

"Hmm." Adam served himself a second helping of potato salad. "What if they decided they missed Alaska or Canada or wherever they originally were snatched from and just started walking? 'The cat came back,' as the song goes."

"Yeah, that was our first theory. A few from every group we've imported *have* gone walkabout, ending up in Utah, or New Mexico or even Nebraska. The males in particular can get restless. It isn't unheard of for a tom to travel fifty miles or more a day for a week, though generally they do that in mating season, looking for ladies. But the satellite searches a wide band. If one of 'em made it to Las Vegas or Laramie, the collar signal would still beam up their location."

"And it hasn't," Adam murmured to himself. "The case of the missing lynx. So…" He cocked a brow at his cousin. "Who's got a grudge against these furballs?"

"Try the Cattlemen's Association and every sheepherder in the state, for starters."

"Lynx kill cows? I didn't think they were that big."

"A big one tips the scales at forty pounds, and they'd eat nothing but snowshoe hares, if they had their druthers. When hares are scarce on the ground, they take pine squirrels or mice or the occasional ptarmigan. I guess a real bruiser might jump a sheep or two a winter, if he were desperate. But this isn't like the wolf packs up in Yellowstone. You could drop a thousand lynx into cow country and never know the difference. They're shy and elusive and they hunt by night. Short of some caterwauling in mating season, you'd never know they were there."

"So why the fuss? I seem to remember some lawsuits, a few years back, trying to stop your program before it started."

"Politics. In 2000, lynx were finally listed as threatened under the Endangered Species Act. And that means, whether the feds want to or not, they're compelled by law to protect *lynx habitat.* And that's where the rubber meets the road.

"The grazers fear that their grazing allotments will be taken away so the cats can hunt in peace. The loggers are scared that they won't be able to cut trees in lynx territory. The Outfitters' Association is worried they won't be allowed to guide big-game hunters where the animals prowl.

"And the ski resorts, well, you remember the rumpus between the environmentalists and Vail resorts when they wanted to expand their ski runs into the Super Bowl area—the last place where native lynx were spotted in Colorado? Remember the Earth Liberation Front burned down twelve million dollars' worth of ski lodges to protest the plan?"

Adam gave a lawman's grunt of disgust.

"Bringing lynx back to the state has pretty well stopped ski development cold. Till the DOW can determine just how much habitat lynx need, and where they need it, we can't allow any more development in the high country."

"So they're popular cats," Adam said wryly. "No wonder they're disappearing. Any cowboy with a rifle…"

"Who's willing to risk a one-hundred-thousand-dollar federal fine and a prison term for killing an endangered species," Gabe reminded him. "And sooner or later, word always gets out. Very few people have the nerve."

"Yet your cats are vanishing, four a month. That sounds like something a little more…methodical than a trigger-happy cowboy. Got any theories who it might be?"

"Nope, but I've got a theory *how* he's doing it." Gabe opened a second beer for each of them. "Somebody's using our own radio collars to hunt them down."

"You can get the equipment to do that?"

"Yep. Buy the tracking antennas and earphones right off the Internet."

Adam whistled softly. "Clever! And cold."

"It's just a notion of mine, nothing the Division has officially considered. But that's when I thought of you. Investigating is what you do. And you've got a cover you could use."

"Line-camp cowboy," Adam mused. Three years ago, after Alice left him, he'd seriously considered quitting police work. While he'd searched his heart, he'd spent a summer cowboying in the high country north of Trueheart, Colorado. "That would allow me to fit in up there, move around some. Are you losing lynx in that area?"

"That's just about Ground Zero, or close enough. But the herds head up the trail about seven weeks from now and…" Gabe glanced at the crutches leaning against the wall. "I hadn't realized, when I first spoke, how badly you were…"

A useful summer in the mountains, rather than stewing and fuming around here, till some doctor cleared him for duty? "Count me in, Gabe. Seven weeks from now I'll be ready to sit a horse."

CHAPTER THREE

LARSON NEVER chose the same place twice for their meetings, but he always picked the same kind of bar, Natwig noted grimly. Ferns and mirrors. Chrome and marble. Micro-brewery beers at eight bucks a pop, and watch the bartender smirk if you asked for a Budweiser on tap.

The clients would be all ski and city types, glossy and blow-dried, with not a care in the world. Those with high-altitude tans had gotten them on the slopes at Telluride and Crested Butte, not packing mules into back-country canyons, or crouching still as a lichen-covered slab of granite, hour after hour, waiting for a line of elk to cross a ridge and step into range.

Natwig's restless gaze touched the mirror behind the bar, where a weathered, squint-eyed face stared blankly back at him. *What's wrong with this picture?* It was he who was out of place here, standing out like a crow on a snowfield. If any of his friends should see him here, they'd know something stunk.

But then, no man he respected would set foot in a place like this. So maybe Larson wasn't dumb in his choices, after all. Still. *Let's get a move on, dammit!* Natwig finished his beer, smacked the bottle down on the polished mahogany and stood.

The drill was, he was supposed to wait till Larson

showed, then follow him out to the parking lot. But down at the far end of the room, Larson was dawdling over his second margarita while he flirted with a giggly blonde who kept tossing her curls, showing off a glittery pair of diamond earrings.

Karen always wore a pair of turquoise studs that Natwig had bought her their last year in high school. *Wonder if she'd like something like those sparklers?*

The way he was going, he'd never find out. Every dollar he earned from this job would go to paying her medical bills and hanging on to the ranch. He shoved out through the door into frosty night air and drew a grateful breath. Too much perfume and aftershave and air freshener back there. *What the hell am I doing?*

What had to be done.

Arms folded against the cold, he slouched against the door of his pickup. When Larson finally sauntered out, Natwig unlocked his door. He scooped the paper bag off the floorboards, then strode across the parking lot to Larson's Porsche—not even a year old, with not a speck of mud to mar its gleaming curves. The passenger door swung open as he approached, and he ducked inside. Set the bag between them.

"How many?" Larson's manicured fingers reached for the parcel.

"Two." He watched with contempt as the city man pulled out the collars, counting for himself. Didn't he know better than to doubt a man's word? Or realize what that kind of distrust said about the worth of his own word?

"Why only two?" Larson inspected the crushed transmitter on each collar, then dropped them back in the bag.

"Like I told you last month. It's harder tracking lynx this time of year. Most of the snow's melted, and what's left is too crusty to take a print." And the one shot he'd got at the big male north of Creede, after three days of hard stalking, he'd missed. But that failure he'd keep to himself.

"My…clients…won't be pleased."

"If your friends reckon they can do better themselves, tell them they're welcome to try."

And just who were Larson's clients? People smart enough to want a cut-out, a middleman, separating themselves from their dirty work. People with deep pockets, to pay the kind of bounty Natwig was collecting.

The Cattlemen's Association could raise that kind of cash. Or the ski developers. Or the timber industry, easy.

The goat- and sheepherders? Somehow Natwig didn't see it. And as a member of the Outfitters' Association himself, he'd heard nothing but the usual bellyaching at their annual gathering. No plan of action to fix the situation, and if there had been, they wouldn't have needed to farm the job out.

"They'll expect better next month." Larson pulled out his wallet, and peeled off twenty bills from a fat wad.

As each thousand-dollar bill was laid upon his palm, Natwig felt the pressure in his chest ease the tiniest bit. Twenty thousand. Before Karen had broken her back, he'd have called that a fortune. A family with a man who could put meat on the table could scrape through a year on twenty grand.

As long as everyone stayed healthy. But now…

"And here are your latest locations." Larson passed over a folded paper.

Imagine a world where a satellite a hundred miles overhead could pinpoint the whereabouts of those soft-stepping ghosts of the forest to fifty yards or less?

Imagine a world where somebody hired to protect all wildlife could be bribed to secretly access the DOW computers, then print out their animals' latest locations, and pass them on to their enemies?

Not my kind of world.

Except he was trapped in it, sure as a lion up a tree. He could snarl all he wanted, but he was under the gun.

"Don't expect too much next month. Lynx tend to travel in the spring," he warned Larson as he gripped the door handle, eager to be out and away. "They'll be searching for mates, looking for fresh hunting grounds." He'd tried a couple of times to explain that just because the satellite pinpointed each cat one day per week, that didn't mean the lynx would then sit tamely waiting till he came hunting.

If these locations were stolen from the computer yesterday, why, by today, every one of these forty-seven cats could be fifty miles to hell and gone across the mountains. Larson's paper only gave him the place to start looking, no guarantee of finding.

But something about all this high-tech bullshit seemed to make a man arrogant, brash as the dumbest horse in blinders. If a computer said it was so—why then, it must be so. Nothing to it. Just reach out and shoot someone.

As Natwig shoved open the door and stepped out into clean air, Larson leaned over to give him a bland farewell smile. "My clients expect better."

THEY'D RENDEZVOUSED outside of Trueheart at midnight, then Liza in her Jeep, with its caged rear end, had followed Tess's pickup, towing its tandem horse trailer, north. Toward the high country.

A horseman could have ridden a straighter and shorter

route to the summer range up through Suntop land. But constrained to travel by vehicle—and in secret—they had to circumnavigate the ranch. Their route wound up through the mountain valleys to the east, then spiraled north, then west, then finally south again.

Sixty slow-going miles of road dwindled from public two-lane to frost-heaved one-lane to muddy Forest Service and logging tracks. The scent of pine and snow blew through Tess's open window. The jewelled eyes of deer gleamed in her headlights, then their graceful silhouettes bounded across the road and into the trees.

"Coming home," Tess half sang aloud, as if the lynx in the car behind could hear her. "Hang on *just* a little longer, baby." Liza had sedated the cat lightly for the drive, but she hadn't dared give her more, since Zelda would have to be knocked all the way out for the final leg of her journey.

It was two hours before dawn when they reached the trailhead east of Sumner Mountain and parked. Just a whisper of cold wind stirring the pines. Stars so big and bright you could pick out colors by their light. "How is she?" Tess asked as she joined Liza at the back of her Jeep.

"*Not* happy." The vet dropped the tailgate to reveal the caged interior, and a low feline moan seconded that opinion.

"But she looks good," insisted Tess, while Liza inspected the lynx by flashlight. "She looks wonderful!"

Once the cat had recovered from pneumonia, Liza had moved her to a large kennel behind her house, west of Santa Fe. Seven weeks of intensive feeding had worked a miracle. Zelda's ribs were no longer visible beneath her glossy coat and, even sedated, she seemed bursting with energy.

"Oh, she's spunky enough," Liza said broodingly, "but I'd still like her to gain more weight. A lot of her bulk is just that fabulous coat."

"But you said she's ready for freedom," Tess worried. They'd discussed this at length.

"Given our schedule, I guess she's got to be."

They didn't dare wait longer. Last week had seen spring roundup at Suntop and all the surrounding ranches near Trueheart. Now that the new calves were branded, within a week or two, the herds would be driven north to their summer range.

Liza and Tess had agreed that it was best if Zelda were acclimated and freed before the cattle arrived in the foothills. Lynx were shy and wary at the best of times. Commotion in the area while Zelda was choosing a den and a territory, might persuade her to seek these elsewhere.

But it was crucial to their plan that Zelda stick around, close to where Tess could feed her, till she'd learned to hunt her own food.

And so this rush to get her settled and happy and accustomed to being fed in a certain place at a certain time before the herds arrived. Cats were conservative creatures who liked dependable rituals, Liza maintained. The fewer surprises, the better.

"Will you tranq her now?" Tess asked the vet.

"Not till you're ready to ride. You don't want her waking somewhere along the way."

"Better believe it! I don't know who'd enjoy that more—me, Cannonball or Zelda." Tess had picked the steadiest horse on Suntop to carry the lynx, and a pack horse that was nearly as sensible. Still, she found her nerves were skittering as she tightened the girths on both saddles, bridled up, then fitted her various packs and bundles into place. Steady or not, she could just imagine how Cannonball would react to a yowling, struggling cat in a basket strapped to his back—her own private rodeo, in the midst of dense forest, or on a cliffside trail!

Liza supported one-half of the collapsible metal cage while Tess lashed it to the right side of the pack mare's saddle. A second four-foot-by-four-foot stack of steel-mesh squares was hung from the left side to balance the load. The mare snorted and rolled her eyes. "How far is it to your site?" Liza dithered. "You're sure you can you find it in the dark?"

"It's about nine miles to the southwest of here, and yeah, I know the trails. And it'll be dawn by the time we reach the point where we really have to bushwhack, so…don't worry." Tess smiled to herself. Somewhere in those weeks of custody and nursing, cat-loving Liza had lost her professional objectivity. She was as anxious as a mom sending her only daughter off for her first time at summer camp.

Not that Tess wasn't worried, as well. If they couldn't give Zelda the wide, wonderful world she deserved—if the cat couldn't learn to survive in that world—neither of them had the heart to stuff her back in a cage. Which left only…another kind of injection. Sleep without waking.

And even if she succeeded in reintroducing Zelda to the wild this summer, Tess still had other worries.

Like the imminent arrival of half a dozen line-camp cowboys, who were paid to keep their eyes wide open for anything strange going on in their territories.

Like the chance of being caught in what they—and her father!—would see as a gross betrayal of their way of life.

If they caught her aiding and abetting lynx, they'd see

her as Tess-turned-traitor. Tess on the side of the tree huggers and the despised government bureaucrats—and against her neighbors, her family, her friends.

And she could argue till she was blue in the face that lynx and cows were perfectly compatible, that the cattlemen had nothing to fear but fear itself. But ranchers were as stubbornly conservative at heart as…cats.

So here she was in the middle, walking her usual tightrope between what she loved and those she loved. Anyway you cut it, it was bound to be a nerve-wracking summer.

And on top of that—in my spare time—I'm supposed to be finishing my dissertation! Tess reminded herself with a grimace. For the past year, she'd studied beavers in a riverine habitat. This summer she needed to analyze her data and write up her conclusions, if she wanted to earn her doctorate, and be qualified for a field biology position with the U.S. Fish and Wildlife Service next fall, which she most certainly did.

"Now, you're going to keep her caged for at least three days?" Liza fretted.

"As long as she and I can stand it." Tess would have to camp near the cage till she freed the cat. It was spring after all, with the black bears awakening from their winter fasts. Though lynx weren't part of their usual menu, bears were omnivorous, and they sure knew how to take apart any container with food inside. Tess wouldn't dare leave Zelda trapped and defenseless.

Thinking of that, she went back to the pickup, unracked her rifle, then settled it into its saddle scabbard.

"What's *that* for?"

Tess smiled at her friend's note of alarm. Liza was from Massachusetts. She'd only come west after graduation from vet school. Apparently, like many easterners, she viewed firearms solely as lethal weapons. Instruments of heartbreak and destruction.

Tess took the view of the tough and capable Western men who'd raised her. A rifle was simply a tool that a responsible person used responsibly. No more or less dangerous than a car or a threshing machine. The only thing *she'd* ever killed with a gun was a tin can, but still… "I brought along some red-pepper spray in case of bears. But I've always wondered if that really works—or just turns 'em into furry buzzsaws. So this is for backup." Which, please God, she wouldn't need.

"O…kay." Liza didn't sound convinced, but then it wasn't she who'd be sleeping alfresco forty miles from the nearest kindly policeman. "And you've got the chickens?"

"Right here." Tess loaded the cooler that held four flash-frozen roasting chickens into the left basket hamper on Cannonball's back. "And I've already stashed another fifty in the kerosene freezer at the cabin."

She'd claimed the highest, tiniest, most tucked-away cabin on Suntop's summer range for herself for the next three months. Her father and sisters were used to her jaunts into the wilderness, so they hadn't been all that surprised when she'd announced that she intended to live in the mountains for the summer, rather than stay at the Big House on the ranch. No distractions or socializing wanted or needed while she hammered out her dissertation, was the excuse she'd given—and they'd bought it.

She'd driven up a few days ago to this trailhead and packed in everything she'd need at the cabin for the period, including a three-month supply of frozen birds. "Well. All we need now is the star of this show."

Liza sighed, nodded, and turned toward the Jeep. Murmuring soothing endearments, she used a noose pole and a pair of elbow-length leather gloves to immobilize the growling lynx, then injected her with the sedative.

She brushed angrily at her lashes as Tess closed the basket lid over the curled-up sleeping cat. "You'll tell me if she needs anything? Goes off her feed or…"

"She won't run too far away," Tess assured her, though she was by no means sure. "Zelda's grown to love her chicken dinners. She'll stick around till she knows she can feed herself."

Or she wouldn't.

But then, didn't freedom always come with risk? Tess had always found the risks worth facing. Three days from now, when she opened the cage door, she figured Zelda would agree.

"So, ZELDA, what do you think? Is it starting to feel like home?" On her way to the pool where she washed each morning, Tess had stopped to check out her charge.

The lynx lay in feline loaf-of-bread position at the front of her cage, fore paws tucked demurely under her breast, back paws folded beneath. With her yellow eyes half closed, she seemed relaxed as any tabbycat, although she was pointedly ignoring her visitor. The comical two-inch black tufts on her ears twitched at the sound of Tess's voice, then her gaze returned to the massive fallen tree beside her cage…to the dark hole beneath its mossy trunk.

"You're right. It would make an excellent den," Tess assured her in a soft voice. "Location, location, location." She'd chosen this site with care—an old-growth spruce forest, because lynx typically denned in such deep, dark places with their excellent cover. A hundred yards to the west stretched a wide swath of younger trees where, years before, an avalanche from the peaks above had scoured the slope. Time had patiently reseeded the scar, and now it was covered with wildflowers and twelve-foot saplings. Tess's research over the past month had told her that lynx favored that sort of terrain for hunting. The smaller trees let in the sunshine, which nourished the flowers and grass, which drew the snowshoe hares. And the lynx who loved them.

"One of these days, if the DOW ever gets its act together and provides you with a boyfriend, this would make a perfect den for kittens," Tess told the cat. "Which reminds me, Liza meant to check you again, to make sure you aren't in a family way." The vet had intended to palpate the lynx after she'd sedated her.

"I remember tucking you into your basket while we were jabbering away about rifles and bears. But I don't remember Liza examining you. Did we just get distracted? Or did she do it while I was fussing with the pack mare?"

The lynx turned to give her a haughty stare over the wonderful double-points of her neck ruff, which resembled a Victorian gentleman's gray-and-white-barred side whiskers, edged in formal black.

"Guess you wouldn't remember, since you were asleep," Tess reflected. "And I reckon you figure it's none of my business anyway."

The lynx stood to stretch magnificently, forelegs, then back. She stalked away on her oversize paws—furry snowshoes that were designed to let the cat run atop the fluffiest powder. Her black-tipped stub-tail stilled as a gray jay swooped low past the cage, then quivered with furious attention when the bird landed on a nearby branch.

"Soon," Tess assured her, standing and stretching, too. She could have chatted happily for hours, but it was safest for Zelda if she lost her tolerance for people. Her best chance for a long, healthy life in these mountains was to shun all humans, friend and foe alike. For that reason, Tess had pitched her tent fifty feet to the west, within easy earshot if a bear came calling, but otherwise out of sight.

She shouldn't linger now. She sighed as she collected her rifle and her kit. "Better get ready," she advised the lynx. "Today's the day."

She'd wait till noon, when a lynx normally would be dozing. This time, instead of giving Zelda her chicken inside the cage, she'd show it to the lynx—then set it at the entrance to her proposed den. She'd open the cage door and walk away.

If all went as Tess hoped, Zelda would step out timidly into freedom. Then, overwhelmed by the sudden expansion of her world, made nervous by the too-bright light of noon, she'd snatch up the chicken and scuttle into cover beneath the fallen tree. She'd spend the rest of the day there, eating and gradually growing accustomed to a feeling of safety and rich possession. The den would begin to take on her scent.

Meantime, Tess would collapse Zelda's cage and carry it away.

By twilight, when her instincts urged Zelda to come out and prowl, maybe the burrow beneath the tree would already feel like a haven, a home to return to. A place where food had been provided before. Where she'd find it again and again, in the following days, thanks to Tess and her cache of frozen chickens.

And so her life in the wild would begin.

Ducking under and around ancient trees, then between head-high thickets, Tess came at last to the stream, which angled across the slope. For most of its course, the brook ran shallow and clear—icy-cold from the snows above, narrow enough to step across. But at this point it paused in its chuckling journey and widened to a pool—another reason Tess had chosen this site for Zelda's den.

She set the rifle and her kit to one side and knelt, then unbuttoned the top button of her shirt. Then the next. An absent smile curved her lips as she pictured Zelda's spotted, big-footed kittens crouching on the rocks beside her, peering fascinated into the pools. Ears pricked as they searched for minnows.

An excellent place to raise a family.

CHAPTER FOUR

YESTERDAY AFTERNOON, Adam had driven his truck up to the trailhead north of Sumner line camp. From there he had made several trips, backpacking a summer's worth of books and supplies two miles downhill to the cabin.

Too tired to head back at the end of the day, he'd stoked the wood-burning stove and stayed on, figuring he'd return to the valley in the morning. There was still plenty to be done before the cattle drive started. Plus, tomorrow night he'd meet Gabe in Durango—go over final thoughts and plans for this investigation.

Sumner line camp was Adam's old stomping ground from three summers ago. Last time he'd lived at this cabin, he'd been mourning Alice. A two-year engagement that should have ended with a wedding had ended instead in betrayal. His ring returned with a pretty apology, and her lukewarm hope that they could still be friends.

But if Alice didn't want to build a home and family with him, Adam could do without her friendship. Without any reminder of her—or what might have been.

Stung by her loss and the part his job had played in their breakup, he'd even considered quitting the police, going back to his Colorado roots to start life over again as a cowboy. He'd spent that summer up here in the high country, relearning that he needed more of a challenge in his life than a herd of cantankerous cows.

That September he'd gone back to New Orleans, back to the force, with a renewed dedication.

And with his heart on the mend, he'd sworn to himself that he'd never risk it again. Since Alice, Adam had devoted himself to loving women well—but never seriously.

Still, sleeping in his old bunk, he found a ghost of that summer's loneliness had crept upon him in the night. Flooded with memories both painful and pleasurable, he'd woken at dawn. Instead of heading back, he'd gone out walking. Wandering miles farther than he'd intended, he came at last upon a stream.

And heard a woman's voice.

Pure wistful imagination, Adam assured himself. Nothing but the babble of running water weaving around the remnants of last night's dreams.

Whatever its source, it trailed off after a minute. He shrugged and walked on, eyes on the stair-stepping run of narrow pools. If a lover was too much to wish for, then maybe there were trout?

A movement ahead caught his eye and he looked up.

And there she was.

A dark-haired woman kneeling on a rock, both hands cupped as she dipped them to the pool.

He sucked in a startled breath and froze.

Her hands scooped water and splashed it on her face. She made a muffled, laughing sound—it had to be freezing—then smoothed her palms over her tousled hair, brushing it back off her brow. Her fingers met at the nape of her neck—she laced them and stretched her spine. Small, high breasts rose with the sinuous movement and Adam bit back an instinctive groan.

Again she bent to the pool. Bathed her face and swan neck. *"Yow!"* Drops of water glistened on her throat and the curves that the flaring halves of her shirt revealed.

Enchanted, he moved closer—

And stepped on a branch. *Crack!*

She didn't glance toward the sound, but turned smoothly away, reached—and swung back again. A rifle swung with her, rising, seeking...

At the sight of that rounding bore, years of hard-earned reflexes kicked in—Adam dived for cover. He hit the ground good shoulder first, then rolled. A bolt of lightning slammed across his chest, sizzling sternum to shoulder point. "Shit! *Merde!*" If he'd rebroken his collarbone! Or had she shot him? But no, he'd heard no retort.

"You're...not a bear." She'd risen to peer into the bushes where he'd landed.

"Dammit!" One minute he'd been whole and well, nothing but flirtation on his mind.

And now? Adam drew a shaking breath and pushed up out of a drift of last year's leaves. Pain played a savage piano riff down his ribcage. *"Hell!"* He *hated* feeling helpless. If she'd shoved him back to the bottom of the hill he'd been scrabbling up with such effort...

"Or maybe you are." She'd shifted her rifle up and away, but not so far it couldn't quickly swing back. "Did you hurt yourself?"

"Did *I*—?!"

"Well, I don't like being snuck up on," his tormentor said reasonably. The corners of her mouth curled, then straightened again. "'Specially not in spring, when the sow bears have cubs." Cradling the rifle across her left forearm, she reached casually for her buttons, fumbled at the lowest one, single-handed.

"Put the gun down before you drop it," he growled, rising stiffly to his knees.

Her slate-green eyes narrowed. Her hand paused in its effort. "No need." A pulse fluttered in the damp hollow of her throat.

So her coolness was a front. The cop in him was glad she was wary of a strange man, even though her grip on the gun set his alarm bells to jangling. "Look, I'm turning around. So set the gun down *nice and easy* and use both hands, okay? Much safer for both of us."

He turned his back and seized the moment to run his own hands up his ribs. Painful, but no new jagged bumps where they'd mended. He fingered his collarbone and winced. Likely pulled a muscle as rebroke the bone, but—the hell with it. If he couldn't cowboy this summer, then he couldn't do the job he'd promised Gabe. He swung around again.

Caught in the act of fastening her top button, she froze as their eyes collided.

The moment stretched out…his breathing quickened. Possibilities spun in the air like dust motes sparked by the sun.

Her fine eyes widened and he knew she read his thoughts, knew she wanted to look away. Was too proud to let him win this silent clash.

With calm deliberation she finished her task, while a dusting of rose painted her high cheekbones.

"What are you doing up here?" he asked suddenly. She hadn't just dropped out of his dreams.

She wore running shoes, not serious hiking boots. He scanned the rocks around her feet and found no sign of a backpack. Just a canvas overnight kit. "You're camping up here?" By herself?

But then, her reluctance to put down that gun showed a woman on her own. If she'd had a companion, a mate, she'd have simply set it aside and called for backup. So…definitely alone. Adam's eyes flicked to her left hand—ringless—and he felt a surge of unabashedly male satisfaction.

"I'm…" She drew a knuckle along her top lip. Her long lashes fluttered as she glanced away, then looked back again.

Adam cocked his head and waited. Whatever came next would be a lie.

"I'm doing research up here. Beaver."

He almost shouted his laughter aloud. "Beaver." A couple of flat rocks made a path across the pool and he stepped across, trying not to grin. *So you can't lie worth a damn. I'll remember that.* "There's no beaver this high up."

"That's what I'm…verifying. I'm a wildlife biologist." When lying, it was best to stick as close to the truth as possible, Tess had always heard. Still, this stranger wasn't buying it. "Doing a thesis on beaver and tamarisk trees," she babbled on. That part was true, anyway, although her research location had been Utah, not the San Juans. "The way one affects the other, and how both affect their environment. Water quality. Bird food. Habitat. Fire conditions."

"Really."

He was so lean and beautifully put together, that his size came as a shock. When he stopped before her, she had to tip her head back to meet his gaze. Eyes blue as a mountain midnight and dancing with laughter. Somehow she knew now he'd never hurt her. Still, that laughter made him… *Dangerous.* As instinct whispered, she stooped for her gun.

Their heads nearly cracked as he crouched along with her. "Allow me, *cher.*"

Like she had a choice?

When they rose again, the rifle was firmly in his possession. "Nice piece." He cracked it open, removed its bullets, closed it and gravely handed it over. "Bit heavy for beaver, isn't it?"

"I *study* beaver. I don't shoot them." And wherever he'd come from—there was a touch of the deep South in his low, lazy voice—it was someplace where they'd failed to teach him that it was rude to confiscate a woman's bullets. Patronizing, if not downright paranoid.

"Ah. And do you have a name?"

She'd liked him grizzly-bear grouchy more than she liked him laughing at her. "I do," Tess agreed airily, then glanced around for her kit, leaned down to collect it. When she straightened, she found her snub had bounced right off him. His smile had only deepened.

The man had a smile to give a woman pause. A lush bottom lip that was finely carved and…mobile. The upper was severe, yet oddly sensitive, as if he hardened it more in pain than cruelty. His angular jaw was blue-black with beard shadow; he hadn't shaved this morning. And, as Tess noted this, the nape of her neck *prickled,* as if those bristles brushed deliberately, deliciously across it. A hot wave washed up her thighs.

She tossed her head and turned aside, cheeks warming, too. *Get a grip, girl!* So she hadn't had a serious relationship—any sort of relationship—for almost a year now; that didn't mean she had to show her lack here. Not to a man who was bound to be trouble.

Trouble in more ways than the usual if he turned uphill, she realized belatedly. Thirty yards of bushwhacking would bring him to Zelda's cage.

A more logical course was to follow the path along the

stream, she told herself. She'd set him an example, heading west along its bank. Once out of sight, she could cut up through the new growth to where she'd picketed her horses. Swinging back to face him, she retreated in a casual backward drift while she asked, "And what are *you* doing up here?"

He had no pack or bedroll, and only an idiot would hike the San Juans this time of year without them. But though he might be irritatingly self-assured, this was no fool.

It was too early for line-camp men. Besides which, cowboys never traveled on foot. So that left—precisely what?

"Spent the night at Sumner cabin." His weight shifted as if he had half-decided to follow her.

"Oh. So you know Kaley and Tripp?" Sumner cabin had belonged to Kaley Cotter's spread, the Circle C. Then a few years back she'd married her neighbor, rancher Tripp McGraw. Their combined grazing allotments stretched to the south and east of this spot. If the McGraws vouched for this man, then he couldn't be quite a rogue, no matter what he seemed to be.

"I do." And she knew them, too, Adam realized with satisfaction as he changed his mind about following her. That meant when he described his rifle-toting babe to Tripp McGraw, he'd learn her name. How to find her.

Because whatever she thought—and damned if she didn't look relieved as she murmured a noncommittal, "Ah," then flipped him a jaunty wave and turned off to the west—this wasn't the end of their acquaintance.

This was only the beginning.

Still, missing her already, he couldn't resist calling after her, "Hey!" *Beautiful!*

She swung back around, her dark brows tipped up like a crow's wings in flight.

"Your bullets, you forgot them."

"Oh…yeah." She dug into a pocket of those snug jeans he'd been trying not to stare at. Held up something in her closed fist that rattled. And gave him her killer smile. "Well, keep 'em. Plenty more where those came from."

So I'll consider myself warned, he promised her silently.

A warning he was bound to ignore.

"Cuz, your taste in dogs is headed south," Adam declared, sauntering over to Gabe's parked pickup. "*Way* south." The big red hound gazing dolefully over its tailgate took his insult for a compliment and waved his tail. "He looks like a melted bloodhound. A sawed-off, melted bloodhound."

"Touch of basset in there somewhere," Gabe agreed, stepping down from his truck. "All those bags and droops. Still, pretty is as pretty does. This is Watson. Belongs to a friend of mine."

"Watson…" Adam presented his knuckles for the obligatory snuffle and sniff, then snatched them back as an enormous pink tongue took a swipe at him. "As in Sherlock's shorter, dumber partner?"

"The very same." Gabe nodded at the cab of his truck. "Care to eat in your place or mine?"

"Mine, unless you want drool all over your rear window."

Gabe had suggested that they meet at a diner in Durango, but Adam had vetoed that, voting instead for this rendezvous at a scenic overlook above the city. Maybe it wasn't as comfortable, but when working undercover, a wise man lived his role from the get-go. A fool broke cover unnecessarily—and sometimes didn't live long enough to regret it.

Not that Adam was expecting that level of trouble here in sleepy southwestern Colorado. Whoever he was hunting was a catkiller, not a mankiller. But all the same, why take a chance on someone linking him to a top biologist with the Division of Wildlife? This part of the state was enormous in size, but not so blessed with population. Strangers were noticed.

So from now till hunt's end, he'd be Adam Dubois, freebooter and line-camp man, just a smiling Cajun cowboy, drifting through life. Not a care in the world. No worry to anybody.

"You babysitting?" he inquired in the truck, while he traded one of the cold Coronas he'd brought for a roast beef sandwich.

"Nope. Watson's for you. He's on loan from a friend in Montana, a biologist with the Forest Service. That hound's the best lynx tracker in the lower forty-eight."

"No." Adam frowned at the dog in the truck ahead. With his chin propped on the tailgate, the brute gazed at them pitifully. His woebegone face was wrinkled in concentration, as if he were trying to levitate a sandwich and call it home. "Thanks, but no thanks."

Adam had had a dog once upon a time. A gangly, knock-kneed yellow mutt he'd found on the street. He'd been a grab-bag of every breed you could name, but brave? Damn, but that dog had been gutsy, and with a great sense of humor to boot. Johnny, he'd named him. Johnny-Be-Good. They'd shared the same bed from the day he'd found Johnny to the day the social workers had dragged Adam off to his first foster home.

They'd promised they'd give him his pet back in a

week or so, but that had all been a soothing lie. By the time Adam had realized this and gone looking for his friend, hunting through every pound in New Orleans a thirteen-year-old could find, the dog was…gone. He blinked his eyes rapidly in the waning light and scowled. "Last thing I need up there is a chow hound."

Last thing he needed was a dog, or anybody else, tripping up his heart. That was one lesson he'd learned and learned very well. First with his dad, then his mom, then Johnny, then most lately with Alice. Alone was the safe way—the only way—to travel.

"Besides," he continued into Gabe's disapproving silence, "the only dogs that are welcome on the summer range are working dogs. Cattle dogs. Any mutt that runs the cows is sure to be shot."

"He minds his manners. Heels, comes, sits and all the usual. When Watson isn't eating or tracking, he's sleeping, according to Tracy. He wouldn't get in your way."

"He'd take up half the cabin I'll be living in, and five'll get you ten he snores. No thanks."

His cousin shrugged and bit into his sandwich. Some hundred miles to their west, the sun was a blood orange, squashing itself past a jagged line of purple mountains. A splash of fiery juice, then it squeezed on down. The ruddy light cooled instantly to blue. Down in the valley, the city twinkled.

"It's a pretty big area you'll be patrolling," Gabe observed mildly, at last. "The lynx are spread out over some two thousand square miles, and no telling which one of them our guy'll decide to stalk next. Reckon it'd be like hunting for an ant in a sandpile, if you don't know where to look. At least Watson could point out the cats, then you'd take it from there."

Adam shrugged and sipped his beer. The dog drooled in the twilight. "Think he's still operating out there?" Adam asked finally, to break the edgy silence.

"'Fraid so. We're down to forty-four animals. Collar YK99M3, a male from our original batch, stopped signaling last week. Last heard from ten miles north of Creede." Gabe sighed and reached for the rolled map he'd brought from his truck. Unscrolling it across the dash, he tapped an inked-in asterisk with a tiny notation beside it. "He vanished right there. And that one really hurt. He was one of the lynx I flew up to the Yukon to collect and bring back here. A big healthy two-year-old with a white bib on his chest like a housecat, and paws like catcher's mitts. Freed him myself. He looked so...*right*...floating off into the woods, the day we let him go. Home and free."

Gabe rubbed a hand across his face. "Dang it to hell! How anybody could bring something that pretty down... Why they'd ever want to..."

Adam grunted his sympathy. That was something a homicide cop often wondered, seeing the aftermath of killings in the city. The good and the beautiful willfully smashed. Ruthlessly brushed aside. Such a waste, such a shame. Any time you could stop it, you felt a little bit better, a little bit bigger. Like you'd done your part, fighting the good fight. Making the world safer for the fragile things that mattered.

Taking the map from his cousin, he spread it over the steering wheel and squinted in the dusk. Checked its mileage scale, then grimaced. Damn, but the West was big! Distance took on a whole different meaning out here. He'd known it already, but looking at it now, peak after peak, range upon range... And roaming out there somewhere in all that craggy wilderness, a bunch of forty-pound cats...

And whoever was stalking them.

"You really think he'd be useful?" The mutt had a home and an owner, after all. He was only on loan. No commitment necessary, beyond opening his cans for the next three months.

"Show you something." Gabe slid out of the truck, strode over to his own, and leaned in its open window. He pulled out a battered Stetson, then offered it to the dog. "*Kitty*, Watson! See the kitty?"

The dog pranced and nosed the hat, yodeling his approval. That hollow banging was the sound of his tail, slamming the sides of the pickup.

"*Nice* kitty. No, boy, sit. *Staaay.*" The dog sat with an anguished yelp and Gabe brought the hat to Adam's window. "Lynx hatband," he noted, pointing to its greasy circlet. "Tracy found it in an antique store. It's got to be fifty years old at least."

"And she trained him on that? You sure he's not chasing mothballs?"

"He's found plenty of lynx in the Mission Mountains. They're doing a census up there and he's accounted for most of 'em, at least in Tracy's section. Distract him for a minute and I'll show you."

Adam sighed, grabbed a bag of potato chips and went to the hound. Stood glumly by while the dog inhaled one chip after another, then wiped his hands on his jeans as Gabe returned from the dark. "Now what?"

"Let's finish our supper."

They ate, talking when the mood hit them, but mostly in comfortable silence. The same way they'd ridden the range as kids, not so far from where they now sat. Adam said finally, "Had my own notion about how we could nail this creep. Most economical way of making a collar."

Gabe turned to prop his shoulders against his door. "How's that?"

"We do a sting. Instead of searching the mountains for the bad guy, we sucker him to us."

"I like it, but how?"

"You said, back in N'Orleans, that the one thing these cats haven't done is have kittens. Is it still that way?"

"So far, I'm afraid so. Oh, we've seen signs of court-ing behavior. According to their satellite signals, the males have been moving around for the last six weeks, searching for ladies. But with only forty-four lynx re-maining, they're spread so thin on the ground, and they only have a one-week window to find each other, while the females are fertile…"

"So nobody's scored yet?" Adam demanded dryly.

Gabe shook his head. "No. Not that we know of. We'll try to contact as many of them visually as we can this summer, especially any females whose signals go sta-tionary. *Maybe* a queen will den up with kittens, though if she does, she'll keep them well hidden. It'll be next winter before we know for sure. We'll snow-track them then. Look for juvenile footprints following a female's."

"But kittens, that's what the pro-lynx camp wants, right? It's the proof that your repopulation program is starting to work."

"Exactly, but—"

"So kittens are the *last* things the anti-lynx camp wants to see in Colorado. There's your bait."

"How are they bait when we haven't got any?"

"You already report on the DOW Web site your cats' latest doings. Their latest sightings." Even their pictures, when someone lucked into a telephoto shot. This was pure foolishness, in Adam's book, drawing attention to potential victims, but try to tell that to a pack of politicians and bureaucrats. He supposed the Division hoped that publicizing the lynx re-intro program would get the public behind it. And maybe that wasn't such a bad notion, considering the DOW was spending a million or more of the taxpayers' money.

"So…" He tapped the map northwest of Trueheart, Colorado. "You post on your Web site that one of your females has moved to this location, where I'll be waiting. That she's been spotted and she's knocked-up for sure. Set to drop a passel of kittens any day now."

"They only have three or four, usually."

"Fine. Four imaginary kittens. You plant them in my backyard, and I guarantee you, your perp will come hunting. If he's smart enough to buy his radio direction finder off the Internet, then he's bound to be checking your Web site for the latest news on his quarry. Heck, if you report every time one disappears, then he can read his own score sheet. Better believe he's tuning in."

Gabe rubbed his jaw. "It might work… I think it would work. Now all I have to do is persuade my boss to try it."

"Your problem, friend." Adam drummed his fingers on the wheel. "Meantime, you gonna show me ol' Watson's stuff?"

He lounged against the hood of his truck, while Gabe loosed the dog and commanded him to *'fetch the kitty!'* Nose to the ground, tail waving, the hound snuffled off into the night.

"Did you lay a drag trail?" Adam inquired. By the sound of his snorts, the dog was circling the parking area.

"No need, with his nose. There's enough of a breeze to carry an air scent. Once he gets downwind…"

"If he doesn't find his hat, you send him back to Montana. How's that for a deal?"

"You're on," Gabe agreed with a smirk.

They waited some more. Adam didn't mind, if it ended this nonsense. He could just picture the other hands' faces if he showed up with Watson in tow for the cattle drive. A dog with ten pounds of ear, and no cow sense? It would take him all summer long to live that one down. Cowboys loved to tease and a newcomer was fair game. *Come on, Watson. Lose the kitty.*

"You know any women over towards Trueheart?" he asked, to pass the time. The Monahan family ranch lay east of Durango, while Trueheart lay northwest, but on the odd chance…

Gabe cocked his head at him. "Lonesome already? Well, there's Kaley Cotter." It was Gabe who'd found Adam the Circle C line-camp job with Kaley's brother, three summers ago. "But you met her. That was the year she came back, wasn't it? And I hear she's married since then."

"To Tripp McGraw," Adam reminded him. He'd be riding for the McGraws this summer. "No, this is somebody else. Met her in passing, but didn't catch her name. Hair dark as…" Wishing he'd never spoken, Adam jerked a thumb at the starry sky. That dark.

That velvety, when finally he buried his face in it, but how did he know that already? He stirred with impatience, then forced himself back to stillness.

"Then there's Lara Tankersly, one of Ben Tankersly's daughters," Gabe continued. "I slow-danced with her once, at a shindig over in Cortez. Didn't sleep well for the next year. But she moved to San Antonio shortly thereafter, and she's a cornsilk blonde.

"Then, speaking of blondes, there's a café in Trueheart called Michelle's Place, and Michelle's—" Gabe broke off as Watson came blundering out of the dark, gripping the hat by its brim. "Well, *well,* what have we here? *Good* boy! Whatta guy, whatta nose! *Good* fella!" He thumped the hound on his side as he accepted the trophy, then straightened with a grin. "And who needs a woman when you've got this for company?"

CHAPTER FIVE

THE NEXT TIME Adam saw her was the last night of the drive.

Following a century-old tradition, the combined herd of all the Trueheart ranches arrived on the summer range at sundown. The cowboys held the cows overnight at Big Rock Meadow. Come morning, the best riders would show off their mounts' cutting skills. The cattle would be sorted by brand, then driven east or west across the foothills, to their own ranch's grazing allotments.

Low, laughing voices rumbled around the campfire, punctuated by the occasional satisfied belch. Tonight was the cowboys' final chance to savor Whitie and Willie's chuckwagon cooking. Grilled steaks and barbecued beans and cornbread tonight, then tomorrow—and for the rest of the summer—it would be bachelor fare cooked in their own solitary camps.

This was their last night to pull a prank, swap a yarn or tell a joke to an appreciative audience, before they rode their separate trails. Starting tomorrow, company would be scant and seldom, not that it bothered this crew.

Line-camp men were chosen for their solitary ways. Solid, self-sufficient men, they were amiable in company and even better apart. After five days of rubbing elbows with sixteen men, most of whom were strangers,

Adam had to admit he was ready for a spell of solitude himself.

"Dubois, this danged hound's 'bout to break my heart! Claims you ain't fed him since Christmas." Across the fire, Jon Kristopherson scowled in mock indignation. Watson stood behind him, with his chin resting on the rancher's shoulder. "He's droolin' down my collar again. Call him off."

"Don't you believe that beggar!" warned Willie. At seventy-five, he was the oldest hand on the drive. Too stiff to sit a saddle these days, he shared the driving of Suntop Ranch's pride and joy, a genuine mule-drawn chuck wagon that was older than he was. And he reigned over the cookfires alongside Whitie Whitelaw. "Worthless bum stole half a skilletful of biscuits this morning, and Whitie's been sneakin' him bacon all the livelong day."

Since Watson had turned out to be terrified of cows, he'd been consigned to ride on the wagon, where the old guys were spoiling him rotten. At this rate he'd be too fat to track a lynx hatband, much less a lynx.

"Watson, get your ass over here!" Adam patted the ground and the hound shuffled meekly around the circle to sit by his side, then heaved a long-suffering sigh. Adam was the only one who refused to be charmed by his "gimme" eyes. "Stay," Adam told him sternly, then glanced up....

And there she was, stepping into the glow of the fire on the far side of the gathering. Slender as a young aspen in her boots and jeans, dark hair gleaming loose on her shoulders.

"*Tess!* What are you doin' up here?" called one of the Jarretts, over a shouted chorus of similar questions and greetings. Faces brightened, bodies shifted to make room

for the newcomer. Adam sat up straighter. At the edge of
his vision, men were rebuckling loosened belts, tucking
in shirttails and wiping greasy mouths. Seventeen men
with a sexy woman suddenly dropped in their midst.

"Now, how could I stay away, knowing this was Last
Night and Willie would be serving his apple pie with vanilla ice cream?" She laughed and folded gracefully
down, to sit cross-legged between Rafe Montana, manager of Suntop and boss of the trail drive, and his stepson, Sean Kershaw. Firelight danced across her vivid
face as she cocked her ear to something Sean said.

She was all he'd remembered and more, Adam told
himself, as she glanced up and over her shoulder, then
reached for the plate Kent Harris had brought her. The
line of her throat lengthened with the movement—
glowed golden in the flames. Adam moistened dry lips
as he pictured himself laying a kiss *there* where her pulse
beat below her ear. Another in that shadowy hollow between her delicate collarbones…

She murmured her thanks, dipped a fork into Willie's
famous pie à la mode, then closed her eyes in ecstasy as
the fork touched her tongue. "Ohh!"

He must be imagining that little moan off her lips. No
way it could carry over the surrounding hubbub; still
Adam could hear it, clear as if she'd moaned against his
mouth.

She swallowed blissfully, opened her eyes, and across
the fire, their gazes met—zoomed together like two oncoming trains, blue light to widening green. Her plate fell
from her fingers—she let out a yelp and grabbed for it as
pie and ice cream slid into her lap. "Oh, darn! *Clumsy!*
Oh, Willie, *what* a stupid waste!" She brushed at herself,
looked helplessly around for a napkin.

Two men rushed off to find one. Napkins weren't a usual part of cowboy dinnerware.

Quicker-witted than his human counterparts, Watson rose, trundled purposefully around the circle, then insinuated himself under her elbow. Slurped greedily at her slender thigh.

Seventeen men watched in thunderstruck envy as the hound licked her clean—while Tess tipped back her head and laughed. "Why, *thank* you, sir. And who is this?" She scratched him between the shoulder blades and laughed again as his tail whacked her in the ribs, then bludgeoned Sean.

"*Watson,* leave her alone! *Come.*"

"Oh, no, he's wonderful!" she insisted, glancing up at Adam, then quickly back to the dog. "Can't he stay here? Clumsy as I am, I'll probably need him." She slid her hands under each of Watson's ears, then lifted them out to the sides. Held their tips. "My! Would you look at these—a three-foot wingspan! Can he fly?"

No, but they would. Together, and soon. As quickly as he could make it happen. Adam hadn't wanted a woman this much in… He couldn't think *when* he'd wanted a woman the way he wanted this one. Or why. She wasn't pretty like butterflies or flowers. Something much better than pretty, with four times the impact, that hit him like a bolt of summer lightning.

She glanced his way again, and her smile faded. She swung her head toward Joe Abbott, who'd brought her a fresh serving of pie, and it returned.

Whatever this is, you feel it, too, Adam told her silently. He turned to his neighbor, Anse Kirby, not quite the foreman at Suntop, but Montana's right-hand man. "Who is that?" No need to point. Kirby's eyes were fixed on her.

"Tess." Kirby was a man of few words and he saved them for those he knew well. Adam would have to stick around a few more years before he'd qualify.

Tess. It suited her. Started strong, ended soft. A good name for whispering in the dark. Adam swung the other way, toward Bob Wilcox, one of the JBJ crew. He didn't know the man well, but at least he was a talker.

"Heard tell she's stayin' up here for the summer," Wilcox muttered to the man on his far side. "Over at the Two Bear camp."

"Well, that oughta liven things up," observed the other hand. "She ain't grown up half-bad."

"They all did. Her daddy had an eye for the lookers, all right. Three outa three."

Two Bear. That was the peak to the west of Mount Sumner; it towered above the Suntop Range. So. Adam drew a satisfied breath. They were going to be neighbors? For the next three months? All right, then.

Something told him he could have cut her out of this herd of friends and admirers if tonight had been his one shot at winning her. But he preferred to take his time. Cool and easy was the best way when courting a woman. Trying to rush the process only made a man look anxious.

"Dubois." Someone touched his shoulder and Adam turned to find Rafe Montana standing behind him. "You're riding herd the ten-till-two shift. Best saddle up." The trail boss moved on around the circle, tapping other men.

Tomorrow, then, Adam promised himself as he rose. Or if not tomorrow, then very, very soon. He shot her a farewell look as he left the campfire.

If she noticed, Tess didn't return it.

"WHO'S THAT?" Tess asked old Whitie as the new guy strode off into the dark.

She'd known most of these men all her life. Half a dozen rode for her father's brand. The rest were friends and neighbors. She'd ridden roundups with them since she turned fourteen, when she'd first flouted her father's orders, running off to tag along on the spring drive. After that there'd been no holding her back. She'd kept right on defying Ben, riding with the hands fall and spring, till she went away to college.

But she'd never seen *him* before. Even at fourteen, she'd have noticed.

"The Cajun? That's Dubois. Riding line for McGraw."

Dubois, she spoke his name silently. If Dubois worked for Tripp McGraw, that would explain why he'd slept at Sumner cabin last week. He must have been moving in. The hairs stirred along her forearms and a warm ripple of awareness lapped up her spine. So… *We'll be neighbors.*

Trouble, that's what would come of this, she knew instinctively. Trouble and excitement.

"Not from around here," she noted casually. "Is he really a Cajun?" Or had the men simply dubbed him that, because of his French surname? Still, that would account for the trace of accent she remembered. And his teasing use of the endearment *cher.*

"He's a Lou'siana boy." Whitie's shrug said, *what more do you need?* He'd brought her a cup of hot chocolate, then stayed to gossip. "I bunked at Sumner cabin with him a few years back fer a while. He was workin' half-time for Kaley and half-time for Tripp, that summer 'fore they came together."

"But a Cajun cowboy?" she mused on a note of mild derision. "What did he learn to ride on? Alligators?"

"Beats me. He was a close-mouthed, smilin' son of a gun back then and he ain't improved much on that count. Seem to recall he said somethin' 'bout having kin over Durango way. Had his share of cow sense."

That was high praise, coming from Whitie. Tess changed the subject before the old man could mark her interest. "I see. So…where's Chang?" Whitie's constant companion was a doddering Pekinese with an evil eye and a worse disposition.

"In the wagon sulkin', if he ain't flopped on his back, chasin' dream rabbits. He's been mad enough to bite his-self ever since we let that there Watson hitch a ride."

The hound was lying with his warm spine propped against her knees. Tess scratched between his ears. "And Watson belongs to…to Dubois?" Funny how momentous that felt, speaking his name for the first time.

Something told her it wouldn't be the last.

NATWIG LAY half dozing on the couch. Any minute now he'd find the energy to get up and stir the fire, he was assuring himself for the third time, when the phone rang. "I'll get it!" He sat and scrubbed a hand across his face.

But Karen was already wheeling herself toward the kitchen. "Don't be silly. It'll be for me." Her big orange tomcat leapt down from her lap and stalked off, tail lashing at this disturbance. The little calico that was draped across her footrest stayed put, staring fascinated at the carpet rolling past its whiskers.

Eight months ago, his lively wife would have grabbed the phone by its second ring. Natwig gritted his teeth as it rang a fifth time, a sixth, while she maneuvered her wheelchair around the center cooking island he'd built her only last year. *Ought to take that out of there, so she can move easier,* he told himself as she snatched up the phone.

Karen had pulled a fit the time he'd suggested it. She was going to walk again—would be riding again by next year—she kept on telling him. *Your lips to God's ear, sweetheart.* But Natwig was starting to doubt it.

"Hello?" she cried happily. She'd left a message on her sister's answering machine just before supper. "Hello? Hel-lo-o-o!" She stared at the receiver with a puzzled frown. "Hung up, whoever it was."

"One of those damned recorded salescalls, most likely."

"But there was somebody there. I heard a rustle."

"Wrong number, then. How about a bowl of ice cream?"

While she tried her sister again and again reached her machine, Natwig dished out two helpings of vanilla. That finished the carton. He scraped up a final spoonful. "This one's got your name on it." He teased the spoon across her smile, then eased it onto her tongue.

As she savored it, her wide blue eyes looked into his. She swallowed, then made a little sound as she licked her lips—his stomach muscles jerked tight. He straightened hastily, turned to drop the spoon in the sink. It jangled against a pot he'd yet to wash.

"Honey…" She broke the charged silence. "Dr. Murray says it's—"

"Yeah, I know he did, but…" But Natwig had hurt her already, allowing her to ride that green-broke colt. Didn't matter that she'd begged him to let her. What kind of fool took a chance with the thing—the person—that mattered most in all his life?

And if he hurt her again, he'd never, ever forgive himself. She seemed so tiny and fragile, trapped in that hateful chair. To satisfy himself at a risk to her? No way. It was better to wait.

But wait for how long? Forever? howled a voice like a lost coyote in the back of his mind. He swallowed around a lump of rock in his throat, then said gruffly, without turning, "want some peaches on top of yours?"

Her answer was a long time in coming. "No, thanks."

"Well, I do." He rummaged in the cabinet, found a can, focused himself on opening it. "How about tuning in the news?"

"I could, sure, but Joe—?"

The phone rang and he snatched it up with relief. "Hello?"

"Ah, you are there. Good."

Larson, calling him at home. Rage washed over him in a boiling wave. *Get out of my house!* They met once a month to conduct their business. That was the only claim Larson had on him, and that was bad enough.

Alarm swirled in anger's wake. *Something's wrong, him calling me here where he never has before!* But whatever it was, Natwig couldn't deal with it now, not with Karen sitting there with her feelings hurt and her ears pricked. "Can't this wait?"

"Something urgent's come up. If you can't speak freely from there, then go where you can and call me back. My usual cell phone number."

"But—"

"I'll be waiting for your call." He hung up.

Natwig stood, his hand clenched on the buzzing receiver. *Bastard! Think you own me, just because you pay me?*

"Who was it?" Karen demanded behind him. "Joe?"

He blew out a breath and his shoulders sagged. Till he paid off their debts to the hospital, laid up some cash against the rehab bills that kept on coming, Larson as good as owned him. There was no other way out but sell the ranch. And if he lost his land, lost his pack animals, then how was he to earn a living?

"That was…" Lying to Karen didn't come naturally to him, but he was learning. He'd had more practice in the past six months than he'd had in the first twenty years of their marriage. "That was Cody, over at some bar in Cortez. Says he came out to his truck and he's got a flat and damned if his spare isn't flat, too. Wants me to come bail him out."

"He can't call his wife?"

"Suzie's not answering her phone," he mumbled. "Anyway, I was feeling restless. Drive'll do me good."

Karen's third blasted cat, the tabby, thumped up onto the counter beside him. He grabbed the animal with a snarl and deposited it on his wife's lap. "Damned *cat!* Tell a dog *once* not to do something and it'll learn, but a cat?"

Beast and woman stared back at him in wide-eyed, wounded astonishment. Then Karen turned her head aside and wheeled toward the living room. "Come on, Posy, let's go watch the news."

He took a minute to cool down, then followed, to set the bowl of ice cream and a spoon on the coffee table at her elbow. Stood, shifting from foot to foot, yearning to touch her. "I won't be gone long."

Her hands smoothed the cat's fur, her eyes stayed fixed on a beer commercial, where a pack of drunken college kids cavorted on an endless, sunny beach. Not a care in *their* world. "Take all the time you please."

HE MET Larson halfway to Durango, at a roadside rest stop. "What's your problem?" he growled, as he fitted himself into the Porsche's low seat.

"*Our* problem." Larson corrected him with a chilly smile. "It shouldn't be a problem, if you move fast. We've learned that a female lynx has finally bred and she's about to give birth. One of the DOW tracking planes spotted her. Four kittens, they're estimating. That works out to roughly three hundred thousand apiece they've spent to achieve that. The taxpayers are out of their minds to put up with this nonsense!"

Natwig nodded grim agreement, though he seemed to recall that the lynx restoration program was financed by a voluntary check-off on the state income tax. Still, that kind of money. He felt a tickle of fear, like a cold breeze on his cheek. No way the damned bureaucrats at the DOW could afford to let all their cats vanish. Sooner or later, somebody would figure out that this wasn't Mother Nature winnowing the weak. Once they did, somebody was bound to come after him.

Let him come. He'd almost welcome a flesh-and-blood enemy for a change. Better somebody he could face— somebody he could pound into the ground—than this formless fear and frustration that came creeping every night to crouch on his pillow.

"—be the Division's media darlings, if we don't watch out," Larson was saying. "Before that happens, before somebody gets photos of the kittens and posts them on the DOW Web site, they need to disappear. Dead. Gone. Eaten by a bear or a coyote or a porcupine or whatever they care to imagine. But out of sight, out of the public's mind— ASAP."

Larson's chubby fingers drummed on the steering

wheel as he glared through the windshield. "We're *just* starting to see the first complaints in the papers and on talk shows that this program is a waste of time and taxpayers' money. Momentum is building. But let the bleeding hearts and the tree huggers have a litter of fuzzy, adorable kittens to rally around and…" He shook the awful image out of his head and briskly turned. "So, get on this immediately."

"I will, but—" Natwig paused. He had a client scheduled, the day after tomorrow. A long-time client, who'd booked a week of fly-fishing and wildflower photography with him every summer for ten years now. No way would he let the man down. An outfitter's reputation was built on dependability, as well as on delivering whatever the client wanted, from a trophy buck to a rare bird sighting.

But try to tell that to Larson, who saw him only as a tool for his own purposes.

"But what? This is crucial. Time is of the essence here."

"Well, it may take a while, running the queen down. If she has a litter, she won't be straying far from her den. And she won't let the kittens out to play for weeks, not till their eyes open and she thinks they're old enough."

"She's not a—a soccer mom, she's a dumb animal!"

Dumb? I'd like to see you up there, with nothing but your claws and teeth and wits to feed your family. You and yours would starve in a week! Natwig dwelt on that comforting image for a minute, then said, "Once she's down in her hole, my equipment won't pick her up. It's line of sight, remember? So if she isn't moving around much, it'll take longer. I may have to circle in till I cross her prints, then track her to her den."

"Whatever it takes. Just do it. My…friends have

authorized a bonus. An extra five thousand per kitten, on top of your usual ten."

Natwig gulped, did the math. Five times ten, plus four times five—seventy thousand dollars, all in one den? That would put him past the halfway mark on his debt. No way could he take this assignment and shove it, much as he'd love to.

"But there's one stipulation to that bonus." Larson gave him an odd look—a twitch of guilty pleasure, instantly buried. "Since the kittens won't be wearing a DOW collar, my clients will need some other sort of proof that you took them."

No way. Natwig let his face relax, the way he did at poker. Not a chance. That would go against everything he was doing. "Like a scalp, you mean?"

Larson pursed his lips. "Or a tail, if that's easier."

What would be easy would be to grab this creep by the back of his greasy neck, then slam his head against his fancy steering wheel—half a dozen times. But how to say "no," without giving his game away? "That would spoil the pelt," Natwig said at last. It wouldn't, but he could trust this city slicker not to know that.

Larson gave a little crow of delight. "With all we're paying you, you're selling their furs on the side?" Greed, now that was something he could understand.

"Why waste a good pelt? I'm tanning 'em and keeping 'em, for now. I'll sell them next year, once the fuss dies down," Natwig added, to head off any objections. "So suppose I take a picture of the kittens when I catch them. As proof."

"You could get a photo at the nearest zoo," Larson noted dryly.

"A photo taken in the wild, not in a cage. Brought to

you at the same time as their mother's collar, with its Division of Wildlife number? It'd be more trouble to fake that, than to bring you the real thing. But if you don't trust me…" Natwig reached for his door handle.

"No, no, I'm sure that will do," Larson said hastily. He drew a folded paper from the pocket of his suit. "Here's her latest coordinates. It's Collar AK00F6."

"That Alaskan hussy? Wasn't she hunting over near Silverton?" Natwig had spent a week on snowshoes, looking for her in February. He'd crossed her tracks a dozen times, without once sighting the sly boots. Finally he'd concluded that she was holed up in one of the mines. The mountains up there were riddled with old shafts, and it would have taken half a lifetime to find her. So he'd gone on to easier prey.

"Yes, but she's moved. You told me they do that."

"Yeah." But why would she abandon a perfect territory for nesting? He shrugged. Maybe she'd hunted it thin this winter and so had to move on. Whatever. "Where is this location?"

"Practically your own backyard. She's in the peaks north of Trueheart."

CHAPTER SIX

A LONG-FORGOTTEN Suntop cowboy had built the three-sided cedar shower stall in the back of Tess's cabin. For some reason—lack of lumber, a fondness for sunshine or sheer laziness, he'd omitted the southern wall.

But then, why not? Modesty hadn't been an issue back then. In what her father fondly referred to as the good old days, the summer range had been an exclusive, unapologetically male preserve, without a feminine eye to be offended in forty miles. Womenfolk were safely confined to the valleys, where half a century before vacuum cleaners, store-baked bread or effective contraception, they had plenty to keep them occupied. A dusty cowpoke could enjoy an outdoor shower without a fear in the world that some gallivanting female would catch him in the buff.

In honor of the changing times—the greatly improved times, in her view—Tess had hung half a ragged sheet across the southern side of the stall. In another break with tradition, she didn't use the original tin bucket with the holes drilled in its rusty bottom, which was suspended in a bracket above her head. Instead she'd brought along a backpacker's showerbag. It held precisely two gallons of water which she heated on her wood-burning stove. As long as she rationed it, that was just enough for her rinse-off. To stretch it further, she always warmed an extra pot of water for her initial drenching.

She lifted the pot, closed her eyes, and poured half its steaming contents over her head and shoulders. *"Ahh-hh!"* Luxurious heat was followed immediately by the sensation of icy fingers stroking her skin—a breeze was wafting down from the peaks this morning. As it sifted through the gaps between the planks, she could smell pine and old snow and wet cedar. Goose bumps rose on her dripping breasts and thighs. Tess poured the rest, then grabbed her bar of soap and hastily lathered.

She had more water heating on her stove. As soon as she'd bathed, she'd brew a fresh cup of coffee, eat a couple of biscuits with honey and butter, then sit down at her desk.

This past week, life had settled into a lovely routine. Each morning she woke at dawn to the cry of the magpies in the pines outside her cabin. She'd gulp a coffee, then ride out to leave Zelda the chicken she'd thawed overnight.

Tess hadn't seen the lynx since freeing her. But every morning when she blew a "your breakfast is served" blast on the supersonic dog whistle that Liza had given her, then walked to the burrow beneath the fallen tree, she'd find that yesterday's offering had vanished. And twice she'd spotted fresh lynx tracks at the pool below Zelda's den. So she wasn't wasting her chickens or her time.

On returning to her cabin, Tess would shower, eat breakfast, then settle in to her dissertation. She'd work till late afternoon, when she'd treat herself to a ride or a hike, then she'd come back to study or write some more. Evenings she'd chop wood for the stove, cook, eat her supper. She'd write a letter or read till the falling temperature drove her to her bunk, where she'd fall instantly asleep—to start the cycle all over again.

A pleasant routine, and with so little to distract her, her dissertation was progressing nicely. All that she lacked in her world was the sound of another human voice. Most days, Tess didn't miss it. Days when she did, like today, she supplied it herself. "I could always go borrow a cup of sugar," she said aloud as she shampooed her hair. No need to specify from whom. Dubois had been much on her mind since he'd startled her into dropping her pie three nights ago at Big Rock Meadow.

Truth to tell, he'd been on her mind before that, though she'd never expected to meet the man again. But since their latest encounter, knowing that he lived only a half hour's ride to her east… "First thing I'd ask you, is what *is* your name? Bob, Bill or Paul? Please tell me it isn't Alvin or Bubba!" She'd spent more time pondering the possibilities, these past few days, than she cared to admit.

They'd never gotten a chance to introduce themselves at the cookout. She'd fallen asleep before he returned from herd duty. Then with the dawn, a line of thunderstorms had rolled across the peaks. All hands had sprung from their bedrolls to hold the spooky cattle, which seemed intent on stampeding straight back to the valley.

Once the squalls had passed and the cows had settled, the cutting had started. Dubois had stayed busy on the far side of the swirling mass, collecting the McGraw stock. The last Tess had seen of him, he'd been driving them eastward to their own grazing allotment. So she'd ridden home to Two Bear with a feeling of unfinished business. At the very least, she ought to know her neighbor's name.

"Could always go fish over that way," she reminded herself, sluicing the last suds off her face. "Trout for supper would be a nice change from—*Eee-yieep!*" she yelped, as something rough and supple swiped the underside of her knee. A tongue? *"Whuh?!"* She spun, bumped fur—something big, red, most definitely alive was in the stall's dimness with her! She flailed out past the curtain, then whirled to look back.

"Oh, *geez! Whew!*" Fist to her hammering heart, she glared at the dog. Watson, sitting down on the wet cedar grate. He gazed up at her with sheepish eyes and thumping tail. Dubois's dog, which meant—!

Tess snatched at the curtain and spun, wrapping its damp length around her. She rotated once more and, dream of the devil, there he stood! Lounging against the corner of her cabin. Arms crossed, a wide grin on his sun-darkened face.

"Sorry 'bout that," he drawled, sounding not at all repentant.

How long had he been standing there, and just how much skin had he seen?

Not that she'd improved her image much, tangling herself in a wet and threadbare sheet. It spiraled down across one shoulder and her breasts, bared her navel, then wound around her hips. Below that, from thigh to toe, she was nothing but drenched skin and mortified goose bumps. Tess glanced down at herself…back up at him—his grin widened as she turned scarlet. Worst of all, one end of her covering was tacked to the plank above her head. No retreat was possible while he stood there smirking.

"If Watson had told me we'd be walking in on a toga party, I'd have dressed for the occasion," he assured her now. "I always did like Mardi Gras."

"I thought the big dope was a—"

"Bear? You've got bears on the brain, Tess." He pushed off from the log wall and strode lazily toward her, his cobalt gaze locked on hers. "Lucky for Watson you don't shower with a rifle."

So…he'd learned her name. One more point to him, as if his being dressed to her naked wasn't advantage enough! Could he see her nipples standing up through this washed-out sheet? The way his eyes darkened as he approached, she knew he could.

Her clothes and her towel were folded neatly on an old chopping block tree stump, which stood four feet to her left. For all the good that did her, they might have been in Trueheart. If Dubois were any kind of gentleman, he'd tactfully withdraw. Offer to wait inside her cabin.

He picked up her towel. "Seems like I always catch you bathing," he mused on a note of husky laughter.

"Lucky me." Her hands clenched on the sheet as he stopped toe-to-toe with her, close enough that she had to tip her chin to meet his dancing eyes. So close, she could feel his body heat. Her skin *ached* with his nearness, with alarm and aliveness.

"Ah, no. Believe me, the pleasure's all mine." He rubbed a corner of the towel gently along her cheek—across her lips as she parted them to protest. "But it's a cold day for prancing around in nothing but a bedsheet and a smile."

You see me smiling, you big—? You… Ohh, you… A little purring sound was trapped below her trembling diaphragm. No way would she release it. The towel's rough texture scratched seductively at her nerve endings. She wanted to follow its caress the way a cat arches to meet a friendly hand.

With tantalizing deliberation, he drew the towel from

her opposite temple to her chin… Stroked it slowly down the side of her throat…to her shoulder…

She ought to slug him. Any other man in the world, she would have. And if he dared to take that towel an *inch* past her collarbone… She widened her eyes in warning.

He laughed at her silently—and brought the towel *up* the nape of her neck, rubbed it through her hair.

"You're Dubois," she told him haughtily as he dried her head. If he could pretend this was nothing but a neighborly gesture, then so could she. "But what's the first name? Fred? Leopold?"

"Adam."

Adam, it suited him. First man. Not *her* first, of course. *But my last?* Ridiculous thought. She didn't think she even liked him! *So* damned sure of himself…

With a lingering fingertip, he traced the wary tilt of her eyebrow. Smoothed a lock of hair off her temple and hooked it behind her ear. "Adam Dubois at your service." His eyes dropped to her lips.

No *way* would she let him kiss her. No way. Not yet. *I don't even know you!*

Somehow, that didn't seem to matter. Something about him…something about her…something about the two of them together…

Who knows where it might have ended, if Watson hadn't broken the spell Adam was weaving. The dog bumped up against her and sat. Leaning heavily against her thighs, he gazed adoringly upwards. Gave a gruff, insistent "woof!"

"Beat it!" Adam growled.

Tess blinked, laughed and retreated a step. Grabbed her towel from his hands. "Why don't you guys go brew us up some coffee? Water should be boiling by now." *My God, what was I thinking?*

SO CLOSE! Still, there was nothing for it but to accept her dismissal with good grace. Once inside her cabin, Adam warned the dog, "you better back off, buddy. I saw her first."

And she almost let me kiss her. He'd seen a 'horse whisperer' once walk up to a wild mustang. Lay his hands on the shuddering mare, then lead her around by a hand cupped beneath her jaw. Magic, Adam had thought that day.

But here was magic, too. As if, below the level of speech, their bodies were talking—had talked from the very start. Pheromones? Kismet? Something strange going on here.

Not that he was about to argue. *Let it come, let it come.* All this past year, he'd been waiting and never knowing it. No wonder he'd come shining through that hailstorm of bullets. He'd been saved for this.

His fingers were shaky as he lifted mugs from the shelf nailed to a side wall, then her can. He boiled a pot of cowboy coffee, found a bowl of rinsed eggshells ready on the rough plank counter. Crushing one, he dropped it into the pot, and the grounds settled.

Color was all around him. Tess's world, glowing richly in the dimness of the one-room cabin. The bold scarlet-and-navy stripes of a Mexican blanket smoothed across her single bunk. The pink and yellow of flowers—a bouquet in a jam jar she'd set on the table at the far side of the room. Another bunch in hues of lilac and lavender graced a windowsill.

Next to a moss-green slicker, her cream-colored hat hung on a wall peg. As soon as he'd filled their mugs, he'd go and sniff it. Not as good as plunging his nose into her cloud of hair to learn her fragrance, but till the moment she let him do that…

As he poured out the coffee, Tess pushed through the screen door. "Find what you need?" She walked over to a battered pine bureau beside her bunk. Moved bright pebbles and a bluebird feather, then a pinecone aside.

"Yep." *You,* he told her silently as she picked up a comb and ran it through her dark hair. With her back turned, Adam could look his fill, and he did. She was built slim but not boyish, with the long legs of a colt. He ached to encircle her waist with his hands, draw those trim hips back against him. Nuzzle the side of her throat, then kiss her till she sighed and turned in his arms. And how would he sleep tonight, after glimpsing her navel?

Combing out her locks, Tess turned to face him, and it was as if he'd shouted those thoughts aloud. She'd heard every one. "So…" She sounded a little breathless, as if he'd kissed her in deed, as well as thought. "How are things over at Sumner?"

"Cows are settling in. First day or so, they were homesick. Wanted to drift down-mountain. But now…" Adam shrugged. "It's a fine year for grass."

"Mmm. We had plenty of snow." She wandered over to the crude kitchen counter, sugared one of the coffees, took it and retreated to where Watson had flopped down on a faded rag rug. She crouched beside him and his tail thumped a cloud of dust from its fraying tufts. "There's powdered milk, if you need some." Lifting one silky ear between her scissored fingers, she drew it out, then let it tumble and fall.

"I take it black, thanks." *And if you want to stroke somebody, then how about me?*

Eyes on the dog, she sipped her coffee, then asked, "Were you just passing by, or is there something I can help you with?"

Oh, sweetheart! Still, Adam knew what she meant. The Code of the West was that when help was called for it was given. Because sooner or later, everyone needed a helping hand. "Nope. I'm just playing mailman. Brought you a letter."

Mail for all hands on the summer range was collected at Suntop. It was delivered once a week, alternately to the east end of the chain of line camps, then the west. When it was driven in to the Sumner trailhead, Adam would pick it up, bring it on to Two Bear camp.

From there Tess would pass it on to her nearest neighbor on the west, who'd carry it on to the next camp and so on, down the line. Besides the incoming mail, outgoing letters to friends and loved ones also would be passed westward this week. At the end of the line, they'd be collected by next week's deliveryman. He'd carry them down to Trueheart and mail them, while the letters he'd dropped off flowed east across the summer range.

It was a system that had worked smoothly for most of a century. Some day soon, cell phones might render it obsolete, but not quite yet. Not while the cowboys around Trueheart called cell phones "electronic dog leashes." They didn't volunteer for this hermit life to be at civilization's beck and call. And thankfully, so far their bosses shared that spirit of cranky independence. Adam had heard that, at Suntop, where old Ben Tankersly fiercely defended his forefathers' ways, a cowhand with a cell phone was a cowhand fired.

He thumbed through the packet of letters he'd brought in from his saddlebag, arranged hers on top. "Ms. Tess Tankersly," he announced, reading from the envelope. He offered the stack with a flourish.

Her beautiful mouth tightened. She looked down at the floor, then back up again. "Thanks."

What had displeased her? he wondered as Tess accepted the bundle. Not her letter itself, since she'd yet to glance at it.

When he'd read her name aloud—her last name. Ah, so that was it! *Right. Now I know you're a millionaire's daughter,* he agreed with her silently. Last name of Tankersly, living in a Suntop cabin? And that explained why Tess had sat with the men from Suntop, then bedded down in their circle, over at Big Rock Meadow. She had to be one of Ben Tankersly's three fabled daughters, lookers all.

Tankersly. Across southwestern Colorado, where wealth was measured in acres and cows and water rights, that name was spoken with envy and grudging respect. There were countries smaller than Tankersly's Suntop Ranch. Tess might as well be a princess, and those cowboys her father's knights.

But so what? he wanted to ask her. It didn't matter. Would have, if he'd had marriage in mind. A man would have to be crazy to marry a woman whose monthly allowance must be more than he'd earn in a year.

Crazy or a fortune hunter.

Since Adam wasn't shopping for a wife, it wasn't an issue. Not for him, anyway.

But for Tess? If she thought he was after her fortune, after anything beyond her sexy self, he'd have to convince her otherwise.

While he stood considering the problem, Tess scanned the envelope he'd given her. Her brows flew together. The return address on that letter had been a woman's, Liza Waltz, Adam had noted. Trouble of some sort?

To give Tess privacy should she care to read it right away, he wandered over to the table she'd fashioned from two planks laid on sawhorses beneath a side window. Piles of papers were neatly stacked. A row of books stood between the rocks which served as bookends. Pens and colored markers were laid out ready to use, and she'd tacked a line of photographs to the window frame. Adam laughed aloud. "Beavers!"

Photos of beavers chewing on the twigs they held in their clever paws. Beavers in a pond, one towing a leafy branch through the water. A beaver kit riding on its swimming mother's back. "You weren't kidding me!" He would have sworn Tess had been lying that first time he met her. "You're really researching beavers?"

"This past year, I've done nothing but live, breathe and sleep beavers." Coming to stand beside him, she smiled wistfully down at the photos. "Seems kind of strange, not having the little guys around anymore. I really miss them. Hanging around with that crew, I felt like Snow White with the Seven Dwarfs."

Beguiled by the emotions playing across her face, he listened while she told him about her critters. For most of the past year, she'd lived by a creek in southern Utah, collecting data, studying beavers in their native habitat, their relations to each other and their environment. "This is Puddleglum, the alpha male, and that's SmackerJack, an up-and-comer." She touched two photos, then went on to describe the rest of her furry tribe, proud as a maiden aunt showing snapshots of nieces and nephews.

"But why beavers?" he prompted, when she seemed inclined to stop.

"Well, why *not* beavers? I had to choose a subject for my dissertation and—" Her voice dropped half an octave as it took on a sultry Mae West lilt. "—they're the only animals that make me laugh."

Whoa! It was all Adam could do not to grab her then and there—demand she say that again, only this time with her lips pressed to his ear. "So…you're in this for laughs." Everybody needed a hobby of some sort, he supposed.

From a clown, she turned serious on him. "For a Ph.D. You have to have an advanced degree these days if you want to conduct any sort of interesting field work in environmental biology. And I do want."

Why would a woman set to inherit millions need to bother with college at all?

"Besides which, beavers are *vital* in the scheme of things," Tess declared earnestly. "There's no other creature on Earth, apart from humans, that shapes the land— the entire ecosystem—the way beavers do. They create lakes, they make meadows, they turn infertile land back to fertile. They build habitats that nourish fish and birds and reptiles. And when you look at the tamarisk problem in terms of beavers—"

"We have a tamarisk problem?" he teased.

She blinked. Paused midsentence. Her brows knit slowly together.

Uh-oh. What did I say?

"I thought you—"

They both started violently as a sound like a ship's horn boomed through the wall.

Ahhh-WOOO!

"Holy—!" Adam glanced around. The blasted hound, of course, but who was murdering him, and where? The screen door stood ajar, no dog in sight. Laughing helplessly, Tess darted past him. He followed her out the door and around the corner of the cabin.

Ahhh-Wooo-ooo-ooo!

A lean-to was built against the backside of the cabin. Within this shed, Watson stood, facing a large, rusty metal box. Some sort of ancient top-loading freezer, it looked like.

"Ahhh-Wooo!" He wagged his tail furiously, glanced up at Adam for support, then turned his gaze back on the freezer. His ribcage expanded in preparation for another Hound of the Baskervilles howl.

Cripes, let him keep on like that, he'd blow the box through the back wall! "Watson, shut up! *Come!*" Adam caught the hound by his collar and dragged him out into the light. "Give us a break, what's got into you? *Sit!* Shut up. Talk about the Last Trump!"

"But thank you all the same," crooned Tess, crouching by the crestfallen hound to rub his ears. "What did you find, boy, hmm? A rat? *Big* rat? *Bad* rat? *What* a good dog!" She laughed as Watson thrust his forehead against her breasts—leaned against her, yodeling and grumbling his woes. *"What* a good boy!"

"You're praising him for bursting our eardrums?"

"Well, clearly he thinks he's done the right thing. Did you train him to chase rats?"

"I didn't train him. He belongs to…a friend of a friend. We're just stuck with each other for the summer. Long story." Adam frowned at the metal box. Gabe had said nothing about Watson being trained to hunt rats. "You've got a rodent problem way up here?" Her cabin was spotless; all her crackers and flour packed securely in glass jars, he'd noticed. "What's in the box, anyway?"

"Oh…" Tess drew a knuckle along her upper lip,

darted a glance at him, then away. She caught the dog's collar as he started back into the shed.

Adam cocked his head. Poker players called it a "tell," a giveaway gesture like that. Next thing she said would be a lie.

Except that the last time he'd assumed Tess was lying—about the beavers—that had been the truth. Still. "Maybe there's a rat in the box?" he prompted when she didn't speak. *I'm starting to smell one.*

"Of course not." Her chuckle was as unconvincing as her shrug. "It's just an old kerosene-powered freezer. I keep extra supplies in there—hotdogs, ice cream and such. A couple of…frozen chickens."

Too many details volunteered for a simple question. "Maybe we should take a look, in case a rat's gnawed his way in from the back," Adam suggested.

"Oh, no! You'd—" She'd grabbed his arm as he started forward. When he paused, she fisted her hands and let them drop. "It doesn't work very well. I'm afraid it's failing fast. So I don't let the cold out, if I can help it. Only open it when I absolutely have to. But if Watson's scouting for a handout, I've got biscuits inside. You hungry, big guy, is that what all this fuss is about?"

The dog trotted away happily beside her. Frowning in thought, Adam followed. Maybe Tess did have a rat problem, and she was simply embarrassed? He'd dated a woman once who'd have sooner attended Sunday School in the nude than admit there were palmetto bugs in her kitchen, even though everyone knew the giant roaches were the state bird of Louisiana.

Well, whatever Tess's mystery was, for the moment their rhythm was wrecked. She didn't invite him back inside. She brought a biscuit out to Watson, then stood with arms crossed, her back braced against the screen door.

Two gulps and the treat vanished down the bottomless canine gullet. Tess glanced at the sky. "Past noon! Wow, I'm way behind schedule. I'm afraid I've got to get to work, so…if you gentlemen would excuse me?"

"Sure," Adam said easily. "Just tell us what night this week you're going to let us cook you supper, and we'll be on our way."

"I…" Again her knuckle brushed her upper lip.

Without thinking, he reached out and caught her wrist. Smoothed his thumb across her racing pulse. "Don't tell me you wouldn't like a home-cooked dinner, macaroni and cheese? I wouldn't believe you." *Not while you're doing that. You want to visit me as much as I want a visit.* Whatever else was going on here, this was unmistakably a two-way street.

Tess looked him straight in the eye as she tugged her hand free. "My schedule's a little crowded this week. Why don't we…leave it for now?"

Push her any harder and she'd just back away. "Ookay. But if you get tired of talking to yourself, feel free to drop on by, any old time. I always cook plenty." *And Tess? Don't kid yourself. It's gonna happen. Pack your pj's when you come.*

As he rode away, Watson loping dutifully at the horse's heels, Adam glanced over his shoulder. Tess remained where he'd left her, slouched against her door. But looking after him, she'd laced her fingers up through her hair. She looked worried, wary, drop-dead adorable.

On second thought, he told her as he lifted a hand and rode on, *you can leave your pajamas at home.*

CHAPTER SEVEN

TROUBLE, trouble, trouble, Tess reminded herself, peering after him. But—darn—why did Trouble have to look so good on a horse? And the back view was as stirring as his front. She could have used Adam's shoulders for bookshelves, half a Britannica set on either side. From there, his torso tapered to a taut and springy waist, then his buns, buns that moved with a horseman's rocking grace with every stride of his mount....

A reciprocal rhythm tugged at her own hips.

"Forget it, Tess, he's bad news." If she put her mind to it, she could come up with a dozen reasons why Adam Dubois wouldn't do for a lover.

But her mind didn't come into this. This was pure, unadulterated lust. Was this how a female lynx felt in springtime, watching an alpha male come over the hill? Just delighted to be found. *"Rrrrowrrr,"* she growled softly after him, as he vanished into the trees.

Tess sighed, shook herself, glanced briskly around. "Speaking of lynx..." She walked back to the shed and cocked her head at the freezer. What had triggered Watson's tizzy?

"He was howling at all my chickens?" She lifted the lid of the freezer, which worked just fine, thank you, and stared down at some four dozen plastic-wrapped birds.

Frozen, they shouldn't have had much odor, though who knew what a bloodhound could smell? She checked the gaskets all around the lid, but they seemed intact.

Tess shut the box and stood, drumming her fingers absently on the metal. Adam had sensed something was fishy when she wouldn't let him investigate. She had never been much of a liar. But how do you explain forty-eight oven-stuffer/roasters? "Gee, Adam, I have this serious chicken addiction. Attend Chicken Anonymous meetings, whenever I can." Yeah, right. Better not to even try.

Next time, she'd have to make sure Watson stayed out of here.

"Who says there'll *be* a next time?" she muttered rebelliously.

Yeah, right to that, too. Tess turned to go, then paused, glancing back with narrowed eyes. "Wa-iii-t a minute." Stepping to one side of the freezer, she pulled out the object she'd stowed between it and the wall.

Zelda's collapsible cage, now folded flat.

ONCE SHE'D MOVED the lynx cage to the roof of the shower house—let Watson find it up there!—Tess concluded that her routine was shot for the day. Might as well deliver the mail while the weather held. Sean Kershaw's camp lay a pleasant half an hour's ride to the west.

With that decision, she remembered her own letter. Liza, now what could she want? "Worrying already," Tess guessed with a smile.

She had written the vet, herself, only last evening. She would take that message to Sean's camp, to be passed on its way. In it, Tess had described Zelda's first week in the wild.

The good news is that Zelda stayed where I freed her, and she's eating her chickens. The bad news is, that I haven't found any sign of a kill yet.

She had spotted no rabbit or squirrel bones near the lynx's den. Still, it was early days for that yet. Give her time.

Tess buttered two biscuits and stood eating them at the counter while she tore open Liza's letter. She scanned its first line—and nearly choked.

Do you have room up there for another lynx?

THE FOLLOWING MORNING, Tess took a thawed chicken from her saddlebag. Leaving Cannonball ground-hitched so he could graze, she walked a few yards into the forest, then put the silent whistle to her lips. She blew three long blasts, three shorts, three longs again—Zelda's breakfast signal—then glanced behind.

The gelding had lifted his head to gaze after her. Wearing a comical expression of interest, he'd pricked his ears till their tips nearly touched.

Tess laughed softly. "I'm glad *you* know it works." For all she could hear, the device might have been broken, but clearly it wasn't.

It had been Liza's idea to train Zelda to a supersonic dog whistle. She'd reasoned that if the lynx ever strayed too far from her feeding station, she might be lured back with a sound that meant "food."

Also, come autumn, if the lynx hadn't learned to hunt on her own, it might be easier to call her to their live-trap with a whistle. Tess blew the signal again, then walked on into the woods.

As usual when she reached the fallen tree, there was

no sign of the lynx. She set the chicken in its customary place before the den, then wiped her hands on some moss. "Breakfast, sweetheart. Are you in there?"

Beyond the burrow's entrance, she could see no movement. "Got some great news, Zelda. You're fixin' to have a neighbor."

Neighbor being a relative thing, in surly lynx terms. Tess hoped to find a suitable den for the newcomer within five miles of this spot. With any luck that arrangement would prove acceptable to both reclusive cats, because—and only because—they were of opposite sexes. In her earlier research Tess had learned that the far-ranging males often overlapped the smaller territories of several females, with no apparent complaints on anyone's part.

A five-mile interspace should give them both ample breathing room, with plenty of game in between. Proximity would also simplify Tess's life, which would be doubly busy with two lynx, instead of one, to feed. Ah, well, how could she object? Her mission was now twice as important.

"I don't think you'll mind, once you see him," she told the log. "I understand he's a stud."

Or so Liza had described him in her letter. At least, a potential stud, once he'd regained his coat and his health.

He'd been seized last week by the Albuquerque narcotics squad in a drug bust that had netted a crack dealer, several pounds of product, and the dealer's own private menagerie. Considering his choice of pets, the guy must have had a serious self-image problem. His macho-man collection had included two pythons, an alligator snapping turtle, three pit bulls, several fighting cocks, a sickly tiger and Geronimo, the male lynx.

Given Liza's reputation as the big cat specialist for all

New Mexico, inevitably the police had dumped the orphaned felines on her doorstep.

"Geronimo's been chained to a stake out at the miserable man's miserable ranch for God knows how long," Liza had reported wrathfully. Not a scrap of shade or shelter for a cat built for northern climes? "Lucky for the jerk—and for me—that the police have him locked up, or I swear I'd scratch his eyes out!"

Meantime, Liza's home kennel was her only pen large enough for an ailing tiger, and he needed all the attention the vet could spare. "I hate to ask this, but could you take Geronimo? I really think he might make it up there.

"Ideally he should have a transition period, as we gave Zelda, but I haven't got space to keep him and Tigger both. And he needs to learn to hunt ASAP—got to be proficient before the snows fall, or he won't stand a chance in the mountains this winter. At least his creepy owner did one thing that may work in Geronimo's favor, even if he did it for all the wrong reasons."

The dealer had been fond of feeding his pets live animals.

Tess grimaced. "So apparently Geronimo knows what to do with a rabbit, and I *don't* mean the kind you find at a supermarket," she informed the darkness beneath the tree. "Maybe he could teach you a thing or two."

Well, enough with the talking. Ever since Adam had dropped by yesterday, she'd been thirsty for conversation. Tess stood. "And speaking of rabbits, princess, are you checking out the possibilities? I saw half a dozen cottontails when I rode over this morning. It's not like I can spend the rest of my life up here, playing chicken delivery girl. Plus the tips are lousy."

No comment from the den. Tess shrugged and headed

west to the meadow where she'd left Cannonball. If she was to find another lynx-friendly location, she had a lot of ground to cover.

ALMOST A WEEK since Gabe had set up their sting and so far?

Nothing. Zip. Adam swung his binoculars through a few more degrees of arc, then waited, eyes unfocused, the better to catch any motion on the rugged slopes below.

Following his suggestion, the DOW had announced on its Web site the sighting of a pregnant female lynx. Since they never released the cats' precise locations to the public, they couldn't pinpoint Adam's fictional cat without arousing suspicions. But they'd dropped enough hints that a hunter familiar with this area could narrow the search to forty square miles or so.

To where Adam waited for him.

He's out here somewhere. I can feel him. A tingling at the nape of his neck. An itching of the palms. The same sensations Adam got back in the city when walking into a dark and seemingly deserted alley. He moved the binoculars another few degrees and paused again. *Come on, show yourself.*

With the ground the guy had to cover, he'd probably be riding rather than hiking when he came. During the heat of the day, when lynx napped on overhanging branches or in their caves, the hunter would scout lower on the mountainsides, if he was smart. He'd use that time to search for paw prints along the water, hoping they'd lead him to a nearby den.

At dawn or twilight, when the lynx prowled, a canny tracker would choose high vantage points, from which he could command miles of alpine meadows and forest at a glance. *I'd climb the lower peaks in the late afternoons, then circle them,* Adam had reasoned. Height was the best way to maximize a radio direction finder, which was strictly line of sight. He'd scan all the terrain he could from one side of the hill, then walk a ways around its shoulder and scan again. Sooner or later he'd pick up the lynx's collar signal.

Or, in this case, where no lynx existed, the hunter would find that this time he was the prey, instead of the predator.

Come on, don't be shy. I can feel you out there. Let's get it on! The sooner Adam bagged the creep, the happier he'd be. He wasn't slated to report for a fitness-for-duty assessment till late September. And he'd still be committed to the McGraws to mind their cattle till the fall. But he could think of better ways to use his spare time these days than lying in wait for some shabby lynx poacher.

Tess. Three days since he'd seen her and it felt like a year.

Will she come visit me? Or do I have to invent some reason to hunt her down?

To heck with excuses, she'd know what he was after. Every time they locked eyes, the air between them shimmered with heat waves. He'd give her one more day to come to her senses, then, if she didn't—

Below the boulder on which Adam sat, Watson lurched to his feet. Facing upwind, he raised his wet nose, then whimpered.

"What ya got, boy?" Adam swung his glasses in that direction. "Hmm?" The hound's bionic nose could be picking up most any scent, he supposed, as he scanned the slopes below. Cattle, a chipmunk in heat, a backpacker's ham sandwich. A mountain lion or actually one of Gabe's lynx, since they were out there someplace.

Watson whimpered again, then his tail fanned the air.

"Somebody we know?" Adam's heart leaped. His binoculars jiggled with the thought, then steadied again.

And there the rider was, framed in his lens. A woman, though the cream-colored Stetson hid her face. But the grace with which she ducked beneath a branch on her trail below was unmistakably feminine.

Tess. Heat shafted through his stomach. "Took your own sweet time," he murmured. But no matter, she was coming at last. And he liked that she was bold enough to admit her own needs, instead of waiting for— His brows drew together. "Hold on."

He brought the binoculars down, but still he could make out the tiny figure, now he knew where to look. Given this wider context, he realized Tess wasn't riding the trail that led from her camp to his. She pursued a roughly parallel track, half a mile above. Let her continue in that direction and she'd skirt the woods north of his cabin. Never pass within sight of it.

"She's lost," he assured the dog, as they hustled down to the pocket meadow where he'd tethered his mare.

Tess, who must have ridden the high country since childhood? Not likely, he had to admit, as he tightened the saddle girth, then put boot toe to stirrup. If she'd chosen a trail that bypassed his cabin, she'd picked it on purpose.

Shy, he supposed. *Or not in the mood for company?* He touched heels to his mount's ribs.

Or she'd forgotten already what sparks they struck off each other.

Or she remembers, but she's out to prevent forest fires?

Whatever Tess's reason, he wouldn't have it. Some fires were meant to burn.

TESS REINED IN Cannonball, then sat, studying the outcrop of sandstone that thrust up through the forest floor. Her trail edged its downhill face, where millions of years of weathering had broken it into a series of ragged red pillars. If the rock split in the same way farther uphill, away from this trail...

"Might do," she allowed, as she dismounted. She dropped Cannonball's reins and left him to crop grass while she picked her way upward alongside the ridge.

This stretch of forest ended a few hundred yards higher, giving way to alpine meadows where snowshoe hares should abound. And not far east of here, she remembered, a tiny spring welled from the rock. Fed from the snows above, it never dried out. So Geronimo would have water and good hunting. Now if she could only find shelter.

"Ah." She paused to peer under a twinberry bush, which seemingly grew from the bare rock, except for that too-dark shadow beneath its overhanging leaves. "Yes!" Behind it, the sandstone had faulted almost vertically, then one layer had slipped down along the other. From downhill, the stone still looked solid. Only approaching from above could you see that fallen rocks had jammed in between the parted layers, creating a roof to a narrow cave that vanished back into the ridge.

It looked too small for grown bears, though she supposed a lion might find it suitable. Tess sniffed, filled her lungs again, caught no odor of decaying meat, or the rankness of predators. And there wasn't the faintest path beaten to the cave's entry.

"But then, there are rattlers," she reminded herself. Backing off a bit, she pitched pebbles into the darkness and listened.

No telltale irate buzzing broke the silence and she let out a pent-up breath. "Okay. This must be the place."

In two days of hunting, she hadn't found better.

And she didn't have time, at this point, to find better. A child of the modern world, Liza hadn't dreamed it could take nearly two weeks for a letter to travel two hundred miles. Knowing that Tess had no way to phone her back, the vet had simply proposed a reasonable date to meet. Trusting Tess to be ready and willing, she was bringing Geronimo to the Sumner trailhead tonight at 1:00 a.m.

"Reckon this'll have to do," Tess decided as she started back to her horse.

Good as the setup was, it still made her uneasy. The cave lay only two miles southwest of the Sumner trailhead, and roughly the same distance northwest of Sumner line camp. This was McGraw grazing land.

Which meant Adam Dubois patrolled it. A tickle of arousal walked her spine as she pictured the cowboy. Those watchful, midnight eyes. That sexy smile of his, half sardonic, half tender. His barely sufferable confidence.

"I'd have to lie low. Very low," she told Cannonball as she gathered in his reins. She meant to follow the same procedure as she had with Zelda. Keep the lynx caged for three days within view of his prospective den, while he calmed down and grew accustomed to the sights and scents around him. And while the cat was caged, she couldn't leave him alone and defenseless.

Could she dodge Adam for three days on his own territory? The meadows where his herds grazed stretched across the foothills, half a mile below. Tess could think of no reason he'd be up here, scouting the trees.

Yet somehow it seemed inevitable that he'd sense her presence. Why, at this very moment, she could feel a shivery prickle of...awareness, herself. A goose wandering over her grave? "Nothing but your guilty conscience," she scoffed aloud.

"Always had a weakness for a woman with a guilty conscience."

"Ooh-*ah!*" She spun, spooking Cannonball as she did so.

In the shadows at the foot of the cliff, Adam slouched in the saddle of his black mare. He'd hooked his right leg negligently over its horn, then crossed his forearms upon his bent knee. His eyes were hidden beneath his hat brim, but below that, his smile gleamed like the Cheshire Cat's. "And if you're aimin' to store up any more regrets, I'm your man."

"Umm, thanks, but I reckon I've filled my quota for this month." *And would I regret you?* Somehow Tess didn't think so. Collecting Cannonball's reins, she led the gelding forward till she could look up into Adam's teasing blue eyes.

Her own face, was it as pink as it felt? But maybe that was good. With any luck, he'd figure she'd been visiting the bushes for the usual reason.

"Ah? Well, it's only one week till July," he said easily as she stooped to pat Watson, who lay panting in the dirt. "So...what brings you over my way?"

She brushed a knuckle across her mouth as she formed a reply. "Oh...nothing much. I'm just out for my after-

noon ride. It's such a beautiful day, guess I strayed a little farther than I usually—" She was babbling. She
tucked a wisp of hair behind her ear, touched her hoop
earring to make sure it was still there. Frowned at him as
his smile broadened to a grin. "And what are *you* doing
up here? Lose a cow?"

"Looking for rustlers, trespassers or anybody who
speaks English instead of Dog. You know there's a toll
for using this trail, don't you?"

Her skin was coming alive under his caressing gaze.
Her heartbeat fluttered in her throat. How did he *do* this
to her with just a look? "Th-there is?"

"Yep. You have to come home and let me make supper for you. And you have to say something besides
'woof,' while I cook it."

"I…don't know if that's such a…good idea," she protested weakly. *Tell him no, tell him no!* shrieked the sane
and sensible half of her brain.

"Goodness never even crossed my mind," he assured
her huskily. "Still, that's the forfeit and it's got to be
paid."

This was crazy. At best Adam Dubois would complicate her life, which was complicated enough already.

And at worse?

His grin was wicked, welcoming; she wondered how
he'd kiss. The half of her brain in charge of Deeds to Tor-
ment One's Conscience had already decided. Still she
wrinkled her nose and said disdainfully, "Macaroni and
cheese? That's a mighty steep toll."

"Or peanut butter and honey sandwiches. Lady's
choice."

CHAPTER EIGHT

TESS FELT JUMPY as a lynx in a dog pound. *Why didn't I just say "no"?* she asked herself, standing awkwardly in Adam's cabin.

She'd had too much time for second thoughts and multiple worries on the ride over. But with Adam loping ahead of her on the trail—a trail too narrow for her to ride up alongside him—she'd had no opportunity to tell him she'd changed her mind. Tess had a sneaking suspicion that he'd chosen their route and their pace to forestall any chance of her begging off. Behind that lazy grin, he was a very determined man, was Adam Dubois.

And where's he gotten off to? she wondered uneasily. As soon as they'd arrived, he'd said something about checking the horses, then disappeared.

Meantime, a wildlife biologist could learn a lot, inspecting the den of a Homo sapiens, variation: cowboy.

"So you're musical!" she murmured, touching the acoustic guitar that lay on his bunk. An old Martin, an instrument for a serious player. And his bed was neatly made, rather than the typical guy's jumble of musty sheets.

And now that she noticed, the floor of Adam's cabin wasn't strewn with discarded clothes. Neither were shirts and jeans and last week's Jockeys piled on the ancient easy chair by the cast-iron stove. "Neat," she concluded with satisfaction. She had always liked that in a man.

Even better, he was a reader. It was no small chore, packing in the supplies you'd need to last a whole summer. Yet the bookcase next to Adam's bunk looked as well-stocked as the shelves in the kitchen area of his one-room cabin. Tess bent to examine the titles.

Like most men, he favored non-fiction. She found books on history, geology, large animal medicine. Astronomy and—she laughed softly. "Dinosaurs!"

"Always had a thing for pterodactyls," Adam agreed, coming through the screen door.

"You did?" she murmured absently. *Aha, so that's what you were up to!* Washing up. He'd slung a used towel around his neck. His hair was damp. His face glowed with scrubbing—no, he'd shaved, that was it.

Heat coiled in her stomach, then descended. *You shaved and washed for me? Pretty darn sure of yourself, aren't you?*

"And stegosaurus," Adam continued, walking so close to her she could smell soap.

Soap and warm, virile man, with just a whiff of horse and leather—a delectable fragrance, to Tess's mind. If she swayed forward, her nose would *just* fit in that hollow at the base of his neck. What would his skin itself smell like?

"Stegosaurus? Not Tyrannosaurus rex? I thought ol' Rexie was every little boy's hero."

"Not mine. Guess I admired all that armor plate. Nobody could ever touch a guy if he was covered in that."

She dragged her eyes up from his whimsical smile to study his eyes. *You needed armor as a child?* She didn't know him well enough yet to ask him why.

And pterodactyls, they looked dangerous and leathery-tough, but they could also fly away. Fleeing from what kind of sorrow and pain? She had a sudden fierce urge to rise on tiptoe and brush his cheek with her lips. To kiss the hurting child that had become this tough, beautiful man.

But he'd take her kiss for something else entirely. Something she wasn't ready to face, not quite yet.

Instead she touched his lean jaw with her fingertips, fleetingly, tenderly. *I'm so sorry.*

Adam stood, gazing down at her. Eyes trapped by his, still she was aware of his breathing. Slow, hot respirations that seemed to drive her own, as if his chest rose and fell against hers. Bare skin to bare skin. Heart whispering to heart.

Soon, maybe. Soon, almost surely. But not yet. *I don't know you.*

You know all that matters. His smile deepened, his eyes beckoned. *Come learn the rest.*

If she didn't break this widening silence, he'd kiss her where she stood. And once they started, could she— would she—call a halt? "*Soo*...peanut butter and honey, huh?" Her words came out chirpy as a schoolgirl's. Before her face went totally pink, Tess hooked her thumbs in her pockets and strolled off toward his "kitchen."

"Mmm, slight change of plan." Adam padded after her, his steps soft as a stalking panther's. He reached beyond her for a small cooler that sat in the sink. "Forgot I caught these this morning. How about rainbow trout instead?"

COOKING TOGETHER isn't that different from foreplay, when two people want each other. Excuses to touch abound. Every touch arouses.

Adam's kitchen was squeezed in between the sink and counter built along an outer wall, and a freestanding cupboard, which flanked the wood-burning stove. Tight quarters.

Tess wasn't so sure it was intentional, the way they bumped or brushed every time they turned around. Adam's body pulled hers, the way the moon lures the tides. "Oops!" she said softly, as she turned from the sink—and ran straight into him. "Sorry."

He'd caught her upper arms to steady her with hands dusted in flour. "Not at all. My fault. But now, look at you. Tess-the-Mess." He brushed the flour off her sleeves with his wrists and forearms, taking his time about it.

Her nerves sizzled as if he'd dragged velvet across her naked limbs. Waves of hot pleasure lapped up her spine. "Th-thanks." She sidestepped past him to stare blindly at the shelf where he kept his spices. *Now what did I want?*

"Find what you need?" Wiping his hands on a dishcloth, Adam came to stand beside her. They touched along the length of their thighs—for a moment seemed to press into each other. Then swayed apart.

Maybe not what she needed—but as for wanting? She was half-dizzy with wanting. "I…ah, yes. Here we go." She chose parsley and lemon pepper to season the rice she was cooking. "And you've got onions, I assume?"

"Does Watson have ears? No," he growled at the hound, who took his mention for a summons. "You sit right back down there. No trout almondine for dogs."

"Where did you learn to cook like this?" Tess marveled as she minced onions. Most cowboys knew their way around a can opener, but the cans usually contained pork and beans, or Dinty Moore stew. A tuna, macaroni and cheese stove-top casserole passed for *haute cuisine* in the high country.

"My Aunt Connie is a woman of firm convictions, one of them being that a ranch kitchen is an equal-opportunity playground. On her kids' weekly chores list, cooking one supper equated to five washing-ups afterward, take your pick. So I learned to whip up an acceptable meal, then skedaddle."

"Good for her." *But where was your mother while Aunt Connie was teaching you?* "You lived with your aunt and uncle?"

"For a while there." His words had the finality of a door gently closing.

No trespassing, Tess warned herself. But why? She sliced a lump of butter into a pan and started sautéing onions. "Whew!" She laughed as the fumes reached her eyes. "Strong."

Adam's hands settled on her shoulders from behind, as he peered past her. "How are we doing, hmm?"

We're trying very, very hard not to notice that if I back up half an inch, my bottom will press against your zipper, that's how we're doing. As Adam inspected her skillet, his cheek brushed hers for a shivery second. Tess's eyes drifted shut. Even clean-shaven, he'd scratch her the tiniest bit when they'd kiss. Delicious, she could hardly wait.

His fingers tightened, then eased on her shoulders, then pressed again, like a big cat's kneading. "Hmm? Should I start my trout yet?"

"Not...quite yet. Give the rice another five minutes, say." She opened her eyes and the rising fumes stung. "Wow, these onions pack a wallop!" She laughed, sniffled, turned her head aside—toward his face.

"Crybaby onions, for sure." His lips brushed through her fluttering lashes. He put the tip of his hot tongue to a tear as it trickled down her cheek. "Want me to stir?"

She was stirred already. Melted as the butter in her pan. "N-no, I'm—" Tess slid out from under his hands, retreated to the sink. "I'm fine." She knuckled the rest of her tears aside, pumped a little water and splashed her face. Dried it with a dish towel and shaky fingers.

Glancing down at the thin blue cotton shirt she wore, she could see where the fabric was tented by her risen nipples. She made a face and glanced over her shoulder. Would he notice?

No question. Adam didn't miss a thing. Darn the man! He looked so...so cool. So in control there, stirring her onions, impervious even to the fumes. If he was going to drive her crazy with desire, she wanted him driven, too. She didn't want to go there alone.

Would not, Tess swore to herself. When the time came, she'd find some way to shake that restraint. To reach the man that lay beneath the armor plate.

He turned away from the stove, and their eyes connected with an almost audible slap. Tess jumped beneath her skin. Even by the dim light of the kerosene lamp that hung midcabin, she could see his pupils had expanded, like a cat's when it sees a mouse. So he *was* moved. She wasn't the only one aroused.

But where she was softening with desire, he was growing harder, more purposeful... Intention in every line of his taut body and in his unblinking gaze.

Can't do this tonight, she reminded herself, fighting the blatant summons in his eyes. Probably shouldn't risk it ever, but most certainly couldn't tonight. An hour past midnight, Liza would be waiting for her at the trailhead.

She'd still have plenty of time, if she ate and ran—left here by nine at the latest—but if she let Adam seduce her into staying… *Can't do it.*

Hadn't the nerve, much as she was tempted.

Couldn't leave Liza, waiting till dawn, wondering if Tess had even gotten her message.

"What?" Adam said softly, trying to read the emotions chasing across her expressive face. Desire and wariness and worry. He wondered if maybe a woman always felt that, felt torn, coming to a man for the first time. Lured instinctively by his size and strength and sheer otherness, but not yet certain whether he'd use his powers for her— or against her.

Don't worry, he wanted to say. Was trying to tell her with every look and gesture. He wanted to gentle her with kisses. Touch her so deeply and deliciously she'd come shuddering into his arms, willing and ready and eager. He doubted if she was as delicate as she looked, still, the first time he'd let her be on top. *Ride me over the mountains and up to the stars, Tess. I know the way. It's gonna be fine, I promise you.*

"I was just wondering…"

Me, too.

"Do you have anything green to round this out? Peas or…" Her voice trailed away as he stared at her. She cocked her head. "Adam?"

"Green beans," he muttered thickly, coming back to the present with a jolt. "Or peas. On the top shelf, to the right. You choose."

They ought to take the pots off the stove and settle what mattered first. Worry about vegetables later, much later. Would he even be able to eat, for wanting her?

But something in her face told him she wasn't ready

yet. She was a funny mix of confidence and shyness. Bold out on the mountain in her own world, hesitant here in his. Like a wild thing brought in from the forest, befuddled by doors and walls. So take it slow, he warned himself. There was no hurry. No hurry at all. It would be all the sweeter when they finally came to it.

"Peas," Tess decided, and swung away from him to briskly open a can.

THEY ATE SUPPER by candlelight.

"Like dining at the Ritz," Tess murmured delightedly, as Adam set two ketchup bottles on the table, with a half-burned candle stub in each.

"Reckon they do it fancier down at Suntop." Adam held a match to the wicks. "Crystal chandeliers and silver and finger bowls?" The flames gilded his angular cheekbones, touched off sparks in his deep-set eyes.

"Christmas and birthdays, sure, but most nights we eat in the kitchen." People who'd never been to Suntop tended to fantasize about her family's lavish lifestyle. They pictured French chefs and Rolls-Royces. Politicians and movie stars coming and going, with champagne flowing like soda pop. Olympic-size swimming pools, race horses and private planes, and—lord—once she'd even dated a guy, a lawyer from Durango, who refused to believe that they'd never had a butler.

In truth, Ben plowed every cent the ranch earned right back into maintaining the business. Paint and cattle feed and salaries for the cowboys. New barns and horse shoes and hay threshers. But the lion's share of profits went to the staggering, terrifying land taxes that rose higher every year.

In the rare season when there was a surplus, either it

was socked away for that inevitable rainy day, or it went to improving the stock. Suntop had the best bulls and studs in the West already, but any time Ben could upgrade the herds with new bloodlines, he did so.

And he leaped upon any chance he had to extend Suntop's borders. Land was the moat between the Tankerslys and a world Ben could do without.

"If you met my father, you'd know we're not into frills at Suntop." Tess remembered how indignant she'd been when she learned that most of her schoolmates in Trueheart received something called an allowance! Ben refused to believe that his daughters needed walking-around money. They never lacked for food or fine, sensible cowponies, new boots when they needed them, or a roof over their heads. What more could a girl want?

Oh, he was generous with his gifts, all right, but they generally came with strings attached. Like the husband he'd tried to buy for her sister Risa. Ben liked to stay in control.

Tess folded paper towels for their napkins, set out cutlery, then cast a critical eye over the battered pine table. "Back in a minute," she called, as Adam served their plates.

She returned with a fistful of daisies and Indian paintbrush from his front meadow. Arranging her bouquet in a Mason jar, she placed it between the candles. "There. Everything we need."

"Everything?" There was a smile in Adam's voice as he held her chair while she sat, then eased her into position.

"Lamplight and candlelight. Fine food and flowers. Call of a nighthawk coming through open windows, instead of traffic sounds?" She tipped her head toward the dog, who sat drooling at her elbow. "An attentive, four-legged vacuum cleaner, if we spill any crumbs?" *And a drop-dead sexy man, who looks as if he plans to have me in place of canned peaches for dessert.* "Heaven must be something like this," she said, at least half-serious.

Might be wholly like this, come to think of it.

Adam laughed quietly as he toasted her with a glass of water. "As long as it pleases you."

In spite of the sexual tension between them, talk flowed like a mountain stream. Another way in which Adam differed from the usual tongue-tied cowboy, Tess reflected as she listened to him. Most cowhands preferred to let their deeds do the talking.

But then, Adam also differed from the academic types she'd been dating since she'd gone off to college. The typical grad student or professor was full of fine talk, yet he was a hapless babe in the real world; all his learning came from books.

But looking at this man—those big, scarred capable hands, and his miss-nothing eyes…

Noticing the way he moved—like a middle-weight boxer prowling the ring. Or a cougar flowing down a scree slope, every muscle in tune and in balance. That impression he gave of force centered—power at rest, but available for instant response on any plane…

Then listening to him—more to the things he left out of his tales than what he put in…

Add it all together and Tess didn't doubt for a second that Adam could back his words and his thoughts with action. *You've got it all!* she realized. *Everything a woman wants in a man.* At least, this woman.

Maybe that's what was scaring her so, in spite of her

attraction. The last thing she needed to find, at this stage of her life, was a man she couldn't do without.

No... No, that was next to last.

Even worse would be to find a man she couldn't live without, that she couldn't attain.

Tess didn't count herself as vastly experienced when it came to romance. Still, some instinct was warning her loud and clear: Adam would give a woman everything she asked for—probably more than she could handle.

But body and soul, he'd be on loan.

One more good reason not to get serious about this man. So far, Tess was heart-whole and fancy-free, and that suited her plans for the next stage of her life. When you've found a winning formula, why risk a change?

WASHING AND DRYING their dishes had been Tess's idea. Adam gritted his teeth—was she deliberately torturing him, or simply a hopeless neatnik? Whichever, he'd granted her this last feeble delay. Endured another ten minutes of standing elbow to elbow with her at the sink, inhaling her scent, imagining how soft she'd be, while he schooled himself to loverly patience. *No pouncing, Dubois. Wait for it. Only three plates left.*

Then two.

He took the last one from her fingers and dried it, eyes locked on her as he did so. *And now,* ma cher...

"Well," she said, with brittle gaiety. "I reckon I'd better be—"

Don't even think it. He ducked his head and kissed her.

CHAPTER NINE

"Oнннн…" she murmured against Adam's lips.

The taste of her! Tess with lemon and butter and peaches, sheer heaven. He set the plate blindly aside—missed the counter. It toppled off to smash at their feet. As she gasped, he took full advantage, sliding the tip of his tongue along the inner dampness of her upper lip.

With a rueful little moan, Tess tipped her head back to meet him.

Yes, darlin', like that. He slanted his mouth greedily across hers. Tentative at first, her lips explored the shape of his tongue—then welcomed it, waltzed with it. *Oh, yeah!* Cradling her head with one hand, Adam hooked his other arm around her waist. He snugged her in and turned her so she leaned against the sink. Crockery crunched beneath their boots and he laughed inside her. *Why did we waste so much time?* Damn, but she could kiss!

She shuddered and sighed. He growled agreement. Her palms flattened against his chest, rubbed hesitantly up and down. "Umm, Adam?"

"Mmm…" He eased his knee between her slender thighs—jolted with the sheer electric surge as their bodies fused. Nudged each other enticingly. Found a rhythm of wanting. Rocking and riding…hard to soft…give to take…

Slow down, he warned himself desperately. This wasn't his usual style. He liked to think he was smooth in his wooing, but tonight, with Tess, he felt like a runaway train, stoked with blazing coal, a full head of steam, no brakes. Just *rumbling*—a downhill grade from here to the coast.

Not that Tess was helping, the way she'd wrapped her arms around his neck. When she arched her spine over his encircling arm, her breasts rose. Brushed his chest. Could *not* be ignored.

But they'd have to wait their turn; he was slave to her mouth right now. He'd been dreaming about sucking her delectable bottom lip for a week now. He was damned if he'd give it less than its due.

"Nooo…" she moaned as he did so. She'd hooked her boot around the back of his leg. Was rubbing him from his calf to his thigh, then down again. One of her hands was laced tight in his hair, the other kneaded his shoulder.

Nooo… The sound echoed dimly in his brain till it formed a nonsensical word. "No?" He came halfway up for air, returned to the surface of her lips and skated their wicked, shiny curves. "No!" He couldn't have heard what he'd thought he heard. Not possible.

"N-no." She kissed the underside of his jaw…the corner of his mouth…his chin… "No, I can't *do* this!" All the while her boot was rubbing him, goading him. Her hips rocked in unmistakable invitation.

"Umm, just who are you talkin' to?" He brushed his nose back and forth across hers. "No, you…or no, me?" *'Cause I'm hearing "yes" all the way from here to the bayou.*

"I…" She froze. Turned her head aside. Blew out a long, irresolute breath. "Umm…"

"Hmm? You don't want to say 'no.'" He nibbled her earlobe and smiled at the yelp and convulsion that earned him. *File that one away for future use!*

"Nooo, but I'm gonna anyway," Tess declared in a wobbly voice. She added on an almost schoolmarmish note, "Adam?"

Surly was not going to cut it here, but *damn,* he felt frustrated! Maybe it was her time of the month? Wouldn't have bothered him, but especially the first time, a woman could be fussy, fixed on perfection. And for all her outdoorsiness, Tess wasn't the earthy type. She was a flowers-and-candles kind of girl.

Still, no way was Adam letting her out of his arms if he had a choice. "We can just cuddle, if you'd rather. I'm a world-class cuddler."

Close as they were entwined, he could feel her shake with silent laughter. "Yeah, right! You're just a big teddy bear—in a wolf suit."

"Scout's honor. Prove it to you. Come lie down on my—"

She smiled, rested her forehead against his chest, shook her head. "I do that and I'll never get up again and you know it. No...I've got to go." She fingered his shirt buttons, sighed her regrets.

Adam counted to ten. To twenty. Found the strength at thirty to shrug and say, "Okay." No way would he beg and he didn't believe in hard sells. She wanted him much as he wanted her. "But if you change your mind, I don't ever latch my door." *Not to you, I don't.*

There wasn't much more to say and he didn't say it while he saddled her horse. Tess wouldn't let him escort her back to her cabin, and though he argued, she insisted. The moon would be rising soon and she knew the way.

Was perfectly fine, thanks. Actually preferred to go alone; riding alone always helped her think.

"Then think about what we're missing," he told her roughly, stepping close when she put one hand to her saddle horn.

She raised her head to meet his kiss and the gesture was so natural, so…right that something clenched behind Adam's breastbone. He fisted his fingers so they wouldn't reach for her.

Only their lips touched—a butterfly brushing, soft as a promise, so sweetly sexy he'd ache all night long, remembering. "*Damn,* Tess…"

She framed his face with her palm. "Thanks for a lovely time, Adam."

"Scoot, if you're not gonna stay," he growled. *Before the wolf unzips his teddy-bear suit and grabs you by the scruff, girl.*

"And you'd thank me for it," he muttered under his breath, as she rode off to the west. *You know you would.*

Graceful and slim in the saddle, she turned for one last wave.

Adam sighed heavily, then stood, his eyes fixed on the gap in the trees where she'd vanished. But she was gone. Wasn't coming back, not tonight. A touch of iron under all that silky softness. *"Damn."*

He turned on his heel—and there was the moon, gold as a sunflower rising over the eastern peaks. Enough to make a man howl.

"OH GEEZ, oh gosh, thank *heavens* you're still here!" Tess cried as her horses burst out of the pines and onto the moonlit trailhead.

Liza opened the door to her Jeep and stepped down. "*There* you are! I was starting to worry."

"I'm sorry to be so late! We came fast as we could. *This* dimwitted jughead here—" Tess tipped her head toward her pack horse, "—had forgotten all about carrying the cage last time. She took a notion that it was a device of the devil, or a horse-eating creature from Mars. Had a heck of a time lashing it on her in the first place. Then halfway here, it must have swung against her leg. You never saw such a Hellzapoppin' hissy fit! She nearly bucked herself—and us—off the side of the mountain." Tess had hoped to stop and leave the mare and her camping supplies at the cave site, but there'd been no time for that detour.

"Well, you made it, and in one piece," the vet consoled her, while Tess dismounted. The women hugged, then led the horses to a nearby tree and tied them. "Now come see what I brought you."

"Oh, wow!" Tess leaned into the back of the Jeep, and laughed. "You sure you didn't bring me the tiger by mistake? *What* a bruiser! Hello, sweetheart."

Geronimo paced his cage, ears flattened to his round skull, stub tail tucked. A low continuous growl made plain his opinion on this midnight escapade.

"Thirty-two pounds when I got him and he's up to thirty-six now," Liza said with pride.

"And what a grump!"

"He's all guy, alright. Clear case of testosterone poisoning," the vet agreed. "Makes Zelda look like a fluffy cuddle-cat. Plus I'm guessing his drug-dealer creepy owner must have teased him. Be extra careful about putting your hands near the cage. He'll swat you, if he can."

Tess made a face. "Oh, he's going to be *fun* to transport!"

"Well, he's had an extra hour to wake up from his sedative. We'll send him back to sleepy-bye land when you're ready to go. But first, I brought a thermos of cocoa."

Leaning against the Jeep, they sipped hot chocolate and gazed up at the jeweled sky, while they talked in low tones. "I'm so glad you showed. I was beginning to think you hadn't received my letter," Liza confessed. "Was wondering if I should go stumbling around the mountainside, looking for your cabin, or what?"

"No, I'm sorry. I started late, was the problem. I got kidnapped for supper tonight, and had a hard time breaking away." Not as hard a time as it might have been. The sensation of Adam's hot, hard thigh moving between hers seemed to be branded on Tess's body. Muscles fluttered inside her; goose bumps stampeded across her skin. The cocoa trembled in her cup.

"Oh-ho!" Liza shifted to study her friend. "Ha! I *thought* you looked sort of...hot and bothered. Let me guess, the kidnapper was male? And studly?"

"We-ell, that's all a matter of taste, isn't it? But he does stand about six-three in his boots. With shoulders out to here." Tess spread her hands as wide as the one that got away. "Deep-set eyes, maybe two shades lighter than the sky up there. Mouth to die for and a five o'clock shadow that must kick in about dawn."

"There can't be twenty men within forty miles of here and you've found one worth a test drive already?" Liza demanded. "And—oh, God—don't tell me! He's a cowboy, isn't he? I smell leather and I *melt*."

"Well, he does hang around with the cows, yeah. And a dopey bloodhound."

"He's got a dog? That's an excellent sign. Pets prove a man's capable of commitment. I hope you ate supper in bed!"

"It's not *his* pet; he's dogsitting. And no…we didn't." Tess gave a wistful sigh, then had to smile with the memory. "Though he was sort of…snapping at my heels, when I lit out of there."

"You should have gone ahead. I'd have waited. *Somebody* ought to get some satisfaction, around here."

"I don't know…" Tess sipped and stared at the moon. "He's drop-dead sexy, but I'm not so sure he's a smart idea. Doesn't fit in with my plans for a Good Life."

"*My* plans for the Good Life start and end with an inexhaustible supply of drop-dead sexy men, one at a time, from now till I'm ninety. You've got different plans?"

Tess shrugged. "Hey, I've got nothing against gorgeous men, but I've told you what I want. To be a field biologist. Live outdoors as much as I can. Travel whenever and wherever, at the drop of a hat. Brazil, Africa, Alaska for sure, as well as throughout the West. I mean to build up a reputation researching and writing over the next twelve years or so, with hopes that it will lead to a full professorship eventually."

"Fine. Nothing wrong with ambitions, but do you have to be a prissy nun while you're at it?"

"Not at all." Tess shook the last drops of chocolate out on the ground and set her mug on the Jeep's hood. "But my best friend from Trueheart, looking at her sometimes… Betsy married the guy she'd been dating since junior high. Her wedding was a week after we graduated high school, then nine months later—abracadabra—she's got a son.

"Then two years after that, she delivers twin girls.

Then about the time I'm getting my Masters, she has an adorable little *Oops*—this one wasn't planned at all. Four kids and she's twenty-five, Liza, and Betsy doesn't know if she's coming or going. She won't get her head up for air for another—what?—fifteen years or so? She can forget about a career."

"Sounds like she's got one."

"Ph.D. in diapers, trikes and car seats," Tess agreed. "And I'm not saying that isn't wonderful. Maybe it's right for Betsy, but..." She shrugged again. "I want something...different. I spent my whole childhood outside, riding the range at Suntop. Watching birds, collecting bugs, observing animals. Being cooped up inside a house full-time would just about kill me."

On top of that, she hadn't had anything like a normal family life, what with her father trading in wives and girl-friends every couple of years, when they didn't stomp off and leave *him*. The closest thing Tess had ever had to a mother was Socorro, the housekeeper at Suntop. With no role models to inspire her, no wonder she wasn't wife-and-mom material.

"So you don't mean to have children?"

"No. I didn't say that. I think a kid or two, someday, would be fantastic. Much as I love kittens and colts and puppies and beaver kits, I'm sure watching a child grow up would be even more fascinating. But a family's on the back burner till I'm established. Ready to settle down at some university or other.

"I figure when I'm thirty-six or seven, I'll take a breather and have my babies. Teach classes and write books while they're growing.

"Then when they're twelve or so, they should be portable. Ready to travel, live outdoors. I'll be roughly fifty by then. Ought to be able to keep on working in the field till I'm sixty or more. Jane Goodall's still researching chimps in her seventies."

"So you've got your life all planned out," Liza said dryly. "But what makes you think a suitable husband will pop up just when you decide you need one?"

Tess shrugged. "If he doesn't, well, there are always fertility clinics full of alpha male sperm. I should be pulling down a salary by then that'll make it possible to afford a kid or two on my own. If a lady lynx can manage kittens alone, why can't I?"

"No reason not, I suppose. But in the meantime, what about *this* alpha male? Why would he mess up your plans? Is he proposing more than a bounce on his bed? You can't enjoy that, then go your merry way?"

"Nooo…" Tess admitted. "He's not proposing more than a good time. And he's not likely to. Something tells me he's strictly a lone wolf."

"Yummy! A rogue, huh? Or what do you biologists call them—dispersers?"

"Nature's version of the wandering bad boy," Tess agreed. "The male that travels. Spreads his genes far beyond the normal range of his species."

"There's something about those dispersers that a girl can't resist," Liza teased. "So why resist him? You cheer each other up for the summer, then about the time you're both cooling off, September's here. He drives his cattle down the mountain. You go back to Boulder to defend your dissertation…end of nice story. How's that for a plan?"

"Sounds sensible," Tess allowed, making a face. "But he—"

"Mmm?" Liza prompted.

"He…scares me, Liza. Oh, not in a bad way, but he's…" Different. *Special*. Reliving the fevered touch of Adam's lips on her face, she felt her spine arching subtly, her heartbeat surging. "I'd hate to fall for somebody I couldn't have."

"Sounds like *having* him's no problem."

"*Ohh*, yeah… But I mean have and keep. I've always been the one to walk away from relationships when they start to get too sticky-serious. But this time…" *If I couldn't walk away from him. Or if he did the walking.* "Well, who needs a broken heart?" She had the strangest notion that Adam could do that to her, if she gave him half a chance.

"You remember that old movie, *Moonstruck,* where Nicholas Cage tells Cher that the point of love isn't to make us happy? It's to drive us crazy and break our hearts?"

Tess laughed. "No, I never saw that."

"Well, think about it." Liza reached into the Jeep and screwed the cap back on her thermos. "Heartbreaker or not, I think you should go for him, girl. Feel the fear and do it anyway. Who wants to grow up making no mistakes? *Can* you even grow up, without taking the wrong turns?"

Tess smiled, shrugged, then walked with Liza to the rear of the vehicle. "Well, I'll tell Adam you're on his side."

"Adam, nice name. But there's one thing, Tess. If you do decide to offer Adam an apple, don't tell him about our lynx repatriation project, right?"

"No way! I'd never do that. If word got around that I was aiding and abetting lynx, I'd be drummed off the range. None of my friends would understand. And Ben— my father—he'd disinherit me for sure."

"Yikes." Liza's amusement had faded to worry.

"Not going to happen," Tess assured her. "As long as I'm very careful. Which I am. And now…" She glanced eastward, to where black sawtooth mountains cut a brightening sky. "We'd better get this circus on the road."

BEFORE HE WENT HOME, Natwig stowed what needed to be hidden in Webster's barn.

The ancient wooden feedbox smelled of molasses-soaked grain as he leaned into it, setting down first the gun, then his radio direction-finding wand and earphones. He straightened, slipped the collar down his forearm and stood, holding it.

A muscle twitched in his jaw. Collar BC02F1. He'd crushed its transmitter with pliers, soon as he'd removed it from the cat, a big wary female. *Ten thousand dollars,* he reminded himself as he placed it in the box, then swung the lid down and snapped its padlock.

He'd taken his tracking gear along on this trip to the Uncompahgre Plateau. His wildflower and fly-fishing client was an older man, easily tired by the elevation. Each night when Cornwell took to his tent, Natwig had walked out and checked for lynx signals. And damned if he hadn't found one, the last night of the trip.

He'd driven his client down to the airport in Cortez, then returned to the plateau. Couldn't pass up that kind of lucky strike. But it had taken him two days of hard stalking to bag the lynx.

Which meant he was forty-eight hours late coming home to Karen. Ought to have called, he told himself. But lying to her was getting to be more and more painful; he preferred not to say anything. Still, he should have phoned from the airport.

And considering that he'd need to leave her again within a day or so to start tracking the pregnant female north of Trueheart... Worrying about that, he forgot to check the road before he walked out of the barn. He locked its door, turned toward the rear of the building where he always hid his truck—and spotted Debbie Jenkins's rusty red pickup just rounding the far bend. Their neighbor and Karen's best friend. Had Debbie spotted him as she drove past?

And that's all I need. Debbie was chattier than a magpie. Everything that went into her eyes fell out of her mouth. "Crap!" he swore aloud. But then, maybe she hadn't noticed him.

He passed her truck ten minutes and two miles later, coming out the drive to his ranch as he turned in. She gave him a cheery wave and what felt like a funny look as she headed on up the ridge to her own place. "Thanks, Deb. That really helps."

He found Karen in the kitchen, putting away the groceries that Debbie must have dropped off. The calico cat crouched in one empty paper bag on the floor, the orange tom in another. Both cats peered out at him from their caves with cool, inscrutable eyes, as if they knew exactly what he'd done.

Karen didn't look round as he closed the back door. Sitting in her wheelchair before the open refrigerator, she was rearranging its contents.

"Hey," he said softly and leaned down to kiss the top of her head. "I missed you." In the old days she'd have ridden along as camp cook, since this hadn't been a hunting trip.

"Missed my flapjacks and pot-washing, you mean."

"That's not what I meant." He brushed his knuckles

down her cheek, but she didn't turn to kiss his fingers as she once would have done. He felt a lump rise in his throat.

"You're late." She moved the ketchup from the door shelf to the top shelf. Slotted a quart of milk in the door.

He waited for her to say she'd been worried. That she'd been ready to send in the marines, or at least ask Cody to ride up and look for him. But she didn't. He cleared his throat and said, "Yeah. Cornwell decided to stay on a couple of days, the fishin' was so good. I couldn't pass up the extra money." She knew they needed money, dammit. How could she blame him?

But if she knew what he was doing to get it…

She took a jar of mustard from her lap, placed it on the middle shelf, then rotated it till its label faced forward. "Debbie said she saw you down at Webster's old barn."

"Yeah." He'd been planning what he could say about that on the drive up. "Been thinking it might be an idea to lease that barn. Those kennels Webster built in there, back when he was going to make a fortune breeding those big white sheep-guarding dogs…"

"Great Pyrenees."

"Yeah, those mutts. But he put a load of money into the kennels. They're first-rate."

Their downhill neighbor had always been full of pie-in-the-sky schemes for making his fortune. Before the dogs, he'd tried breeding llamas and potbelly pigs. He'd been talking about importing yaks from Tibet when his house burned down last winter.

Now he'd taken a job driving a school bus way over in Colorado Springs while he waited to hit the jackpot—by suing his own insurance agent. Something about the man not getting him the fire coverage he'd claimed he had. Of course, the broker claimed Webster never sent in his premium check. Looked like the case would drag on for years, with no one the winner in the end.

Meantime the barn sat vacant and Natwig was already leasing it. Had done so since January. Webster thought he wanted it for his tractor and to store the hay he'd harvest this summer.

"Sturdy kennels like that, just sitting there, goin' to waste. Thought maybe I'd start raising Mountain Curs again." Natwig's old man had been famous in these parts for his hunting dogs, thirty years ago. There was no demand for a good dog now, not in a world that had forgotten what mattered, but... "It's just a thought," he added lamely when she sniffed.

"Well..." He shifted from boot to boot. *And aren't you going to ask me if I'm hungry? If I had a good trip?* He'd saved up all kinds of stories to tell her about Cornwell and his doings since she'd seen him last. The old guy was nearly family. "Well...reckon I could use a shower." He stepped over a cat in its bag, then paused hopefully in the doorway as she called.

"Joe?" Eyes cool and wide, brows raised, not a hint of a smile on her lips when she finally looked at him. "Is there...something you need to tell me?"

Back when they were engaged to be married, Natwig had gotten his first outfitter's job—working for a man who guided lion hunts.

As soon as she heard, Karen had returned his ring. Told him she could never love a man who'd kill cats.

He'd tried to convince her a cougar was something entirely different from her lap cats, a wild and vicious animal. But he could have shifted a mountain easier. To Karen, a cat was a cat was a cat. She'd shared her cradle with a moth-eaten old tabby. She'd learned the word *kitty* before she'd learned *Daddy,* Natwig's father-in-law had confided once. Her sister owned cats. Her mother owned cats. Karen had never had less than three house cats padding at her heels since the day he'd met her.

So he could hunt lions or he could love Karen, but he sure couldn't do both. Not in the same lifetime.

The day he'd promised he'd never hurt a cat again, she'd taken his ring back. They'd married within a month and that had been thirty days too long for him. He felt the same way still.

And now you want to know if there's something I ought to tell you? If he'd found any other way out of their troubles, he'd damn sure have taken it. "No," he said gruffly and turned away. "Don't reckon there is."

CHAPTER TEN

"So, CRABBY-CAT, are you ready to go it alone?" Tess knelt a few feet away from Geronimo's cage and set the chicken down beside her. "Better be. I'm ready to head back to my cabin and have a nice hot shower. Then cups and cups of hot coffee. And a grilled cheese and tomato sandwich."

Her stomach rumbled fierce agreement. The lynx flattened his tasseled ears and growled without turning to look at her. Tess laughed softly. The big cat had flung himself down on his brindled side, with his back resting against the cage door. His black-tipped stubby tail twitched a slow tempo of feline displeasure. "Yeah, a lot you care if your babysitter's done without hot food or fires for two long, cold nights, you ungrateful dude!"

Tess had decided not to light her camp stove in Adam's territory. Though Geronimo's cave lay two miles northwest of Sumner line camp, the winds had been fluky, swirling up and down the mountain slopes. She didn't dare risk their carrying the smell of cooking to Watson's ever-questing nose.

Instead she'd subsisted on cans of Boston brown bread, a jar of peanut butter and a bag of apples, these past three days of lying low. Now, on this final morning she was dying for a hot meal, followed by an unbroken nap on a real mattress.

"Of course, first I've got to ride over to Zelda's and drop off her chicken," she told the tom. "Can't have her thinking I've totally abandoned her."

At dawn on the day she'd had supper with Adam—could that be only three days before this one?—she'd left two birds on Zelda's doorstep, instead of her usual one. "Do you figure she rationed herself, or pigged out the minute I turned my back?" she asked Geronimo. "Nah, probably she cached one; she's not a dumb dog, now, is she?"

The lynx growled again, so low she could hardly hear him.

"But by now she's probably wondering what happened to the chicken delivery girl, and I'm sort of worried, too."

This hiatus was actually part of the original schedule Tess and Liza had devised. Feed Zelda daily for the first week or so while she grew accustomed to her den and her territory. Then begin to cut back on her food, leaving her a chicken three or five times a week for the next month.

In the wild, predators went without till their hunting paid off. Hunger whetted the instinct to find prey and bring it down. And the sooner the lynx shifted into stalking mode, the better. By August, Tess hoped she wouldn't need any supplementary feeding.

"With luck, I'll get back there and find her all fat and sassy, with a rabbit-eating smile on her fuzzy face."

Or possibly, like a house cat whose source of food has been cut off, Zelda had already packed up and wandered away over the mountains. Tess bit her bottom lip. "Hope not." She'd grown fond of the dainty female. This big-footed grouch was more of an acquired taste, though given his previous owner, how could she blame him?

"So if you'd consider shifting away from that door, we could get with the program."

No way was she opening it till Geronimo had moved to the back of his cage. He'd taken several swipes at her during feeding these past few days. Normally lynx were shy—much less aggressive than their bobcat cousins. But this one was intensely territorial. And he was fast as a rattler.

Tess crawled a foot closer, then paused. Edgy as he was, her proximity should get on his nerves soon enough. "Now we know you're not afraid of people, not in the least, but I hope you're going to be careful up here." The corners of her mouth tipped up as she heard herself. Like a mom, giving her son last-minute advice the day she left him at his freshman college dorm. "'Cause Liza told me somebody may be hunting lynx."

Among the many cat-related sites on the Internet, the vet monitored the Colorado Division of Wildlife's Web site for the lynx restoration project. The same day that Liza brought Geronimo, she'd found a posting there, announcing that a female lynx, telemetry collar number BC02F1 had stopped signaling over on the Uncompahgre Plateau. "That's not that far from here. The DOW says this doesn't seem to be an accidental death, since they can't find the body or its collar. They're suspecting foul play, and are asking anybody who knows anything about it to contact them."

The lynx lashed its tail against the mesh.

"Liza says there's a rumor going around among the big cat folks." The vet belonged to a network of eco-activists who promoted the interests of American wild cats, every species from the Florida panther to the Arizonan jaguar, to the shy little margay. "They're starting to think that too many lynx have gone missing these past few months here in Colorado. They're saying that maybe it isn't just encounters with cars or starvation or disease that's accounting for all the disappearances. That maybe somebody is picking you guys off."

An ugly thought. Tess wasn't sure she believed it. People often imagined conspiracies to account for plain old bad luck. "But all the same, I want you to be careful out here. Trust no one."

The lynx flowed to its feet and glided across the cage, then turned to glare at her.

"Yeah, that's the attitude. Not me, not anybody who walks on two legs. Trust these chickens I leave you, but beyond that, you're on your own, sweetheart." Tess held up the plucked bird and brought it near the mesh, twitching it to hold the cat's attention. "So…see the nice yummy chicken? Watch where I put it now. That's your new home."

She backed away to the nearby cave and wiggled the chicken again as she set it down before the entrance. "Right here, baby, come and get it. It's your housewarming gift."

The lynx's eyes were locked on the bird. Good. Tess drew in a steadying breath and returned to the cage. Crouched before it. "So go and God bless, sweetie." She opened the door. "Let me just back on out of the way and you can—"

The lynx charged.

Tess had one glimpse of oncoming golden eyes. Reflex beat thought by a mile as she dropped, face in the dirt. Razor-sharp claws hooked her back—dug in—as a weight and shadow lunged over her.

The cat was gone.

"Whee-ewwww!" Tess breathed, contemplating a pebble not an inch from her nose. Was that the last thing a snowshoe hare ever saw, incoming eyes like blazing comets? Starting to laugh, she sat up shakily, and reached her fingers back to where it hurt.

They came away covered in blood. "Oh, *thanks,* you bum!"

She glanced toward the cave. No sign of the lynx, no sign of the chicken. Well, that was something, anyway. And she *had* told him to trust no one.

Tess stood with a wince and a groan, and set to folding up the cage. "Yeah, and when I grow up, you know what I want to be? I'm gonna be a wildlife biologist. Bet they have all the fun."

ADAM KNOCKED on the door to Tess's cabin. "Tess? Tess, are you in there?" When she didn't answer a second knock, he twisted the knob.

Still locked, just as it had been when he tried it yesterday. Frowning, he turned to study the meadow where her horses should have been grazing.

They'd been missing the day before, too. Which would lead a detective to conclude that, at least, she'd left here intentionally. She hadn't taken a hike and fallen down a cliff somewhere.

He shifted restlessly with the thought—jerked his hand away as Watson nosed him from behind. He turned to growl at the dog. "So where'd she ride off to?"

And why? She'd said nothing, the night she came to supper, about going away. "Did I come on too strong? Scare her off?"

The bloodhound gave him a mournful look, then sat to scratch his ribs.

Maybe Tess had left for good. She could have packed up, headed down the mountain to Suntop. A hard day's ride and she'd be home. "But if she thinks I won't follow her there…" Guarded by her legendary hard-ass old man, with two dozen cowhands to back him up. Suntop might be enough to humble the average cowboy come-a-courting, but Adam would have no problem riding up to her door. Demanding she—

"Getting ahead of yourself," he muttered. Just as likely she'd gone for a ride. Had been off riding yesterday, too, and he'd simply missed her. Adam walked around to her showerhouse, swept its curtain aside and stooped to feel the cedar grating.

Bone dry. Tess hadn't showered for days. He felt a nerve twitch in his cheek as he stood. If she'd ridden out somewhere, for whatever reason, then taken a fall… Her horses might well have homed to Suntop, instead of here. He clenched his fists as an image of her flashing smile swept through him. Not half as tough as she thought she was. A night or two, exposed out on the open mountainside… *God, what if something happened the night she left me?*

No, get a grip, Dubois. Her pack horse was missing, too. That meant she'd reached home that night, then left again later, taking both horses.

But he wasn't going to rest easy till he was sure she was safe. A washcloth and a towel hung on a clothesline stretched from the showerhouse to her cabin. These also showed no hint of dampness. Adam unpinned the cloth and offered it to the bloodhound along with the command Gabe had taught him. "*Find.* Find Tess, ol' boy. *Find* her!"

The dog nosed the cloth and yodeled his excitement, his tail waving frantically. Now here was a game a dog could play! Dropping his dewlaps to the ground, he started circling.

"Yeah, I *know* she lives here," Adam snarled when Watson stopped to paw her front door and bark. "Problem is, she's not home. *Find* her. *Find Tess.*" He offered the rag again. The dog whimpered and snuffled away, circling wider. With an enlightened yelp, he headed northeast.

The direction she'd been riding when Adam had intercepted her three days ago. He hurried for his mare, then swung around as the bloodhound bayed.

Stopping where the trail vanished into the trees, Watson bellowed again. "*Ah-woooo!* Wooo-ooo!"

And a rider jogged out of the woods with a pack horse trotting behind. Tess!

Adam drew a long breath. Stupid, getting worked up like that. Lust had a bad way of clouding a man's judgement. She was fine. Putting on a cool, casual face, he strolled to meet her.

His eyes narrowed as she neared.

Normally graceful in the saddle, Tess rode with a telltale stiffness. She smiled at him as she approached, but the smile wobbled and wavered. Beneath the hat, her face seemed too pale. Adam closed the last few yards quickly and frowned up at her as she reined in. "What happened?"

"N-nothing. What are you doing here?"

I've come for you. These past few days, he'd thought of nothing but the taste of her lips. Told himself all the while that he was a fool, that he had to be exaggerating her impact. That he'd simply gone too long between women. That any willing female would do.

Looking up at her now, he knew this yearning was

more than simple need. But never mind that now, some-thing was wrong. "You're hurt," he said roughly.

"N-not really."

"Huh." Gripping her waist, he lifted her out of the sad-dle.

She winced as she caught at his shoulders, then her boots touched ground and she laughed at herself. "I'm fine. Really. Just…was doing some bushwhacking. Didn't duck in time, when we loped under a branch. Got scratched a bit." She brushed a knuckle across her lips and glanced aside.

Lie, Adam noted absently. But most of him was focused on the curves of her waist beneath his fingers, so incredibly slender, so enticingly warm. *Mine.* He'd known it from the first time he met her. "Show me." He turned her in spite of her resistance, then sucked in his breath. *"Shit!"*

The back of her shirt was shredded and stained. The blood had dried, sticking the cloth to her shoulder blade.

"REALLY, Adam, I can handle this myself," Tess tried for the third time, a short while later.

Not that her previous protests had done a bit of good. He'd built a fire in her stove. Then, while the water heated, he'd scissored her shirt away, tossing the parts of it that weren't stuck to her wound on the floor.

Attuned to the whisper of his breath behind her, she'd heard it quicken as her shirt fell away. He'd unhooked her bra with shaking fingers, then skimmed the straps ten-derly down her shoulders. His eyes had darkened to black when he wrapped a towel around her and walked her to the shower house.

While she'd scrubbed herself, Adam had unsaddled her horses and boiled more water. All her assertions that she was okay, that she could doctor herself, had been ignored.

Now he sat on the edge of her bunk, where she lay facedown, wrapped in a towel. "*Darn* it, Adam, it was nothing but a tree branch!" She'd said it often enough to almost convince herself. "Happens all the time."

"If you say so. But then we've got to worry about splinters, don't we? Let me have a look."

Trapped by her own lie. And blast the man, he sounded as if he was smiling! "Oh, go ahead," she said sulkily and gave up her grip on the towel.

He eased it down almost to her waist.

As the terry cloth grazed her skin, goose bumps scurried along her arms and thighs. Though she'd worn swimsuits that exposed more than she was presently showing, never had Tess felt *this* naked. She could feel the solid weight and heat of him looming above her. He'd braced one hand on the far side of her bunk, so she was surrounded, going nowhere till he permitted.

She ought to have felt tense. On guard. Instead she felt bonelessly limp, her muscles all loose and lazy, stunned by the heat of her shower and by Adam's almost tangible attention. A shudder of awareness flickered through her. "It's n-nothing, I tell you."

"Uh-huh." He traced the edge of her shoulder blade with a work-roughened fingertip. "Gonna have to soak this some more. This bit of shirt's still stuck."

Closing her eyes, Tess surrendered herself to sensations—the drenching heat of his washrag, his deft and soothing fingers, the honeyed flow of arousal between her thighs. As Adam eased the cloth away from her skin, inch by careful inch, the tiny bursts of pain only sharpened her awareness.

"Ow!" she cried suddenly.

"*Sorry,* sweetheart." Adam leaned so close she could feel the air compress between their bodies. His lips found the nape of her neck, brushed back and forth, making delicious amends. "I know it hurts. Hang in there… Just a little more and we're done."

She drew a ragged breath. Her hips pressed against the mattress in a slow-motion rock. But realizing he'd see this, see it for what it was, she stopped—at the height of her pendulum swing. Desire spread out from that point of pressure in tantalizing ripples. She *needed* to move. Itched to move.

Shouldn't.

"Once more," Adam warned, then made her wince again. She let out a shivering gasp. "I'm sorry, Tess." Nuzzling through her tousled hair, his lips found the rim of her ear.

She whimpered as his teeth closed on it, nibbled her gently.

"Just to distract you," he assured her on a note of husky laughter.

Consider me distracted. Devastated. Oh, don't stop!

But Adam sat upright. "Now, let's see what we've got here." He reached for a flashlight, switched it on and played it over her back. "Hmm. No splinters that I can see… Looks more like you tangled with a major cat than a tree."

"It d-does?" Tess was glad her face was buried in the pillow.

"Yep." A fingertip stroked her tingling skin. "We've got three punctures here. Then…four gashes, couple of inches long and fairly deep."

Where Geronimo's front paw had landed, then he'd

hooked in with his rear and pushed off, using her for a launch pad. "Oh?" she murmured, striving for innocence.

"Could use some stitches, I'd say. I see you've got needles and catgut in your first aid kit. I'm not a bad hand at this."

"Those are for sewing up cows and horses and other folks! I *hate* needles. Would you just slap some ointment on, then tape it, please?"

His lips touched her skin just north of the pain. "Could do—it's what I'd do for myself. But a back as beautiful as yours? 'Fraid it'll scar some."

"I don't care. Scars show where you've been."

"And the no good you've been up to." There was rich amusement in his voice as he bent again to nuzzle her nape. "Tess, scratched by Life."

But it was Adam she wanted to be marked by. Liza was right. Her life would never be complete if she let him come this close then no closer. Whatever he had to give her, pain or pleasure, she *needed* it. Would have it.

So when he'd completed her bandage, it was Tess who clutched the towel to her breasts, then rolled gingerly over, to lie looking up at him with wide, wanting eyes.

His dark brows drew together. "Sure you should lie like that?"

"For now…" It did hurt, but the first time, she wanted him face to face. She walked her fingers up the placket of his shirt, hooked a finger in above a button. "Thanks for…taking care of me." She smiled, tugged on his shirt—

And down he came, like a big tree toppling. "Oh, Tess!" Bracing his weight on one forearm, he framed her face with a hand.

Soft as a sigh, their lips met, clung, danced in slow, sweet hunger.

What she'd been wanting from the very start. Humming her pleasure, she opened to him. Closed her eyes and aimed all her senses inward, to the liquid dance…the dark, hot-velvet thrusts of his tongue. Her hips rocked upward, which pressed her shoulder into the mattress; she whimpered, more in need than in pain.

But he tore his mouth free. "Can't do it like this." Hooking an arm around her waist, Adam lifted her and rolled till she lay full-length on top of him. "There, that better?"

Oh, that was the best! A raft of rippling muscles beneath her. The fragrance of his skin surrounding her— whiffs of sage and sweat and leather and soap. Tess molded herself to his surging shape. Nuzzled her face greedily into the top of his shirt. Cried out with pleasure as he dragged the towel from between them, then splayed his hands on her writhing hips.

"My sweet…"

They found each other's mouths again. Kissed deep and long and laughing with the sheer delight of it. There was too much wonderful to touch all at once. Their hands caressed; their arms and legs twined and tangled like two starfish trying to connect every point.

Except that she was naked and he was not. "No fair! All these *clothes*," Tess complained, tugging his shirttails free of his jeans. Did he have chest hair? Could she love a man who didn't? But a button went flying as he yanked his shirt open and she let out a cry of triumph. Dark, silky whorls on his tanned skin and—

"*Oh!*" She hadn't expected scars. "Is that a—?"

Had to be. Nothing but a bullet would leave a mark like

that, there above his collarbone. And it was recent. Tracing it with a fingertip, Tess glared at him with flashing eyes. *Somebody hurt you? Show him to me! I'll shoot him myself!*

"Yeah, but I can explain." Adam caught her waist and dragged her upward along his length, till he could reach her breasts. *"Later."* His tongue flicked her nipple, then circled its aching peak, slowly, wetly, with luscious deliberation.

When he sucked, all sane thought flew away. Worries were for later. Questions for some other lifetime. Moaning deep in her throat, she arched to give him better access. Ruffled his thick hair with restless hands.

"Like that, do you?" Adam laughed softly—and turned his attention to her other breast. Lips…tongue…then his teeth closed delicately upon her.

Yes, oh, yes, oh, please, please, yes!

LATE SUNLIGHT slanted through the window when Tess woke from enchantment—to find her cheek pillowed on a hard brown arm. She lay spooned to Adam's length, cradled by his warmth. His other hand was flattened on her belly; the tip of his forefinger nestled possessively in her navel. She sighed in dreamy contentment. They'd made love twice, dozing between times, and if the first time had been thrilling, the *second!* For sheer sweet lingering perfection…

"You awake, there?" Adam murmured behind her. He lipped the rim of her ear.

"Might be…but if I'm not—" Tess purred, stretching back against him. "Don't you *dare* wake me." She licked the hard swell of his bicep, savoring salt and man.

Silent laughter vibrated against her. He outlined her bandaged shoulder blade with kisses. "And how does this feel? You're not hurting?"

She had a deep, well-earned ache between her thighs, as if she'd galloped bareback over the Rockies. But she wouldn't have traded the feeling for all the gold in the West. "I feel fine." *Wonderful.*

"'Bout a million miles beyond fine," Adam drawled, his hand smoothing from her belly to her breasts. He skimmed his palm across a peak, found it risen, teased and tantalized till her hips nudged his swelling hardness and she hummed with helpless desire.

Shouldn't do this with him a third time, she warned herself. Twice was pure magic, but another could be downright dangerous. Three made the charm. If he cast a spell she couldn't break…

Any woman with an ounce of sense would get up, get dressed, start fumbling her way back to reality. She should comb out her hair. Make sandwiches and have him talk to her. Ask him things she ought to know, like where he'd learned to make love like a fallen angel? And just what gave him the notion to stick a couple of condoms in his pocket this morning? Or, what she was really wondering: *Who shot you, Adam?*

Twice. He had a second bullet scar on his thigh.

But while he touched her like this, she was going nowhere…asking nothing. It was all she could do to draw breath, with her heart hammering so.

"Woof!" Over by the door, Watson surged to his feet. He padded to the nearest window and reared to stand, paws propped on the sill, gazing out. He snorted and shook his ears. "Arr-*ooof!*"

Outside in the meadow, Cannonball whinnied. Another horse answered in the distance. Adam's hand stopped its magic. "Hell and damnation! Company's coming."

CHAPTER ELEVEN

THE MORNING SUN had yet to clear the peaks when Tess reached the new-growth hillside to the west of Zelda's den. Swinging a leg over Cannonball's rump, she winced, then smiled to herself. She couldn't put that man out of mind for five minutes before he reminded her, one way or another.

On the ground, she clenched a fist between her breasts and tipped her head back, remembering. Savoring. Adam's lips, the strength of his hands—a shudder shook her from boot heels to Stetson. That wild, wonderful feel of him moving inside her!

Maybe it was just as well that Sean Kershaw had barged in, needing help with a cow that had fallen down a ledge. If the kid hadn't intruded, they'd be in bed yet.

As it was, she'd felt the strangest reluctance to see Adam go. A feeling almost like homesickness. Anxious to postpone their parting, she'd volunteered to ride along and help. Sean was working for Suntop, after all; this was his first summer down at White Rock line camp. So his problem cow was her cow, in the end.

But Adam had been immovable. She was injured. In no shape to go messing around with panicked cows after dark, and anyway, two should be plenty for the job. Sending Sean out to catch his horse, he'd slid his hands into the back pockets of the jeans she'd thrown on, and hauled her close. "Don't tell me you couldn't use a nap right now," he teased, his lips on her temple.

"Really, I'm fine. Not tired at all," she insisted, leaning against him.

"Say that one more time and I'll start thinkin' I wasn't as thorough as I thought I was." He ducked to catch her mouth, and kissed her till an after-explosion of ecstasy sent her shuddering and arching. When he lifted his head, his mouth curled at the corners. "A man doesn't want to leave his woman fresh as a daisy. Maybe I better come back, once I'm done—finish what I started?"

Oh, absolutely!

But she couldn't quite admit it. To want a man as much as she wanted this one was dangerous. Not in her plans, and yet... Torn between desire and worry, she brushed a knuckle across her lips and glanced aside, then looked up—to find him wearing a wide, self-satisfied grin. She frowned, gave a haughty little shrug. "Whatever."

He wasn't rebuffed in the least. "'Whatever' sounds good to me."

And to her, even if he was too darned sure of his welcome. So after he'd gone, she'd showered again, made a sandwich, then climbed into bed, but left the lamp burning and her door unlatched. She'd meant to stay awake till he returned, but Adam had been right; she was spent, both physically and emotionally.

She remembered waking once in the night to the sound of thunder. A big storm was rumbling across the peaks. She'd felt a longing sharp as a lightning bolt, wishing he was there, making love with her while the storm raged.

Then the next thing she knew, it was dawn. And he hadn't come.

And Zelda hadn't been fed in four days! "So get on with it," Tess muttered now, as she pulled a wrapped chicken from the saddlebag.

Wading through the dew-drenched grass, she walked around a wide shaggy fir—then froze, one foot in the air.

A ghostly gray shape glided across the slope below. Zelda. Her head was tipped back, so that the limp rabbit she carried didn't drag the ground. She turned to cast a golden-eyed glare upon Tess, then stalked on, ears warily reversed to monitor any sounds of pursuit. Reaching the shorter grass at the edge of the older forest, she bounded into the shadows. Vanished toward her den.

Tess blew out her pent-up breath and sat. *"Well!"* Sad for the rabbit, happy for the cat, she blinked and found tears on her lashes. A sight as primeval as that...so fiercely innocent...so ruthlessly right... She hugged herself and tipped her face toward the rain-rinsed sky. This was the real reason she had to be outdoors. Simply to witness and be thankful. Some people sought God in church, but she'd always crossed His trail in the wild, with sights like that one.

"Thank you!" she whispered, and touched a blue columbine that waved in the grass beside her. A drop of dew caught the first rays of sunlight as it rolled onto her fingertip. She put it to her tongue.

Adam...if only she could have shared this moment with Adam.

RIGGING a primitive block and tackle, then using horse power to haul the cow up the ledge had turned into quite an operation. She'd landed in a bush and hadn't been hurt by her fall. But she was indignant and scared and her calf's bawling from the cliff above only made her more frantic. Adam and Sean had finished the rescue near mid-night. He'd been tempted to ride straight back to Tess, but by then thunder was rolling up from the west.

Lightning out on the mountainside was not to be messed with, so he'd bedded down on Sean's floor. And dreamed of loving Tess.

This morning she was still the main thing on Adam's mind. But Sean's problem cow had reminded him of his duties. He ought to head straight back to his own range and check how the herd had weathered the storm. Still Tess's cabin was only a short detour from the route home, and he didn't want her thinking he took her for granted. So he'd stop by, kiss her dizzy, then be on his way, he promised himself.

And make sure of his rain check. *Tonight!* The hours between were going to move like molasses.

By the time he swung down from the saddle, he was nearly exploding with impatience. "Sit," he warned Watson; he wasn't in a mood to share her smiles with a dog. He rapped on her door. "Tess!" He rapped again, then swung it open. "Tess?"

The cabin's emptiness found an echo in his heart. Reminded him of all the cold bare rooms of his childhood. *She's gone.* Hadn't waited for him.

Scowling, he turned to scan the meadow. Her pack horse grazed on its picket line, but he'd been too dis-tracted to notice that her big, rawboned gelding was gone. "Now where the hell did you ride off to?" The sun wasn't an hour above the horizon.

He laughed as it hit him. She'd gone to find him when he didn't return! Doubtless Tess was waiting now at his cabin, maybe fixing herself a cup of coffee, or— *She's lying on my bed?*

He snapped his fingers at the bloodhound, sprang into the saddle and galloped sunward.

RIDING BACK to her cabin, Tess found her breath coming quicker, her toes curling in her boots. Adam must have slept over at Sean's place, but by now? Surely he'd returned as promised. Cannonball gave a little jump as her thighs tightened in reflex. He flicked his ears back at her and snorted when she reined him in to a walk. "Sorry." She patted his neck. "Just thinking."

About Adam. Oh, this was no good! She'd never met a man before who took up so much space in her mind—and on such short notice. She wasn't sure she liked this. Still, as Tess rode out of the trees, she looked eagerly toward her cabin.

Her smile faltered. Adam's black mare was nowhere in sight.

She waited breakfast for an hour, hoping he'd join her, then scrambled the last of her fresh eggs, fighting an impulse to bang the pots on her stove as she cooked. It was silly to be hurt. Most likely he'd hurried straight home to check his herd, what with all that thunder last night. The man was a cowboy, after all, and conscientious was good. Still, her cabin wasn't that far out of his way, was it?

After eating, Tess determinedly hit her books. Her campout with Geronimo had put her behind in her dissertation work. But her heart wasn't in it, and neither was her mind. She read one statistical survey of beaver populations in the Cascades three times, not absorbing one word of it, finally giving up and tossing it aside.

"Okay, okay." She'd write Liza instead, brag about Zelda's triumph, confess her barbed encounter with Mr.

Claws. After that it would be time to visit the tomcat, see if the big jerk had stuck around.

And she had better collect the folding cage, which she'd left hidden near his den. She had been in no mood to wrestle it onto her pack mare yesterday, with her shoulder hurting so.

THE HERD had weathered the storm alright, though it had drifted before the wind. Adam spent most of the day moving it back west to better grass. While doing so, he'd spotted four cases of pinkeye. By the time he'd returned to his cabin for the medicine, then ridden back and roped and treated every infected calf he could find, the sun was a red ball, sinking fast.

He'd showered, shaved, saddled a fresh horse from his string. Now he stood in the blue twilight, his smile fading an inch with every unanswered knock on Tess's door. What the hell? What game was she playing—hide and seek?

He blew out a frustrated breath. All day his spirits had been spiraling down from yesterday's stupendous high. From this morning when he'd found her not waiting for him at his cabin, they'd descended through a day of hard work among contrary cows to…this. No welcome waiting.

No Tess, welcoming or otherwise.

And—he scanned the meadow and blinked. This time she'd taken both her horses! Which meant she'd returned, since his morning ride-by. Then had gone out again.

"You've got to know I'm looking for you." *Wanting you.* He stirred irritably as what he was feeling now reminded him of the way he'd felt that last month when Alice was making up her mind to leave him.

Alice hadn't been up-front with him.

She didn't tell him straight that she'd decided she didn't want to be a cop's wife, after all. That she'd concluded Adam wasn't worth all her long hours alone or the worry she felt whenever he was out on the streets. She didn't tell him that, all things considered, she'd rather marry a handsome dentist who earned three times a detective's salary plus he'd make it home every night by six, with never a bullet hole to show for a day's work. Instead of telling Adam this bad news, Alice had simply faded out of his life for that last month or so.

She would make charming excuses when he tried to ask what was wrong, then she'd drift away a little more. "But I didn't want to hurt you," she'd protested in her spun-sugar drawl, when he'd finally pinned her down.

Which showed how little she'd ever known him. He'd always been one for ripping the tape off a wound, rather than drawing out the pain, bit by cowardly bit.

Thoughts of bandages brought him back to Tess. "Are you ducking me?" There was no law that said she had to fall for him, simply because he'd taken her to bed.

No guarantee that she'd even want a repeat.

Yet something—not just her laughing little cries during, but the look in her big eyes afterwards, or the way her lips had quivered and clung when she'd kissed him? *Something* had made him assume that Tess was feeling what he— He slammed a fist into her door and swung away.

Aw, to hell with it. He was beat. Hungry. In need of a bed, and he'd damn sure sleep all the better if he was the only one in it.

In his black mood, it didn't occur to Adam till he'd ridden halfway back to his own cabin: if Tess was dodging him, then why would she need a pack horse?

And if she wasn't?

Then what was the woman up to, with all her roaming around?

TESS FOUND no sign of Geronimo when she checked his cave just before sundown.

Possibly he was catnapping inside. No way would she crawl in to inquire! Or maybe he'd stalked off by his own surly lonesome, never to return. All she could do was leave a thawed chicken on his doorstep, then check back tomorrow.

With supper delivered, it took her a good hour of hearty swearing to load the folded cage on her skittish pack mare. Perhaps it smelled more and more of lynx? The stench of a big cat could hardly be a comforting odor to a horse in mountain lion country, but at last she got it lashed in place.

Returning through the dark, Tess kept her ears pricked for sounds of a horseman's approach. This wasn't the direct trail from Adam's cabin to hers, but if for some reason he chose it instead—? "Don't suppose he'd believe I've been trapping beavers," she muttered, glancing back at the slabs of silver mesh that swung from the mare's sides.

On the other hand, maybe she had no need to worry about bumping into him. While waiting for Adam all day, she'd started to wonder. With his curiosity slaked and his urge satisfied, maybe the man had taken everything from her he wanted?

Or maybe it hadn't been as good for him as it had been for her?

"Whatever." Tess raised her chin and squared her shoulders. It wasn't as if she'd been looking for a man in the first place! With two lynx and a dissertation to juggle this summer, who needed a hot, sweet, heart-stoppingly sexy affair?

Her mouth tipped up in spite of her mood. "Yeah, right!" Touching her heels to Cannonball's ribs, she urged him to a jog.

But maybe this was too early to sing the blues. If Adam had found his herds scattered by the storm, then it might have taken hours to put things right. Easily all day. Still he could hardly work in the dark, which meant...

Her hopes scattered like dandelion fluff on the wind as she reined in at the edge of the forest. With the moon riding high, she could see clearly. There was no strange horse staked out in her meadow.

Besides, she'd left her door unlocked, just in case. But if Adam was waiting for her, he'd have lit the kerosene lamp.

Her cabin windows were black squares, dark and empty as an unloved heart.

ADAM SAT BOLT UPRIGHT as a phone rang.

For an instant he was back in New Orleans, in his own bed, where a call after midnight meant a death in somebody's family. And a night of grim duty for him.

Another chirp—his damned cell phone! He shook his head to clear it and found himself in Sumner cabin, with a wild hope dawning. Tess! Could she be calling him? Demanding that he come on the double to warm her bed?

On my way! He threw the blanket aside—tripped over Watson, who yelped and shambled off across the cabin. Cursing a blue streak, Adam fumbled for his cell phone, which he'd hidden behind a book on his bookshelf.

Can't be Tess, he realized, and his mood blackened to match the pitch-dark room. He was the only cowhand in the high country with a phone, as far as he knew, and he hadn't admitted he carried it to anyone on the trail drive. Or to Tess.

There was a fourth ring as he snatched it up and barked, "Yeah?"

"Adam. Did I wake you?"

Gabe. They'd agreed Adam should carry a phone for emergencies or crucial updates. Communication was often the difference between case cracked and case failed. "It's a bit late even for you. What's up?"

"It's only eleven, but sorry. Forgot you'd be sleeping with the cows."

Adam snorted and sat on his bunk, ruffled a hand through his hair. "Not that desperate yet." *And if I sleep with anybody again this summer? She'll have green eyes, not brown.* "What's up?" he repeated.

"Just got back from the Uncompahgre Plateau. We lost a lynx over there five days ago. We got the death signal for Collar BC02F1 on Monday."

"And today is?" Adam asked as he noted the number. He'd add this data to the map of crime scenes he was compiling. Sometimes the date was significant in predicting a perp's patterns.

"Ah, the carefree life of a cowboy. Dad was right. I should have stuck with ranching. It's Saturday, sliding into Sunday."

"So…" Adam scratched his chin. "He didn't come straight for our bait. Wonder why not?"

"Beats me. But I thought you should know he's still out there and active."

"And hunting not too far from here. My guess would

be he'll move the Trueheart area to the top of his list now. Maybe he's thinking a pregnant female might stay near her nest. Be harder to find till she's dropped her kittens."

"He'd be thinking right."

"And whoever he is, he's an experienced hunter. Knows his prey well enough to keep bringing it down."

"We've got to bring *him* down, the cold-hearted bastard! I want to see him in a federal prison, doing hard time. All those prime lynx in six months! He's dismantling our program single-handed."

"We'll get him," Adam promised. He'd taken his eyes off the target the past few days. But no more. He'd promised to do this job and he would. Time to stop chasing the elusive Tess, and start chasing the killer.

CHAPTER TWELVE

ANOTHER DAY passed and still Adam didn't come. But by the following dawn, Tess's spirits had rebounded.

At least, she was working on a rebound. "So what that he never returned?" she said aloud, as she rode toward Zelda's den. She'd been an idiot, taking their afternoon together for anything more than a romp.

A female lynx would never be so foolish. She'd know a disperser for what he was—and was not. She'd take the lusty pleasure he offered, then get on with her own life, no grudges, no regrets.

No romantic daydreams or expectations for the future.

Of course, a lynx queen in heat might mate with her suitor two dozen or more times over the course of a few days, Tess recalled with a grimace. Maybe it was easier to see the last of his hairy face, after *that* much fulfillment.

"So what's the solution?" she muttered. "Go demand my other twenty-two times, and then I'll forget him?"

Yeah, right. Better to quit while she was ahead.

When she reached the slope of young trees, she took care creeping through it, on the lookout for the huntress. She'd stayed away for forty-eight hours since Zelda's kill, in the hope that the lynx would grow hungry and go stalking again.

But if Zelda was on the prowl, Tess failed to spot her. Approaching the den beneath the fallen tree, she blew Zelda's food signal on her silent whistle. Then she placed the chicken in front of the burrow and backed away.

Something stirred in the tunnel's dark entrance. Tess froze. Blinked. Her mouth rounded to an *"oh"* of utter astonishment as a tawny kitten wobbled out into the light. A second spotted baby galloped behind it, bumped into its sibling and both went sprawling.

"Oh, you wonders! You *miracles!*" Tess crooned under her breath, backing away. Though her every instinct insisted that she sweep up the fuzzy darlings and hug them, her wildlife training demanded otherwise. Some animals abandon their young if a human interferes with their scent. Tess had no idea of lynx policy in such situations. But she'd no intention of wrecking Zelda's new family.

"Adorable!" she whispered as the kittens sniffed at the chicken. They were too young for solid food; still they were interested.

An imperious feline chirp sent the babies scurrying into the darkness. Tess turned to a guilty statue.

Ears flat to her skull, Zelda ghosted out of the downhill bushes. Most likely coming from the pool, since her neck ruff hung in damp points. Icily ignoring her trespasser—though the lynx's outraged ears spoke volumes—she snatched up the chicken and vanished down the hole.

"You should have seen them! Oh, I wish you could have seen them!"

Tess exulted to Liza in her letter later that morning.

"They can't be more than two weeks old—must have been born within a day or two of Zelda's release. Guess we were both wrong, assuming she and her cage-mate had neither room nor inclination. Plus I realized the other day that we got to talking, and forgot to check her for kittens one last time the night you brought her to me."

Sitting on her cabin stoop with her notepad balanced on her knees, Tess leaned back against the doorjamb, and sighed contentedly.

"Anyway, all's well that ends so well, but do you realize what this means? We've midwifed a miracle! The poor Division of Wildlife has been trying and hoping for lynx kittens for four years now with no luck."

Not that anybody was about to congratulate them. Tess's smile turned wry for an instant. They'd helped make a miracle, yet they couldn't brag or pass out cigars. Dared tell no one but each other.

The DOW would be highly disapproving—to say the least—should they discover that a couple of amateurs had encroached on a federally authorized, Endangered Species program. And worse yet, that they'd succeeded where the professionals had failed.

As for Tess's family and friends in the cattle industry? Yes, she could imagine what her father would say if he learned that not only was she freeing lynx on his range, but that they were multiplying!

Still, still and still: lynx back in the San Juans, and she'd helped make it so! Tess hugged herself and laughed in delight.

HE SHOULD HAVE STAYED home till Karen was talking to him again. But Natwig couldn't afford to wait. Not while seventy thousand dollars in bounty money was denned up in the mountains north of Trueheart.

A queen lynx with four kittens, Larson had said. By now Natwig figured she'd be nursing her litter, which meant she'd be constantly hungry. For the past few nights he'd camped high and slept little. Spent hours sweeping the slopes and valleys below with his radio direction-finding antenna. To keep her milk flowing, she had to find meat. Sooner or later, he was bound to catch the signal off her collar as she hunted.

But two nights passed with not a beep in his earphones to show she was out there.

While he stood in the dark, rotating the wand slowly, Karen's face loomed large in his mind. The way she'd looked when last he'd seen her. Tears in her stormy blue eyes and her pretty mouth thinned to a trembly line when he'd told her he needed to ride out again so soon. Just for a few days, he'd pleaded. He needed to scout the elk herds. Spot the trophy bucks, so he could plan his guided hunts for this coming fall.

"Like you needed to drive up to Wyoming last month, or the month before?" she'd muttered and rolled herself down the ramp to her garden.

"I told you, there was a horse sale, some likely animals," he'd protested, following her.

"Which you didn't buy!" she pointed out, cutting a dead rose off its stem and flinging it across the lawn. The calico cat leaped down from her lap to crouch, eyes fixed on the spot where it fell. Tail-tip twitching, it stalked toward the "bird."

"And the two times before that, you drove up there?

An old friend in trouble, then a shotgun that was sold before you got there? *Ha!*"

He could have been smoother with his lies, he saw now. But he'd grown so used to her trust over the years, some part of him had figured she'd believe whatever he told her.

Or maybe some part of him wanted to get caught.

"Like you need to hang around Webster's barn all the time? Well, whatever you're looking for, Joe Natwig, you go right ahead and get it. Who's stopping you?" She threw another dead rose after the first, then another. Bombarded by "birds," her cat shot into the bushes.

I'll make it up to you, baby, he swore to her silently now. *Stick with me like you've always stuck. I'll make this last score and then—*

But he had an uneasy feeling that it wouldn't be that simple, telling Larson he'd had enough. That if he kept on this way, he might lose his wife before he settled their debts.

Except for those flat little snake eyes, Larson looked soft. Yet something about the man put Natwig in mind of one of his grandma's old sayings. *He who sups with the devil better bring a long spoon.*

Well, he'd settle that problem when he came to it. Meanwhile, there was the lynx—or there wasn't.

Finding no trace of her from the heights, he began seeking her during the day, as well, burning the candle at both ends. If he couldn't catch her signals hunting, there was always water. A nursing female would be thirsty.

So he checked every spring for miles around. Followed every stream. Scanned their banks for prints, and the surrounding bushes for tufts of snagged hair.

She wouldn't den far from water. Every dawn, every twilight, she'd come to drink—she had to. Just let him find her tracks and the rest would be easy.

THE AFTERNOON of the fourth day, Natwig's luck finally turned. He was cutting back west on a trail that ran north of Sumner line camp.

Mostly he stayed at higher elevations than the cattle grazed, since he figured the lynx would do the same. But he'd remembered a spring lay along this trail and he meant to check it.

Slumped wearily in his saddle, he kept his eyes peeled and his ears tuned for hoofbeats. Line-camp cowboys were a nosy bunch, jealous of their territory. Interested in anyone who passed through it. Though he kept his direction-finding equipment broken down and hidden in a fly-fishing rod case, still, he didn't need that kind of attention if he could dodge it.

He reached the spring, just a trickle down a cliff that pooled in a basin he could have stepped across. Dismounting, he held his roan gelding back when the animal would have pushed forward to drink. Eyes narrowed in the late-afternoon light, Natwig swept his gaze over the likely approaches.

Then he let out a grateful sigh. At last, there in that patch of mud! One perfect print and half the other paw, where the cat had crouched to lap water.

Groaning with relief, he stooped and drifted his fingers just above it. Big for a lynx. Big enough for a yearling mountain lion! *"Shit,"* he muttered, then his face relaxed. No, look at the blurring around the pug marks from all the fur that turned the lynx's outsize paws into snowshoes for winter traveling. "Gotcha."

Well, she was as good as got.

Behind him, the horse's bridle clinked as he threw up his head and whickered under his breath. Ears pricked, he looked westward along the trail, to where it vanished beyond a ridge of sandstone.

Hell! Somebody coming.

By the time his own ears could make out hoofbeats, Natwig stood fifty yards off the path, peering through a gap in a stand of sumac bushes. He kept one hand clamped on the gelding's nose, ready to pinch off his air if he tried to call. "Ea-a-a-sy," he crooned, rubbing the animal's jaw and the muscled arch of his neck. "Not a sound, ol' boy."

The rider wasn't a cowboy, but a girl. Or young woman, Natwig decided, watching her tensely. What the hell? Pretty as this one was, she wasn't likely riding alone. There'd be a man sniffing around here someplace.

But nobody else showed, while she loosed the reins to let her horse drink. Taking off her hat, she shook a cloud of dark hair out on her shoulders. "Shouldn't do this," she said aloud, apparently to her big, hammer-headed gelding.

With his nose in the pool, he ignored her completely.

She stretched her arms wide, laughed softly, then settled her hat back in place. "On the other hand, we're two-for-two—no, better than that—and there's not a drop of champagne at my place. And who wants to celebrate alone?"

Not that one, Natwig concluded, amused in spite of his worry. And whatever she needed to toast, she was too happy to notice the tracks at her horse's feet. Reining her mount away from the pool, she loped off to the east. Toward Sumner line camp.

When the hoofbeats had faded to silence, Natwig studied the rosy sky. Not an hour till sundown. The lynx should be stirring in her den. Nursing her kittens one last time so they'd sleep while she prowled. Then she'd come to water before she went hunting.

And find him waiting.

WATSON LURCHED up from the grass and shuffled to meet her, tail waving, as Tess rode toward the cabin. "Hello, sweetie." She dismounted to rub his silky ears, then thump his bony shoulder. "Where's your pal, huh?"

Adam's door stood open to the cool evening air. The glow of a lamp gilded the room beyond. *You shouldn't have come,* she told herself, as she dropped Cannonball's reins in a ground hitch. *The man doesn't want to see you. Can't you take a hint?*

But this was the second day without him, and she was missing him. Wondering. How could all that blazing passion have turned to ice overnight? Could there possibly be another, less painful explanation for his negligence?

Like he'd caught a foot in a bear trap. Or contracted malaria and taken to his bed? She smiled at herself and took the tip of the bloodhound's ear, the way one might hold hands with a child. Strolled with him toward that beckoning door. "Might as well find out the worst, huh, guy? Can't start getting over him, till he's said 'so long' for sure."

She stopped at the doorway and peered in—and drew a long, slow breath. God, but he was beautiful!

Wearing nothing but a pair of jeans, Adam sat at his table. The bold angles and planes of his profile were lit by the lantern beyond. Its light swooped and played on the bunched muscles in his shoulders, stroked gold along the generous curve of his lower lip. He was studying a large, curling paper he'd pinned to the tabletop with his brawny forearms.

"Hey, neighbor!" she called, her voice husky with shyness. "I was wondering—"

He jerked upright, glanced around frowning. Then a smile lit his face.

Nobody could fake a welcome like that—a grin like she'd just announced Christmas. Ignoring her wobbly knees, Tess walked in. "Wondering if I could borrow a cup of sugar. Or salt. Or…" *You and that smile.*

Adam swung entirely to face her, and his paper—it looked like a map—curled to a cylinder. "How about honey?" He didn't rise to greet her. Tonight there was nothing gentlemanly about the way his eyes climbed her body and stopped on her lips. "Or lemme think…" His voice had dropped to a smoky drawl.

Her heart was fluttering against her chest the way a moth batters the chimney glass that keeps it from the flame. She bit her bottom lip so she wouldn't smile, or worse, laugh for pure joy. *Oh, you are glad to see me!* Unable to stop herself, she drifted closer—then let out a startled squeak as he leaned. Hooked two fingers over her belt and reeled her in.

"Come here!" he demanded as he slid a foot between her calves. His other foot followed. Another tug and Tess landed astride his lap, laughing helplessly. "*Yeah.* I believe we've got something better than honey 'round here." He laced one hand up into her hair and tugged her head back to meet his descending mouth.

"You didn't come!" she blurted against his lips, though she—she was near to coming already, sensations exploding out from their point of contact. Rising from her parted legs to her nipples in jagged, electric jolts. He cupped a big hand on her bottom and snugged her in against the welcoming bulge in his jeans.

"I did." Adam nipped her bottom lip, gave a dark and hungry growl, then added, "Came by twice, the day after, and where the hell were you?"

"You d-did?" Then all her pain and sadness, the awful humiliation at the way she'd let loose with him, shown him what she'd felt—that had all been for nothing? Simply foolish pride and fear? She laughed shakily as he kissed his way up her throat. Shuddered when his lips found her earlobe.

"Damn right I did. Sat there and howled on your doorstep a while and finally figured—" He plucked at her collar. "Oh, cowgirl with a pearl-snap shirt! I'm in heaven and it looks like Colorado." The snaps snicked and gave way as he bared her to the waist.

Adam stared down at her breasts, then up into her widening eyes. His own had gone black with desire. "I figured you were reconsiderin'...*this*..." He skimmed a rough fingertip over the nipple that swelled against the sheer cup of her bra.

Rocking against his hardness, she shivered. Shook her head. "No." No reconsiderations at all, as he circled that peak of gorgeous sensation, then bent his head to suckle her through the silk. She let out a throaty little cry and buried her hands in his hair, pressed him closer.

When he drew back at last, he laid an open-mouthed kiss on the curve of her breast, warming her with a damp sigh. "Thought maybe I'd rushed things. That if you needed some space, I'd give it to you." Lifting his head, he rested his forehead against her own. "Hmm?"

Silently she shook her head. She smiled and found

tears were gathering on her lashes, shattering the light to shards of gold, as he cupped her breast. He kissed her deep and long and so slow she'd have sworn she could feel the earth turning. "No, I don't want more space from you. I want less!" she whispered when he let her breathe again.

"Ah." His smile was hot and dangerous as a bed of raked coals in wildfire weather. "Well, that, *ma cher,* can be arranged."

REALLY OUGHT to get up, shut that door, Adam thought around midnight. Not that they'd have noticed a bear cruising through, helping himself to all the jam and crackers, then lumbering out again. Not for the past hour or so. *You are something else, Tess-my-green-eyes.* Braced on his elbows, he savored the sight of her.

Something else entirely from any other woman he'd ever known. He couldn't figure why or how she could touch him clear down to bedrock. But maybe *why* didn't matter, as long as it was so. Who questioned or complained when the sun finally rose? Dipping down, he stroked her kiss-swollen lips with the tip of his tongue.

She made a small, purring sound way back in her throat. It turned to a whimper of protest as he started to ease away. "No! Don't go." She caught his buttocks and held him where he was. "Stay."

"I'm too heavy for you."

Her muscles clenched him as she rippled like a wave. "You're perfect."

"No, that's you." He bent again to kiss her chin, the corner of her drowsy smile. "Thought I better shut the door before a bear or a cougar comes calling."

"You'd protect me," she assured him blithely, walking two fingers up the path of his spine.

And he would. From any and all comers. *You're mine now.* For this blissful while, anyway. Ought to have scared him, feeling like that, but it didn't. More of the rightness she brought with her.

Her fingers arrived at the point in the back of his shoulder, where the bullet had exited. Tess stroked the raised welt and gazed up at him. "Tell me about this?" She brushed her nose above his collarbone, where the same shot had entered. "And this?"

Adam sighed and dropped his face into the fragrant hollow of her neck, thinking, *I don't want to lie to you.*

But only a fool broke cover. And confessing to a lover was always the biggest temptation. The greatest danger. *She's a cattleman's daughter,* he reminded himself, *and friends to the rest.* Whoever was stalking the lynx might very well be a cowhand, her childhood sweetheart or neighbor.

While he, he was just a stranger passing through, however good and right this felt. No way could he figure to claim her loyalty, expect her to side with a stranger against her own kind.

"Mmm?" she coaxed, as her fingers sauntered back down his spine. Reaching his buttocks, they delved between, to stroke his inner thighs, one of them scarred. "And this?"

He felt himself stirring inside her, hardening more when she responded. He cocked his hips and drove into her one wet and satiny inch.

She let out a feathering gasp and gripped his hips to keep him there. "Don't...don't try to distract me, Dubois."

He grinned. "Think I couldn't?"

"I know you could, but don't. Who shot you?"

Half the truth then, since she insisted. "I walked in on a holdup one night at a corner grocery."

He'd had to go in without waiting for the reinforcements he'd called. After four months of mopping up after the Ski-Mask Killers, he'd known what was in store for the clerk, and anybody else unlucky enough to be shopping inside, if he didn't do something—and do it quickly.

But backup would have been nice. Just his luck that, after setting traps for those sadistic clowns all winter, they'd fall into his lap when he was off duty. Driving by on his way to pick up a pizza. Fate had a nasty trick of sending you what you'd prayed for when you were least prepared to handle it.

Tess sucked in her breath. "Oh, *Adam!*" She framed his face with slim fingers. "You could have been—"

"Yeah." It had been close. He'd decided it was smarter to go in with his weapon concealed. Let them think he was just one more hapless shopper to toy with, till he could see the setup and how to blow it apart.

But this stickup they'd been less playful and more hurried, and he'd just about missed his chance. Had had to take some punishment before he'd rolled free of their boots and gone for his gun.

"Was…was anyone else hurt?"

"Yeah." He'd had to hurt them all the way. There hadn't been space or time for finesse and the clerk was bleeding out, needed an ambulance yesterday. Not that three hopped-up teenagers were good candidates for negotiation anyhow. Not when they knew they'd already earned the Louisiana death penalty five times over.

Still he wasn't proud of what he'd had to do. "I'd just as soon talk about anything else." *You.* He stroked the upper swell of her left breast with a fingertip. "Like where you got this brand?"

"Brand!" Tess glanced down at herself in alarm. "There's no—"

He laid a scorching kiss on the spot, closing his eyes as her softness, her taste, the exquisite shape of her, burned his mouth. "There is now."

CHAPTER THIRTEEN

SOME TIME LATER, Tess awoke. Flattening her hands on Adam's broad chest, she raised her head.

"Hmm?" He reached up to ruffle her hair. "S'matter, sweet?"

"Cannonball! I never unsaddled him."

"Ah. I'll do it." Adam rolled with her toward the wall, disentangled himself, then slid away.

"Don't be silly. I'll—"

"You'll let me take care of it." He dropped a kiss on her stomach. "Go back to sleep."

"Bossy," she protested, though she had to smile. He was such a guy. Almost arrogantly at ease in his own skin. In giving orders. His high-handedness should have made her indignant, yet somehow it made her feel softer, more feminine. A woman could get used to his instinctive gallantry.

Don't, she reminded herself. He was a fabulous interlude, but no part of her plans.

Restless without him, she rose, decided to visit the outhouse. She found Adam's shirt-of-the-day tossed over his easy chair and slipped it on unbuttoned, amused when it brushed her knees. Another thing she liked, the difference in their sizes. As a child, she'd always favored large horses; she'd been thrilled by their power and speed. *And their endurance,* she reminded herself. To gallop all night with the wind in your hair? If that wasn't heaven, it was close enough.

When she returned, Adam still hadn't come back, so she prowled his cabin. It hadn't changed much since her last visit. Still neat, except for— Tess stooped to collect the tube of paper off the floor. He'd been studying it when she'd arrived. Smoothing out its curled edges on the table, she saw a topographic map. The San Juan Mountains—the whole southwest quadrant of the state.

Someone had added asterisks here and there, with notations in pen beside each star. She bent closer, trying to read the tiny letters in the dim light.

"Ho, raiding my closet already?" Adam's hands clamped on her waist.

"*Yikes,* don't sneak up on me like that!" As he nuzzled her nape, she laughed and let go the map. It snapped back to a cylinder. "*Mmm...*" Arching her neck, she reached behind to rub the back of his head. A wave of erotic heat rushed through her as his beard bristles scratched. "What's this you were doing?"

"Just a little geography." He rotated her to face him. "Calculating the distance between you and me." He lifted her up to the tabletop. Rested his hands on her knees. Slanted a dark brow in question.

"H-how...how far was it?" Between her thighs she could feel a pulse throbbing, a moist clenching and fluttering. Her heartbeat surged in expectation. Her hips rolled upward an inch and he didn't miss the instinctive response.

His smile deepened. His hands exerted a gentle, undeniable pressure. "Too far."

"Maybe...this would help?" She parted her legs so he could step forward between them.

SOME TIME near dawn, Tess plundered the kitchen. She found a bag of apples, some hard cheese wrapped in a vinegar-soaked cloth, his stash of crackers. Brought them back to the bunk, along with a glass of water.

";Should have fed you," Adam observed as she cut the apple into wedges.

"You did." Her soul was past satisfied, full to overflowing, but her stomach was starting to whine. "This is just to fill in a few gaps."

"Come over here and I'll fill in the gaps."

"Ha! I believe I've heard that before." She leaned from the chair she'd dragged over to feed him a slice—sighed as he kissed her fingertips. No holes in *her* contentment tonight. It was downright scary to be this happy. Anything so breathtakingly perfect couldn't possibly—

Shut up, shut up! she warned herself, and topped a cracker with cheese. Why spoil something wonderful with worry?

She turned instead to study his bookshelf and smiled as she saw the book on dinosaurs. Right, Stegosaurus Man. He hadn't shown *her* much armorplate tonight. "What were you like as a boy?"

Adam's face didn't so much darken as close. "A brat. Wise-mouth. Typical kid."

"Oh?" So here was the armor. She poked it just to be sure. "Drove your parents crazy, I suppose. Are they both back in New Orleans?"

"Guess they're no place in particular, bein' dead." He kicked off the sheet and rose, magnificently naked. "Thought I heard the horses. Back in a minute."

She fisted a hand and rapped it against her skull. *Good, Tess. Very good.* So much for not messing with perfection! Scowling, she constructed another cracker sandwich and munched it, all the while thinking: *Back off, girl.*

Easy to say when she wanted to know it all. Everything from his childhood, to his middle name, to a life list of his girlfriends.

Think of him as wildlife, she advised herself. *You wouldn't rush a beaver into accepting your scent and sight. A guy's no different.*

It was just that she'd felt so close to him tonight. Never this close before, to a man.

Funny how he could blithely, ruthlessly enter *her*—know her from the inside out—yet lock her out of his head and his history with no remorse. Men. *Ha!* Her irritation was building instead of fading. She bounced to her feet and paced, glaring at the table as she stalked past. Feeling an oven-blast of heat with the memory. Her nipples rose to brush painfully against the coarse cotton of Adam's shirt.

And what they'd done on the table reminded her of that map she'd been looking at just before—Tess paused, glanced around for it. Must have rolled off onto the floor?

But if it had, the map wasn't there now. She turned in place, eyes roving the cabin as she frowned. It was nowhere in sight. Now that was odd. When had he—

Her gaze came to rest on a rounded white object, placed on a window ledge. A rock? Except that the softly shadowed hollows suggested...

Crossing the room, she reached for it. Found it much too light for stone. Her gasp hissed loud in the silence. A skull—the sunbleached skull of a cat! Its cranium was too large for a domestic feline, to say nothing of those two-inch frontal fangs, yet too small for a grown mountain lion. Also the bone plates were fused, which meant it was a mature animal, no cub. Her heart was hammering painfully in her throat. She spun as a boot scraped in the doorway. Adam.

"What's this?" she demanded as he came to her.

He took the skull and put it back in its place. "Some kind of critter. Found it down by the creek."

Her heartbeat was calming, as much as it ever calmed around Adam. "It's some sort of cat." But not a fresh kill, as she should have realized by the whiteness of the bone. Nothing to do with *her* cats. A foolish, late-night worry.

"Mmm," he agreed. "I figured a bobcat." Spreading a hand on the back of her waist, he eased her toward the bed. "Now…I'd say we've got an hour or two till sunrise, and I don't know about you, junior. But me, if I'm going to be worth my salt tomorrow, I need a nap."

"Yeah, I can see you're tottering," she teased as he pulled her down onto the mattress and into his arms. "Just how old *are* you, Gramps?" She winced as she realized she was prying again.

But this time he didn't rebuff her. "Thirty-six," he growled against her hair. "And you? I reckon now's when you tell me you're jailbait."

"Flatterer." She molded herself against his heated length, sighed with sleepy bliss. *I could lie like this forever.* "I'm twenty-five."

"Twenty—!" Adam groaned as he nudged a leg between hers. "No wonder I feel rode hard and put up wet."

Well, that makes two of us. And lying like this would never work. How could she be utterly exhausted, yet totally aroused? Pondering that riddle, Tess kissed his collarbone just below the scar. She blessed the bullet that had spared him—and slept.

ADAM WOKE as he always did, at first light, but with a warm weight pinning his arm. His head snapped around, then his muscles eased and he laughed under his breath. Tess! Limp as a sleeping kitten, she lay curled into his side, with her nose buried in his armpit. From this angle she was a welter of glossy dark hair, a series of elegant curves.

A starburst of happiness around his heart.

Gradually his brows knit together. A dangerous feeling, that. Lust fulfilled was one thing, but "happy" could be the slippery slope toward "unhappy."

Lust was something a man could control, indulging or ignoring it as he pleased. Last night he'd been pleased to indulge.

But happiness, that heart-rise caused by one special woman. How did a man control it? Channel it? Guarantee that it would always be there when he needed it?

And if he couldn't, then it became the lever to pry his soul out by its roots. Nothing to be trusted. Something a wise man avoided.

As if to argue, Tess muttered darkly in her sleep. She squirmed around to her other side, snuggled her tight little bottom against his thigh.

Half-erect already, Adam found himself wholeheartedly saluting. Smiling wryly in spite of his worry. *What's not to enjoy here?* Only a damn fool let the future wreck the present. He eased over onto his side, fit himself to her heated curves. Spreading a hand across her silky stomach, he touched his lips to her nape and waited to see if she'd respond.

Tess sighed in her sleep, a dreamy contented sound that set off those fireworks in his chest again. But no further reaction. Adam brushed his smile through her hair.

Had your limit, huh? He might be eleven years older, but he was also the tougher.

Eleven years. His smile faded away. A wise man would be wary of that, as well. Around the police department, he'd seen plenty of forty-, even fifty-year-old men chasing twenty-something women, and it never ended prettily. Even if the man was as fit as he believed he was—and that was rare—rarer yet was a meeting of minds. Or intentions.

Which was fine for the short-term, Adam supposed, but for the long haul?

But then who's thinking long? Not he. Not for a minute.

And he was going to make a pest of himself if he stayed like this. That or he'd explode. *Till next time, sweetheart,* he told her silently as he slipped from the bunk. He stood for a while looking down—then tore himself away and headed outside for a shower. A cold one would be just the thing.

WHEN TESS wobbled out of the cabin, she found Adam saddling his black mare. "Where are you…?" She sank down on the stoop and brushed her hair back from her face. "It's not…" Well, okay, it was past sunrise, but what was his hurry?

He came to her in ground-eating strides. Held her chin and kissed her briskly. "Gotta check something out, Tess." He hooked a thumb over his shoulder, toward the southeast. "Might be trouble."

High in the shell-pink sky, she could see a black bird spiraling on wide ragged wings. Then another, and above that, another. "Vultures!" Which meant something was dead and its scent must be drawing them.

"Might be clear over on Kristopherson land," Adam said, "but again, it might not."

"Of course. Go." His first duty was to his herd. And the scavengers could also be drawn by an animal in trouble. If so, time was of the essence.

"Will you be here when I come back?"

"Umm, no…" Since she'd learned Zelda had kittens, she'd reverted to a daily feeding schedule. It was essential that the lynx have enough nourishment to care for her babies, and herself, as well. The mother's best chance of surviving the winter snows would be to start the season in prime condition. "I've got work to do, too."

"Then I'll saddle up your ride." He returned from the shed with her tack draped over one forearm and Watson shuffling eagerly alongside. Every few feet the dog would sniff at her saddlebags and whine. "What's he after?" Adam growled as he passed. "He was doin' this last night, as well."

Trust a bloodhound to zero in on the scent of raw chicken. By now it must permeate her leather bags. "Umm…" Tess brushed a knuckle across her lips. Lying to Adam, she hated it. But what could she do? The man was a cowboy. No way would he be sympathetic to the cause of lynx restoration. "I left a sandwich in there yesterday. Reckon he smells it."

"Ah." Adam shot her a piercing glance over the back of Cannonball, as he settled her saddle in place. "Shall I take it out, so you don't forget?"

"*No!* Umm…no, thanks. I'll clean out my bags when I get back to the cabin. You'd better run, Adam. Let me finish that."

"It's done, but don't forget to tighten your cinch before you ride." He led the gelding to her and dropped the reins so he'd stay. "Sure you've got to leave? I might be back in an hour or less."

She had a furry family to feed. "I'm sure, but anyway, I had a—" She felt herself reddening. The standard phrases of politeness didn't begin to describe what they'd done. What she'd felt.

Adam laughed softly as he locked both hands behind her waist and bent her backwards in a heart-stopping kiss. "Me, too," he teased. "I had a 'lovely' time, loving you.

"And Tess?" He drew a fingertip along her bottom lip. "Look for me…soon." *This isn't over. It's only begun,* was the unmistakable message in his midnight-blue eyes. He turned away, swung into his saddle and set off at a brisk lope, with the bloodhound running at his heels.

Hugging herself as she watched him go, Tess couldn't have said what she was feeling. Delight? Alarm? Utter confusion?

"Mix all three of the above in equal parts," she muttered aloud. "Then stir—right down to my toes."

THE VULTURES marked a mountain lion kill. A yearling elk, dragged down on the border between the Circle C allotment and Kristopherson land. By the time Adam arrived, Jon Kristopherson stood, scowling at the remains.

"Who needs this?" he growled as Adam dismounted beside him. "We had a young cat workin' the valley last summer. Took a coupla calves over on your boss's home range. Then a few weeks after that, he jumped a blood colt over at Suntop, and mauled a dog. Ben Tankersly's grandson waded into the ruckus, and was damn lucky he wasn't gutted for his trouble."

Adam glanced up in interest. Tess had a nephew? So

much he'd yet to learn. "They ever get him?" he asked idly as he circled the bush, beneath which the meat had been cached. It looked as if coyotes had found the cat's hiding place and dragged bits of the prize back into view.

"Nah. They brought in Jarrett's beagle pack and chased his butt on up to here, then over the peaks to the back of hell and beyond. Figured he'd find enough elk to stay there. Could be he's wandered on back, or this might be a new one entirely. Either way, who needs the trouble?"

"Mmm," Adam agreed. A lion stalking their herds was the last thing they wanted.

"Reckon he'll come back for seconds?" Jon wondered. "If we staked out this carcass tonight…" He glanced around. "Cover's not bad."

Adam shook his head. "If he comes, he'll come in the dead of night. We'd never get off a shot."

"Reckon you're right. 'Sides, once he smells us and your hound, he'll lose his appetite. Turn and walk."

Watson explored the site, nose to the ground, inhaling lustily. Tail waving with wistful passion.

Adam rubbed his unshaven chin. "In that case, maybe we could encourage him to walk a little sooner and a lot farther. Watson," he called as the bloodhound circled near. "*Find.* Find the kitty. *Find him!*"

IN THE END, they'd done a lot more following than finding. For the first few hours as they bushwhacked behind the dog, Adam had wondered with mounting embarrassment if he hadn't proposed a snipe hunt. Maybe Watson was backtracking the cat, rather than tracing his progress since he'd left his kill.

But about the time he decided to call a halt to this nonsense, Watson led them to the banks of a creek. Two perfect front-paw prints showed where the lion had stopped to lap water.

A very large cat indeed, from the size of its pads, and the distance between them.

Then, not long after that, Watson bayed a tree with a wide horizontal limb, some twelve feet off the ground. It was where the animal had laid up for the day, Jon concluded, looking up. That he was no longer draped there suggested he'd heard them coming and fled.

With Watson trailing so slowly, they hadn't a chance of catching their fleet-footed quarry. Still they'd harried him past sundown. If they could persuade him this neighborhood wasn't a healthy one, that he should seek his elk on the far side of the mountains, that would be sufficient unto the day.

Much better than shooting a magnificent predator, in Adam's book, though he knew better than to voice this opinion to a cattleman.

When it grew too dark to avoid low branches, they'd called it quits and headed home to their respective cabins, which by then lay miles to the southwest. Adam trudged in his door at nearly midnight.

He stood motionless while his eyes adjusted, looking toward his bed. Hoping to make out a curvy shape beneath the covers. Half persuading himself he saw one. If Tess had finished her business, whatever it was, then returned… His heart was beating hard with hope as he walked toward the bunk. Shouldn't care this much, one way or another, he told himself.

But who cared? This was a matter of wanting, no more than that. What man wouldn't crave an armful of long, laughing woman in his bed?

Still, as his fingers swept the mounds of bedclothes and came up empty, he heard an echo of that emptiness tolling in his heart. Missing her, was that what he was doing?

"No way," he said aloud as he shrugged out of his shirt. No way at all.

Couldn't be that.

CHAPTER FOURTEEN

ADAM SPENT the next day treating more calves for pink-eye. It was a bad year for it. He was running out of ointment.

Late in the afternoon, he rode above the timberline to scout for Gabe's poacher. He spent hours combing the slopes below with binoculars, till his eyes stung and his shoulders creaked. "Burning the damn candle at both ends *and* in the middle," he told Watson, who lay on his back beside him. "Me, not you."

Clearly. The hound made a whuffling noise in his sleep and twitched a front paw.

But Watson's companion had bitten off a mouthful this summer. That was the problem with working undercover. You needed a life to mask the underlying mission—but to appear genuine, it had to *be* genuine. You talked the talk, and walked the walk. Which meant you were doing double duty as you led your double life.

Being more than a cowboy, that he could handle. But throw a woman into the mix and suddenly there wasn't quite enough of him to go around. Just when he wanted to spend all of himself in one place.

Tess. She was taking up way too much of his mind. When he wasn't reliving every texture and taste, every sensation and sound of their night together, he was think-

ing about the next time they'd be together. Things he'd
like to say to her. Things he meant to do with her. *To* her.
His hips tightened against the ground he was lying on;
the blood jolted in his groin. Damn. "This isn't good."
She was turning into a serious distraction.

He'd promised Gabe he'd solve his lynx problem, and
he intended to keep that promise. He was taking the Mc-
Graws' money to mind their cattle, so that duty couldn't
be set aside. Yet it had been almost thirty-six hours since
he'd held Tess, and that was thirty-five too many. "Could
go see her tonight," he told the dog, while he peered
through the lens.

Or was tonight too soon? He didn't want to look
needy, or—much, much worse—to feel that way. Wanting was one thing; he wanted her till his back teeth ached,
and that was acceptable. All part of the mating dance.

But need? He'd be damned if he'd *need* Tess, or any
other woman, ever again. "Wait another day," he decided
with a grimace. Anything that hurt this much was bound
to build character. "Right. One more day—we can do it."
Watson could do it with four paws in the air.

That settled, Adam lifted his head from the glasses to
scan the valley below. The sooner he caught Gabe's problem boy, the more time he'd have to spend with—
"Ho-old on." He studied the flash of movement below,
fixing its location, then lifted the binoculars, focussed
in—and laughed aloud, a husky sound of pure happiness.

"Well, well, *well*." Dream of the angels and here one
came riding! Tess. Adam chuckled as he watched her
brush a wisp of dark hair off her cheek. God, but she was
beautiful! A bit of heaven, headed his way.

Just can't stay away from me, can you, sweetheart? If
Tess needed *him*—beneath the binoculars, Adam's mouth

relaxed in a dreamy curve—somehow that didn't trouble him in the least. It made him feel…safe? *Good,* he amended instantly. Tess wanting him was all to the good. The way it should be. A man could deal with his lover's needs. Would be delighted to oblige.

Laying down the binoculars, he sat upright with a groan. Rolled his cramped shoulders. Glanced to the west. Barely enough daylight left to make it down the mountain. She'd beat him to his cabin by a good half hour, but he'd posted a note on his door, in case she dropped by, telling her to wait.

Tess waiting for him when he rode in. That same little starburst of happiness blossomed in his chest. A man could get used to the feeling.

Adam lifted the glasses for one last glimpse of her before he went for his horse—and swore aloud. Fatheaded fool, he'd made the same mistake all over again! Tess wasn't riding the trail to his cabin, but the one north of it. The same one he'd found her on before.

"What am I missing here?" If she wasn't coming to visit, then what the devil was she up to? He settled back down on the turf and brought the glasses to his face. She'd vanished into the trees, just west of that sandstone outcrop that loomed over the trail. But once she rode east of that ridge, near the spring, she'd be back in view.

"Supper!" Tess caroled, then underlined her announcement with four short blasts and one long on her silent dog whistle. "Come and get it, you brute!"

With a wary glance at the surrounding bushes, she ducked under the limb that hid Geronimo's cave and set his chicken down. A swift scan of the sandy entrance to his den brought a smile to her face. Cat tracks going in and coming out. He still was in residence. "Two out of two," she murmured happily. The Tankersly/Waltz lynx restoration program was still on track. She'd have to write Liza tonight.

Or maybe tomorrow, she decided as she walked downhill to her horse. She'd covered two-thirds of the way to Adam's cabin already. Could be there in half an hour. At the thought, a shiver started in her boots and climbed. *Oh, Adam.* How could she miss him so? Less than two days had passed, yet it felt like forever.

Well, enough with the waiting and the yearning. If a strong woman wanted something, she should go and get it. Settling into her saddle, she turned Cannonball east.

THE BLASTED CAT had proved to be jumpy as a tarantula on a hot stove. For the past two days she'd come to drink after sunset or just before sunrise. With no night-vision scope on his gun, all Natwig could do was sit downwind and wait, and strain his eyes till he saw a lynx in every shadow. One or two of his glimpses might have been the actual beast. But he'd gotten nothing like a clear shot.

Till now. For some reason she'd come early tonight. One minute there was nothing but the pool on the slope below him. Then, between one blink and the next, there she stood at the water's edge, nervously sniffing the evening air.

Damn, but that was a big cat! Biggest female lynx he'd ever—

Natwig's lungs emptied in a silent *whoosh*. The animal had turned to scan the bushes to the west. As he swerved, his equipment swung below his stubby tail. Balls that clanged—a tomcat!

Crap, shit, hell and damnation! No kitten bonus here,

after almost a week of hard hunting! A week of leaving Karen home alone. He should have known, from the size of those prints.

Still… Natwig sucked in a slow breath, lifted the gun, brought its stock smoothly to his cheek. A lynx was a lynx. Any one of 'em earned Larson's ten-thousand-dollar bounty.

Black tasseled ears twitched—the lynx faded into the bushes.

Natwig lowered his gun and swore, silently and long. Then he leaned back against the tree. Something had spooked the cat; still, he might return.

Five minutes later Natwig heard hoofbeats.

No SOONER had she resolved to see Adam, than all the reasons she shouldn't came winging like bats through the twilight. "He said to look for him soon," Tess reminded Cannonball while she let him drink at the little spring just above the trail. "That implies he'd be coming to me, right?"

The gelding flicked his ears backward, but kept on sucking water.

"Right. But then what, precisely, is 'soon'? It'll be forty-eight hours come morning." She was starting to lose perspective here. Though that felt like forever, in reality, it wasn't long since they'd been together. "I'd *hate* it, if he started thinking I wanted him more than he wanted me!"

Cannonball lifted his head, shook his mane till his bridle jingled, then blew a sputtering sigh. Tess sighed, too. "Last time, I went to his place." She frowned as she gathered her reins. "If I drop in a second time, without an invitation…"

She'd look…too eager. Oh, she didn't doubt Adam would smile when he saw her, and bundle her straight into his bed. But what would he be thinking? "That I'm desperate. Or over-sexed. Or—" *Much* the worst of all. "—that I'm taking this for more than it is?"

Because this wasn't serious. No way she'd let it be. It was simply a summer flirtation. Fun.

At the moment, it felt oddly painful for fun. She felt…torn, instinct demanding one thing, and her reason quite another. Usually she preferred to listen to her feelings, but this time?

Maybe it was better to be safe than sorry. A woman had her pride, after all. "It's *his* turn. This time he should come to me." If she gritted her teeth and waited, sooner or later he was bound to do so—when his idea of "soon" came round.

"Damn, damn, oh, totally damn!" To go from skyrocketing excitement to black depression in five minutes flat? Whatever this was, it wasn't worth it. She swung Cannonball around and tapped her heels to his ribs.

"WHAT'S TAKING so long?" Adam growled when Tess didn't reappear in his glasses. It wasn't a hundred yards from the west side of the outcrop to the east, yet somewhere in that blind spot, she'd vanished. He'd been squinting hard in the gathering dusk for ten minutes or more. Perhaps she'd ridden on, and somehow he'd missed her?

"Ah!" There she was at last, just coming into view. She swerved her horse uphill to the spring below the cliff. Let him lower his head to the water.

Maybe his first impression had been the right one. Maybe she *was* headed to Sumner line camp. Where the trail branched ahead Tess could still cut down to the southeast, the same route they'd taken when he'd extracted his toll of cooking her supper. *Let it be so.* His heart turned a pirouette in his chest.

But mysteries had a way of making his brains itch, an occupational hazard for a detective. Even if she did angle southeast, ending up at his place, that didn't explain why she'd chosen this trail, instead of the direct and shorter path to its south.

"Considers this one more scenic?" he suggested to the dog. Tess was one of those people whose strings could be plucked by beauty—a sunset or moonrise or clump of wildflowers.

Below, she was swinging her horse away from the pool. "Go east," Adam urged. "East, sweetheart, you won't regret it."

Cannonball set off west at a trot. "Damnation. Hell! What is *with* you, woman?"

Tess couldn't be aware she was torturing him, so either she had never intended on stopping by—or she'd changed her mind. Whatever. For a moment the night ahead had lit up in his mind, bright as a Japanese lantern, a globe of flame and laughter. Now it collapsed in a heap of ashes.

"Yeah… Well…" He stood and shrugged his stiff shoulders, then put away the glasses that it was now too dark to use. If Tess had changed her mind about seeing him, well, maybe she had been wise to do so.

A woman like that deserved…everything. Children. A safe and beautiful home. A happy, secure future with a dependable man.

A man she could count on not to get himself killed. Not a cynical, street-hardened cop, but a cheery optimist. One with a decent income. Look at Alice with her dentist; she had known what she needed.

But what was he offering Tess, beyond a night of mind-bending pleasure? Adam pulled a face. "Sixty nights?" This was only the start of July. Still, though sixty nights in heaven might be all a loner like himself could ever hope for, a woman like Tess had every right to expect more from life.

"Ride on, Sunshine," he muttered grimly as he trudged downhill. If he were any kind of gentleman, he wouldn't bother her further.

WELL, LITTLE Miss Jabber-Mouth had spoiled this hunt for sure! The lynx wouldn't be back for hours. Might avoid the spring for days, after her intrusion on his territory. "Shit," Natwig said, watching her ride back the way she'd come.

Tomorrow. He'd give himself one more chance to score then, either way, it was home to Karen. He'd been gone too long.

He frowned, glancing back at the bushes where the lynx had vanished, picturing the animal as he'd last seen him. Something was wrong with that picture, besides his sex being wrong…

Natwig grunted as it hit him. *The radio collar.* No wonder he hadn't caught any signals for all his monitoring! "Well, I'll be *damned!*" The cat must have slipped his collar at some point. At least two lynx had done so, in the early days of the DOW program, Larson had told him. This must be one of those.

So there was no other choice as to how to get the critter, but stake out his water hole. Couldn't track his collar signals back to his lair, as Natwig had done with most of the others.

On the other hand… Maybe he'd come to depend too much on technology. Funny how it could corrupt a man's skills, without his even noticing. *Use your brains,* he reminded himself. The lynx came to drink here, morning and night. Which meant he denned nearby. Tonight, when he'd been spooked, he'd vanished to the northwest.

Could mean nothing—or all. Natwig turned in that direction, peering with his memory more than his eyes through the dark. A hundred yards thataway the slope was broken by a long outcropping of sandstone, a rock that weathered, cracked, eroded frequently to… "Caves," he said softly. If he hiked both sides of that ridge in the morning, when the lynx should be sleeping, what might he find?

"I'VE BEEN THINKING," Adam said, the moment Gabe answered his phone.

"Useful habit, in moderation," his cousin conceded cheerfully. "How are you?"

"Fine, fine…" Bluer than gun bluing. Maybe he'd just wanted to hear a friendly voice tonight? "But this is going…slow. I've been watching for days and I haven't seen a sign of our guy."

When he'd imagined their original sting, he'd been thinking like a cop with a car. Though he knew the mountains, still he'd failed to appreciate how vast forty square miles could be on a horseback scale. "Either we're just not intersecting each other, or he's not out here. But either way, I've thought of a refinement." Something to bring this to a close so Adam could focus on more important things.

Tess. Because he wasn't a gentleman. No way could he stay away from her for long.

"Anything that nails that bastard, I'm in favor of. What's your idea?"

"If he's doing what we think he's doing, he's sweeping for radio signals for a pregnant female, AK00F6."

"By now, of course, our imaginary lynx has delivered," Gabe pointed out. "We posted on our Web site three days ago that she was spotted by one of our field biologists, and that he caught a glimpse of a kitten. We speculated that probably she has several. I'm really sticking my neck out here, by the way, doing this."

"Once the end justifies the means, you'll be a hero."

"Sure, bring me the creep and we'll both be heroes. But till then…"

Yeah, Gabe had to be sweating it. The last thing a scientist enjoyed was diddling the facts. But even so. "If we assume he's still looking for a radio signal, why don't we give him one? Let him home in on it. Could you get me a working, broadcasting lynx collar?"

"To draw him straight into your arms?" Gabe thought for a minute. "You are considering that this guy will be carrying a rifle? And that unless he's entirely a fool, he'll realize he's got a lot to lose here?"

Hello, Bo-peep. That's just dawning? "I'm taking that into account," Adam said patiently. "That's what makes police work so rewarding. All the interesting people you meet."

"Yeah, yeah, but…" Gabe grunted. "Guess I was picturing you popping up out of a bush and getting the drop on the guy. Not that he'd be beaming in on *you.*"

Adam glanced across the cabin, to where the hound was blissfully absorbed in licking a forepaw. "You forgot the Bionic Nose. He'll keep me apprised of visitors." Provided he could stay awake.

"Maybe so, but he's a smell-hound, not a guard dog. Watson was home the time somebody broke into Tracy's place, and she suspects he helped the guy carry her TV to his car."

"Strictly a consultant, not a player," Adam agreed. "But about that collar?"

"Give me a day and I think I can arrange something. Any chance you could meet me in town?"

BLOOD. Adam had seen too much of it over the years to mistake that stomach-twisting stain of reddish-brown for anything else. Fingers hooked through Watson's collar, he stood, staring down at the drops.

Its source could be most anything. Spatters from a coyote kill. A lion kill. Possibly a hawk strike?

Whatever its source, Watson was enchanted. He whined and reared, fighting to be free. "Easy ol' boy. At crime scenes, we start with the eyes. See what we can see, before we mess up the site."

Though truth to tell, it was Watson's nose that had led them here to the sandstone ridge on the northern trail.

Late this afternoon something had snapped. Adam had decided to ride over to Tess's. Tomorrow he'd be down in the valley meeting Gabe, and to wait till the day after was unthinkable. He needed to hold her…now.

All the same, any hint of need made him edgy. Irritable. So to justify that urge, he'd taken the long way 'round. He'd ride the trail that Tess always chose. See if he could solve that mystery, anyway. What kept drawing her here.

They'd stopped at the little spring to the east and suddenly Watson had been electrified. Nothing would persuade him to abandon a scent. When he refused to heel to Adam's horse, finally Adam had followed the dog. He'd been trained to track lynx, after all. Maybe at long last he'd gotten a whiff of one?

Whatever he was tracking, it had moved from the spring to the ridge. Up through the thickets along its eastern face, then over and down along its west, leading at last to this clearing before a bush, where they'd spied these drops of blood.

"Calm down and sit. *Sit,* Watson. *Sta-ay.*"

The dog sat with an almost human sob.

"Sta-ay." Below an overhanging branch was another splash of rusty brown. Then beyond the leaves, could that shadow be an opening into the rock? Cautiously Adam lifted the branch to peer beneath. Bingo! A small cave, too small for a lion, he hoped.

But whatever lived in there, it had either dined well— or come to a bad end. A large splash of blood stained the sand at the den's entrance.

Watson yipped in frustration.

"Stay, there's a good boy." Adam crouched and crept closer, half expecting something clawed and furry to come rampaging out of the darkness. He didn't normally pack his gun, but this time he wished he had. "Sta-ay," he repeated under his breath, though any predator with ears would know he had visitors.

Hunching over his bent knees, Adam studied the ground. Some sort of struggle had kicked up the sand, as well as spilled blood. And then there— "By *God!*" He'd been starting to wonder if Colorado lynx weren't a figment of Gabe's imagination. But here was his proof at last. Two hind-paw tracks at the base of the rock, as if the animal had backed up, then stood at bay.

If Gabe hadn't coached him, he'd have figured the

prints belonged to a half-grown cougar. But the spacing between them was the tip-off. Huge feet on a forty-pound cat. With a lynx, the wheel base was narrower.

So… Adam scowled. What had happened here? Lynx eating? Or lynx eaten? No way was he crawling in to find out. Grabbing hold of a human killer might be part of his normal job description, but going nose-to-nose with a wounded, pissed-off cat…?

"Your turn," he told the dog, as he scrambled out into the open. "But strictly voluntary."

The bloodhound was delighted to oblige. While Watson snuffled and snorted and vanished into the dark, Adam searched the ground beyond the bush. Most of it was too hard to take a print. But in a patch of dirt where a stone had been dislodged to roll down the slope, he found a single clear impression.

A human boot track, which was just what he'd feared. Because judging from the continuing silence, there was nobody home in that cave. Tot up all the clues and it looked like Gabe's poacher had added another notch to his belt.

Adam set his own size twelve alongside the print and grimaced. The killer he was chasing wore a size-six boot! "If he's male."

Or roughly a seven female.

Adam blinked. Only woman in the high country was— He shook the thought away with a jerk of his head. No, not possible. Tess loved animals.

He studied the marks again. No way to tell the difference between the pointy-toed track made by a man or woman's Western boot. "Teenager," he muttered. That was more likely than… A thousand times more likely. So much of the crime in this country was perpetrated by juvenile males. He could easily imagine a rancher's kid taking it upon himself to rid the range of lynx. Telling himself he was protecting his own kind against the dreaded tree-huggers and eco-freaks.

Adam jumped as something nudged his knee. Watson, his chocolate eyes gleaming with the thrill of the chase. "Nobody in there, huh?" But there had been, and recently.

"Just how good is that snout, anyway?" If the bloodhound hadn't found a body, then the hunter must have carried it away. To bury it where no one would ever find it? Or to show off to his friends. Or as a trophy, stuffed or otherwise? Homicide detectives were grimly aware that some killers kept souvenirs, to remind them of the pleasure they'd taken.

But if the creep had carried the lynx away on horseback, could Watson follow? Only one way to find out. "*Kitty,* Watson. *Find the kitty!*"

CHAPTER FIFTEEN

AN HOUR before sundown, Tess tied her horse in her usual spot at the base of the ridge. Dismounting, she drew Geronimo's chicken dinner from her saddlebag and walked up the slope. Her nerves were jumping with an odd mix of anticipation and worry. Once she'd fed the cat, she meant to ride on to Adam's line camp. Because today she had an excuse—no, two excuses. The mail must be delivered, plus there was Sean Kershaw's unexpected invitation to be passed along.

"So I'll see you tonight," she murmured. But she wished Adam had come to her instead. It had been— what?—two and a half days now. *Men.* Didn't he care? Or maybe Adam was determined to *seem* not to care?

Either way, his neglect stung. "I'll bring you the mail," she said aloud, "but who says I'll stay?"

Her lips quirked. A wave train of sensation shuddered up her spine with the memory of his hands, his lips, what they did to her. Could do again tonight. "Yeah, right." Something told her she wouldn't be sleeping at home this evening. Maybe not even sleeping. She gave a little skip of joy and found herself before Geronimo's den.

"Supper," she sang out. "Chicken *again,* you brute, and I hope you're sick of it!" A couple more feedings and she'd cut him back to three per week. It was high time the tom started fending for himself. Zelda had caught another rabbit only this morning. If a working mom could do that well… Tess blew his signal on her supersonic whistle, then stooped to duck under the bush.

And froze. *Two branches broken, there, right before her face.* The hairs lifted along her nape. A cat would never do that! Something big and careless had passed this way—and recently; the leaves had barely wilted on their twigs. "Geronimo?" she whispered. "Sweetie pie?" She swallowed and ducked under the bush and dropped to her boot heels. "Oh, no!"

The earth before his cave was gouged and scuffled and— *"Noooo."* That splash of reddish brown—blood! "Oh, Geronimo." It looked as though some animal had rooted at the stain, snuffled it. Biting her lip, she bent closer. Blurry bits of tracks marked the trampled dirt, then there—a clear one. A perfect print.

Canine. Too big to be a coyote. But no wolves hunted these mountains. "A dog, dammit!" A sizeable dog.

"Damn and *blast* and—oh, *geez,* baby? Are you in there?" She crawled closer to the mouth of the cave. A lynx as large as Geronimo would be a fair match for a single dog, especially if he could fight with his flanks and back protected. "Talk to me!"

Except that he'd be talking—growling—already, if he was holed up in there, scared and possibly wounded. She sighed, picked up a handful of sand, tossed it into the darkness. Listened. Sighed again. Nobody home.

But possibly he'd simply leaped right over the dog? Slashed and run, then retreated up a tree somewhere?

That was the best she could hope for, Tess supposed, but if so, it wasn't likely he'd return. Not to a den that had proved dangerous. Still, hoping against hope, she set his chicken down in the spot where she always left his meal and backed out into the open.

"Oh, kitty…" She knuckled the tears off her lashes then glanced around. As for the worst that might have happened? She scowled as it hit her. *Dogs didn't roam the high country alone.* There'd have been a hunter behind the dog.

But if so, there should be some sign. Tess fisted her hands and started circling.

FOR THE FIRST two miles Watson led the way west along the trail. Toward Tess's cabin.

Which proved nothing, Adam assured himself. For ease of travel below the timberline, you had to follow a trail. The poacher could have ridden in that direction, then easily bypassed her camp.

Still, he let out a grunt of relief when the dog broke north, cutting up through alpine meadows toward the ragged crest of Two Bear Peak. For just a bit there he'd worried… Tess was a rancher's daughter, after all. It wouldn't be so strange if her loyalties lay with the grazers. Her family's fortune was built on cows, not cats. Ask her to choose sides and, of course, she'd choose her own.

But, blood in the sand. Not Tess's style, he'd have sworn.

And now he didn't need to, with the track leading northwest. There was a pass over the peaks in this direction, with a trailhead beyond it, Adam recalled. Reining in to give his mare a breather, he glanced south over the descending miles. Was startled to see the roof of Tess's cabin from where he sat. Plus that shed built off the back, where Watson had howled the first time they visited.

Adam's brows drew slowly together. *The same god-awful racket the bloodhound had made today, on finding the lynx cave.*

"Proves nothing," he muttered. The dog could have been howling at...something. Most anything else. A rat.

Except he'd never seen signs of rodents around her tidy cabin. "Forget it." An occupational hazard of hunting killers was that somewhere along the way you forgot how to trust. Alice had complained more than once that he was too suspicious. Too cynical.

Well, forget Alice. Whatever he'd once felt for his fiancée, it was nothing compared to the way he felt about— Adam sliced that thought in half. Glanced uphill to where the dog was nearing the ridge line. "Keep your mind on business," he warned himself.

But as he rode after the bloodhound, he looked wistfully back over his shoulder. And realized. With the peaks to the west blocking the last rays of the sunset, darkness had fallen half a mile below. So why couldn't he see lantern light at any of her windows?

"ADAM?" Tess knocked again, waited, then opened his cabin door. "Hey! Anybody home?"

Nobody. She wheeled on the stoop to count his string of horses, grazing in the long meadow. The black mare he favored was missing. "*You're* working late," she muttered. The sun had dipped below the peaks.

Her mood was as murky as the shadows. From the cave, she'd galloped here, meaning to have it out with him. Demand to know if he and Watson had gone hunting, bagged a lynx? Because she'd found boot and horse tracks when she'd circled the den.

Man and beast, the size of the prints was a close match

to Adam and his hound. Besides, who else kept a dog within ten miles of here? Oh, she supposed the tracks could have been made by a passing hunter. But in all probability...

She crossed to his easy chair and sank into it, then bounced up again to pace the darkened room. She felt like a tea kettle, boiling with adrenaline and sorrow. Chagrin at her own stupidity. Somehow she'd gotten ahead of herself—she now cared for a man she couldn't quite trust.

This was what came from taking a lover on instinct, rather than waiting till you knew him. *Would* Adam break the law and shoot an endangered species?

Lots of cowboys would, if they thought the animal threatened their own way of life. They considered the feds and even the state environmental bureaucrats as intruders in God's country, heavy-handed outsiders, who didn't respect the ways of the West.

Knowing plenty of good men who felt that way, Tess could sympathize, even though she couldn't agree. But that didn't mean she'd forgive Adam if he'd shot Geronimo.

"Where are you, where are you, come *on!*" She needed him to come. To tell her that he wasn't a man who could turn all that silken savage beauty into a pile of bloody fur. Such a waste, *such* a pity. "*Come on*, Adam." She wanted him to say it wasn't him, then she wanted him to hold her.

Tess blew out a breath. "Calm down." Fumbling around the kitchen, she found his box of matches and lit the lantern. She wanted to bury her face in his shirt and weep. She crossed to his bed, toppled over to press her face into his pillow. Inhaling his scent, she murmured, "Oh, Adam..." *Tell me you didn't do this.*

She sat up, hugging his pillow to her stomach, and scowled at the door. What could he be *doing,* out this late?

Could be most anything. A calf in trouble. His horse had stumbled and gone lame on the far side of the range. He might be burying a lynx carcass, where no one would ever find it. "Oh, shut up, shut *up!*" she chanted, and turned to his bookcase for distraction.

She pulled out his book on dinosaurs and looked up a picture of a stegosaurus. Smiled in spite of her bleak mood, then closed it, put it back. Selected instead a thick volume of the collected stories of Sherlock Holmes that she hadn't noticed before.

Something in the space behind the books winked in the lantern light.

Tess pulled out two more books, dropped them on the bed, and reached into the gap. Touched cold metal. Drew out a gun.

WHATEVER Watson had been tracking, he lost its scent on the far side of Two Bear, at the trailhead. "Good job," Adam told him, swinging down to pat the disconsolate dog. "No, come back here," he called, when the bloodhound started along the dirt logging trail. "*Sit.* We can't chase a car."

Or a pickup, he amended, after inspecting the area by flashlight. A truck with one pattern of tread marks on its front wheels, then a second kind on its rear. Towing a tandem horse trailer. "He parked here. Rode up and did his dirty work, then went out the way he came in," he told the dog, who wagged his tail politely.

And took the lynx with him when he went, since Watson had discovered no grave along the way. Adam was gaining a grudging respect for the hound. What he nosed, he knew.

"So that's how the guy operates." How he covered such a range. There were trailheads all over the San Juans. The poacher could leave his truck and trailer at the nearest site to his quarry. Ride in, bag the cat, then be gone in a matter of hours.

"So we're looking for someone with a truck and a horse." He could tell Gabe to start pursuing that line, but every cowboy in southwestern Colorado fit the description. Adam, himself, had a pickup parked over at Sumner trailhead.

Thinking of which, he glanced at the glittering stars. Must be near midnight by now. Too late to drop in on Tess, and his own cabin was miles beyond hers. Maybe it made more sense to ride straight to Sumner trailhead. By the time he drove the sixty rough miles down to the valley, then on to Durango, it'd be dawn. He could grab an early breakfast, run a few errands, then meet up with Gabe.

CONCEALED ALONGSIDE the gun in Adam's bookcase, Tess found a cell phone. She sat, frowning as she turned it in her lap. The automatic was strange enough. Most of the line-camp men owned rifles, but she'd never known one to use a handgun. This was the new West. No cowboy outside of Hollywood wore a pistol in a holster.

Nor did they carry cell phones.

She stood, glanced nervously toward the door, paced around the cabin. "Who *are* you, Adam Dubois?" He'd told her so little about his past. His presence was so distracting, so utterly overwhelming, she'd let him get away with that.

No more. A Cajun cowboy with an automatic and a cell phone—and a hound who was afraid of cows? What else was wrong with this picture? Her steps slowed, her gaze sharpened; Tess stopped by the window sill to pick up the skull. Rotated it and frowned. A bobcat skull, he'd said.

"Or lynx?" she mused. Not one of hers, but there were other lynx in these mountains, the Division of Wildlife imports. What had Liza said, that a rumor was going around, that someone was systematically sabotaging the DOW program by killing their cats?

"No, no, no, you wouldn't *do* that, Adam... Would you?" Yet there was an essential toughness at his core. A certain...ruthlessness.

She set the skull back in its place and prowled on, searching for she didn't know what. Praying not to find it. "The map," she recalled. A map that had disappeared after she'd asked about it. She'd thought it was simply evidence of Adam's wide-ranging interests, but could it be something more?

In a back corner she found a built-in cupboard that held his fly-fishing rod, a rifle, some dusty slickers and a battered, greasy old hat. No rolled-up paper cylinder. Tess shut the crude plank door with a frown. Where else to look? And if the map had an innocent purpose, why would Adam hide it? Drifting back to the center of the cabin, she braced a hip against the table as she scanned her surroundings.

She glanced wistfully down at her perch, smoothed a palm across its scrubbed pine. Here they'd shared a meal, laughing and talking. That was when she'd first fallen for him, she supposed, captivated by his conversation. Later, they'd loved each other here, just about set this old table on fire.

And now? "What am I *doing?*" Suspecting him of this awfulness.

But still… Geronimo's blood on the sand. That wasn't something she could stomach. She had to know, even if it meant knowing the worst.

Her gaze swept the room, finding no place for concealment; it came to rest on the phone she'd tossed on his bunk. Liza. The vet ought to be told. Geronimo had been her baby before Tess had taken him on.

She sat on the stoop where she'd see Adam coming—and punched in the number. "Liza?" she said, when the vet answered. "You'd better sit down."

"I'm sitting and driving, as a matter of fact. What's wrong? And how did you—"

"Adam has a cell phone. But Liza, I've got bad news."

"Oh, *no*—the kittens?"

"No, they're fine—thriving. Absolutely adorable. Nonstop wrestling matches and pouncing contests. I took some photos that you're going to love. No, it's Geronimo… I'm afraid somebody shot him."

After Liza had scorched the airwaves with her swearing, she added in a weary growl, "So the rumors were right. Somebody up there *is* killing lynx."

"Looks like it," Tess agreed. "Which brings up a question. Do you know where and when those other cats were killed?" Knowing the dates and locations, perhaps she could prove that Adam had an alibi.

"I could look it up on the DOW Web site when I get home, get back to you. They've posted a map of last-known locations for each animal that has vanished. Last time I looked, the latest disappearance was a female lynx over on the Uncompahgre Plateau, roughly two weeks ago."

Tess gnawed at her lip. Roughly two weeks ago she'd lost track of Adam. That was when she'd camped out beside Geronimo's cage, while he grew accustomed to the mountains. During that three-day window, could Adam have driven to the Plateau, bagged a lynx, then returned?

"And I believe the one before that was a male, north of Creede, some time around the end of May," Liza continued.

Before Tess had ever met Adam. No help there.

"Whoever shot Geronimo, it's *gotta* be the same guy," Liza said bitterly. "Looks like somebody's hired a lynx hitman. Oh, I'm so mad I could *spit!*"

Tess closed her eyes, trying to visualize the markings on Adam's map. There'd been a notation over on the Uncompahgre, hadn't there? She jumped as Liza spoke again. "What? I'm sorry, you're a bit broken up."

"I said, what's the number of Adam's phone?"

"Umm, I don't know it and he's not around to ask." Somehow Tess couldn't share her suspicions with Liza. Telling her might make them true. "Oh, hang on, here it is." With a fine disregard for its sleek design, Adam had printed the number on the phone's backside in indelible marker. "But you know…" If Adam took a call for Tess, he'd know she'd searched his cabin.

Whether her fears proved false or true, she didn't want that. "You'd better not call me. I think his battery's almost dead, and I won't be around here anyway."

"Oh, I thought you and he were—"

"It's…we're…on hold for now. Everything's sort of…well, I'll tell you later, okay?"

The first half of Liza's reply was garbled, though its tone was warmly sympathetic, then she asked a question ending in "Zelda?"

Tess raised her voice. "I guess you're moving out of range. But listen, Liza, if you can hear me. I'll be watching out for Zelda and her babies. Anybody wants to go after them, he'll have to go over my dead body."

"Don't *say* that!" the vet protested. "I mean, do your best, sure, but don't—" Her voice faded off into the ozone.

Phone to her ear, Tess stared up at the stars for a minute, then she sighed and switched it off. She stood and peered out at the darkness. Normally she felt at home in the dark. At one with the night and all its roaming critters. Tonight, she felt...alone. Lonely. *Adam, where are you?*

And who are you?

Exhaustion rolled over her in a leaden wave. She'd entertained too many conflicting emotions in too short a span. Tess glanced longingly at his bed, then shook her head. Not while she didn't know.

In which case, she'd better be gone before he straggled in. She moved toward his bookcase—then swerved toward his table, and unbuckled her belt. With a pen she found there, she inked in his phone number on the inner side of her belt. An old habit of hers, for numbers and codes she wanted to conceal, but not forget. That done, she put the automatic and phone back in their hiding place, and smoothed out his bunk.

She found a notepad and scribbled a note.

"Adam, Here's everybody's weekly mail as you can see."

The day after tomorrow was pick-up day for the mail at Sumner trailhead.

She tapped the pen to her lips, frowned in thought, then shrugged and added,

"And Sean Kershaw asked me to pass on an invitation to you. He's hosting a potluck supper at White Rock, sundown tomorrow night—a sort of belated Fourth of July cookout. It's his first year in line camp and I reckon he's getting lonesome."

She made a rueful face. Well, that made two of them. And now…if Adam was a lynx killer, she had no desire to ride over to Sean's in his company.

But if he wasn't? Maybe those dog prints hadn't been Watson's. Maybe her case against Adam was mere rampaging paranoia, plus a few oddball, unrelated facts.

"Oh, I hope so!" she prayed aloud, then added,

"I figured on leaving for his place about 5:00, if you're interested in coming at all, and care to stop by."

She studied her words and grimaced again. The tone was pretty cool, but it would have to do. She closed the note with neither an endearment nor even a "Yours Sincerely," signing it simply "Tess."

With a sigh, she stood, stretched, turned to go—then swung back, scanning the cabin one last time. That map…if Adam had nothing to feel guilty about, why had he hidden it? And where?

Something about the cupboard—something *in* the cupboard?—nagged at her mind. With a swift glance toward the open doorway, she crossed the cabin in quick strides to the little pantry. Found no map all over again. "*Dope,*" she muttered aloud. The only thing it contained out of the ordinary was that hat, which looked old as the mountains and twice as moldy. Some cowboy must have hung it on its nail long before World War II.

Grasping the brim by two fingertips, Tess brought it out into the light. Its hatband was disgusting, made from some sort of greasy— Her gasp echoed in the stillness. She brought it over to the table to hold it up near the lantern.

The pattern on the matted strip of pelt was one of brindled, broken stripes. Black on long-haired gray.

Lynx fur.

NONE OF Karen's cats came trotting when Natwig let himself in the kitchen door. Sniffing stale air, he stood in the darkened room and knew: *She's gone.*

The pain pills they'd given him at the Durango ER must work for heartache, as well. Or maybe he was too tired to feel anything but numb.

He trudged to the light switch. Blinking owlishly in the overhead glare, he found the note she'd left on the center island.

"We're at Anna's,"

his wife had written in her rounded, schoolgirl hand.

"Can't say for how long. If you want me, maybe you should call. Or maybe—"

The rest of that line had been obliterated with a fierce black line, a tiny whirlwind of emotion.

If? "Oh, baby," he muttered wearily. Gone to her older sister, in Cortez.

At least she'd signed her note "love, Karen."

That was something. Was what would carry them
through, he prayed. The bottom line beneath all this doubt
and trouble. *Just keep on loving me, baby. Without that—*

He shook his head and glanced up at the wall clock.
Too late to call her now. He'd lost as much time sitting
in the emergency room waiting for a damned doctor, as
he had riding out of the mountains.

In the bathroom he stripped with care, wincing as he
worked his sleeves past the bandages. "Blasted cat," he
mumbled.

Searching the sandstone ridge, he'd stumbled on the
tom's cave around noon. He'd brushed a branch aside and
there it was. But the lynx within had heard him coming.
Warned him off with a low-pitched snarl.

Natwig decided he'd better bag him then and there.
The only other choice was to lie in wait till the lynx came
out at twilight. But if he missed his shot, the cat might
take off and never return now that his den had been discovered.

So he crawled till he blocked the entrance, figuring his
flashlight would mesmerize the animal long enough for
him to take aim.

Glowing green eyes and an eerie sing-song snarl,
crouched way back in the darkness. Natwig darted him in
the flank, breathed a sigh of satisfaction as he started to
count. A minute was usually all it took, then he'd crawl
in—

And the brute charged. Who said lynx were shy? He'd
caught the critter by the scruff, figuring the tranquilizer
would kick in any second.

That's all the time the cat needed to twist like a snake
and wrap himself around Natwig's arm.

Natwig studied himself glumly in the mirror. Fifty-seven stitches in the right arm, the doc had said with a smirk, and thirty-something in his left. Plus the fang wounds in his left forearm and that swipe across his cheek. Ten seconds of hanging on to that hellion, and he was ribbons. Shreds. While the cat...

The lynx had gone limp and dropped to the sand, and Natwig could have sworn he was smiling in his sleep.

"Blasted *cat*," he muttered. If it wasn't for Karen...

He sighed heavily. Hollow-hearted as it made him feel, coming home to an empty house, maybe it was just as well. He'd figured he'd spin her some version of the tale he'd given the doctor, about breaking up a dog fight. Now he didn't have to lie. Not till she came home.

And when will that be?

A question with more claws than a cat. Maybe tomorrow he'd be brave enough to ask her. Stumbling out of the bathroom, he hit the lights—and fell facedown across their bed.

CHAPTER SIXTEEN

PUSHING HARD, Adam made it back to Sumner line camp by five the following afternoon. Which meant he was too late to ride to Sean's cookout with Tess, he figured, upon reading her note. "Great," he muttered to the bloodhound, who was eyebrows-deep in his food bowl. Any itch for conversation he'd had, he'd already scratched, visiting Gabe. After flogging the truck all those dusty miles back from Durango, the last thing he wanted to do was ride ten miles to a party.

But the thought of Tess spending her smiles on half a dozen lonesome cowboys spurred him to wash up, change his clothes and head out again.

In the hope that she'd waited for him, he rode past her cabin. But only her pack mare grazed in the meadow. Adam sighed and rode on.

Halfway to White Rock line camp, they crossed an open slope. An old avalanche scar had turned to grass. New trees grew about the same height as a man on horseback. Watson ranged on ahead—tracking Tess's gelding, Adam suspected—when the dog stopped short to bury his snout in a bush.

"Whatya got?" Adam inquired as he rode alongside.

"Ahhh—wooo!"

Adam's mare shied violently sideways. *"Whoa,* easy

there!" Adam reined the snorting horse to a standstill, just as the bloodhound let out another yell. "Watson, shut *up!* Sit!"

Nose to the ground, the dog headed downslope, angling off toward the deep woods to the east. "Watson, *come!* Get back here!"

"Ruh-ooooo!"

In the end, Adam had to leash him with his lariat and haul him away. "We'll check it out tomorrow," he assured the whining hound. Could it be another lynx?

Whatever had enticed him, Adam had no intention of chasing it into the forest half an hour before sundown. "We're off duty tonight," he reminded his prisoner. Even undercover, you had to take a break now and then.

But nearing Sean's cabin, Adam's ears pricked to professional attention. *Gunfire.* He reined in with a scowl— then swung down to unleash the hound. "What the devil?" he muttered, remounting as the noise continued. The pattern of shots was slow. Deliberate. Didn't sound like a shoot-out, but still, with Tess involved... He touched his spurs to his mare's ribs and flew through the twilight, stopping under cover of the trees that overlooked the line camp.

A cluster of cowboys stood near a blazing bonfire. A slim figure stepped from the group, raised a rifle, took aim at a distant treetop. Adam blew out a breath of relief as Tess fired.

A pinecone fell and the men called praise, or teasing comments. Tess aimed again, fired—another cone tumbled to the ground.

Mighty fine shooting, Adam realized, as he walked his mare across the clearing. Tess kept on firing till she missed a shot.

"Nine!" somebody called out her score. Jamie Sikor-sky, who rode for the JBJ, stepped up and took aim.

So you shoot as well as you make love, Adam thought as he reached the fire. *Why am I not surprised?* Half a dozen men called greetings, but he didn't answer or glance aside. There was only one person here he'd come to see.

Watson nudged her hand. Tess turned, laughed, smoothed his ear, then, holding it, looked up to meet Adam's gaze.

Her smile faded, her big eyes widened.

No smile for me? he wondered silently. Seeing *her,* he felt as if the sun had risen in his chest.

She looked down at the dog and bit her bottom lip.

ADAM DIDN'T COME to her right away and for that Tess was grateful. She didn't know what she wanted, didn't know what she felt.

Half of her longed to walk straight into his arms. Dark and vital, he eclipsed all the others around the campfire. They simply faded away beside him, nice men every one, but none had his force, or his depth, or that wicked glint of intelligence in his miss-nothing eyes. None had his controlled grace of movement, nor that ironic curl at the corners of his sexy mouth. No one had shoulders as wide, nor hands half as clever.

And though several of the other men looked at her with warm approval, her body rang like a bell to Adam's glances and his alone.

Half of her was smitten all over again at the sight of him. But the other half of Tess coldly noted that every quality that made Adam stand out from the others was a cause for wonder.

And worry.

If he was more than a cowboy—then what was he?

Well, she wouldn't get her answer tonight in the midst of a rowdy cookout. And till she had an answer, she'd be wise to keep her distance. Each time Adam drifted her way, Tess gave him a cool smile—then threw herself into the nearest conversation. She didn't mean to let him cut her out from the herd, not tonight.

"Have you seen any sign of him since?" she asked Jon Kristopherson, who'd been describing the mountain lion he and Adam had tracked.

"Not a whisker," Jon said with satisfaction. "Nothing over your way, Adam?"

As Adam shook his head, Tess moved on. "So, Sean, have you taken many pictures this summer?" The stepson of Suntop's ranch manager, Sean Kershaw was a brilliant young photographer, hoping to make a career of it. For the past few years he'd recorded the events of spring and fall roundups, gaining himself statewide acclaim.

"I snapped some shots of a wildcat last week that are gonna be dynamite," he assured her. "It was fishing off a rock along Crystal Creek."

"Huh!" snorted Bob Wilcox, who rode for the JBJ, farther to the west. "It was probably one of them damned lynx the government's dumped on us. You should've shot him with your gun, not a camera. Endangered species, my ass! *We're* the endangered species! Let those cats get a toehold up here, and we'll be out on our butts before you can say 'scat.'"

"Pshaw!" Brady Mann spat in the fire, then glanced apologetically at Tess. "Whole lynx program's nothin' but another excuse for the politicians to spend our money.

They ain't never gonna survive in these mountains. I hear none of them cats have bred. Give 'em a few more years and they'll all fade away, and we'll have nothing but holes in our pockets to show for it."

"Not what I heard," Adam said easily. "The Division of Wildlife claims there's a she-lynx with a litter someplace right around here. And once they start multiplying, look out! In no time, they'll be thick on the ground as rabbits."

"And each of 'em will have his own damn bureaucrat to hold his paw and protect him," snorted Jamie Sikorsky. "You watch, before we know it they'll be fencing off the summer range, declarin' it lynx habitat. Fine for cats, off-limits to cattle and cowboys."

"I think this was just an ol' bobcat," Sean observed mildly. "Didn't have those crazy ear points."

"Much more likely," Tess hastened to agree.

"Oh, I don't know," Adam said with a shrug. "I hear only an expert can tell the difference. Though if you make a mistake and shoot the wrong one…"

"Yeah! That sheepherder down near Durango who shot one last year, thinking it was a wildcat?" growled Bob Wilcox. "They were talkin' about prison time, maybe, and fines to break a man. I say we ought to lock them worthless cats and the damned bureaucrats in the same boxcar and ship 'em all back to Alaska!"

"We ought to do *something*," Adam agreed.

Tess dug her nails into her palms. *Do you really believe that, Adam?* Worse, was he acting on his beliefs? Or was he simply stirring the pot here, just for the fun of it?

"Oughta blow every one we see to kingdom come," declared Wilcox with a vigorous nod. "They want to declare 'em endangered, we'll *give* 'em some endangerment!"

Sean punched his arm. "What's in danger is those biscuits you're cooking." He nodded at the cast-iron Dutch oven, half-buried in the coals. Steam was swirling from its lid.

"Aw, *shoot!*" Wilcox snatched at a poker to jab at the coals.

"Reckon I'll go get my salad." Delighted to end the conversation, Tess hurried off to Sean's cabin, where she'd stored her potluck contribution.

As she stirred vinaigrette into her black-eyed pea salad with carrots and onions and bits of canned ham, Tess realized that the blues she'd brought with her to Sean's cookout had returned. *I don't belong here.* As comfortable as she was around men, as fond as she was of cowboys in general, she was a hen in the duck pond. Always had been.

They were so bent on defending a threatened way of life—a wonderful way of life—that they didn't see that every piece of it needed protecting. Cows weren't God's only creation. His flowers and trees and birds and beasts needed looking after, too. There was room enough for all up here, she was sure of it. Cats, as well as cattle and cowboys.

But Adam? What did he think? Somehow she'd fooled herself. Let herself hope that he might share what she cared about—or at least, not oppose it. But the way he'd talked out there? Why, he'd been egging them on, it had almost seemed like!

Whoa. Get a grip, she warned herself. She'd long ago learned not to argue environmental causes with cowboys. They'd stop taking her seriously. All it ever got her was teased. "Tess the Tree-hugger" they'd called her in her teens, till she'd learned to shut her mouth and keep her causes to herself.

But she didn't want to keep herself from Adam. She needed to share what mattered to her.

But if he really believes the lynx should be shot?

That didn't mean he'd killed Geronimo. Some people enjoyed playing devil's advocate, she reminded herself as she picked up the bowl and headed back to the party. Maybe that was all he'd—

He was waiting for her as she shoved out the screen door. "Hey, stranger." Adam caught her arm, halting her in her tracks. "Sorry I missed you."

Oh, I missed you, too! she realized, looking up into his midnight eyes. More than she'd have dreamed possible. More than was good or wise, given what she'd thought she wanted from all this. From him.

"Had to drive down to Durango to pick up some more pinkeye ointment." He'd also purchased condoms, a ridiculous quantity, though holding her, Adam wondered if he'd bought enough. "Got back too late to ride over with you." *But I mean to ride back.*

If Tess wanted him to. He'd been wondering, ever since his arrival, given the way she seemed to be avoiding him. Had something changed between them?

No way could she know that he'd suspected her, for a while there, of being his lynx poacher. So maybe she was simply shy in public? Fearful that he'd be a heavy-handed, possessive lover, embarrassing her. Claiming her for all her friends to see.

And damned if he didn't want to. He felt like punching each and every cowboy who dared to smile her way. But a man didn't own rights to a woman, just because the two of them had gone to bed a couple of times. He wasn't asking for that—and she hadn't offered. And at this stage, whatever they had between them was private.

But compelling. "I try to hold a picture of you in my mind," he confessed huskily as he reached for her. Brushed a knuckle along her bottom lip where he needed to kiss her. "But every time I see you, I'm surprised all over again. Like the full moon when it rises." That beautiful. His heart banged in his chest. He could hustle her off into the shadows right there and then and—

"Forgot the salt," Sean grumbled, dodging around them, into his cabin.

"And don't forget ketchup!" Tess called over her shoulder, "and— Oh, I'd better—" She thrust the bowl she was holding into Adam's hands. "Here, I'd better go help him. Would you take this over to the table?" She nodded toward the fire.

Adam obeyed with a thoughtful frown. Something *had* changed between them. But what? And why?

Well, whatever, this wasn't the place or time to sort it out. *Tonight,* he promised himself. And he hoped she'd let him do his sorting with actions, not words.

NATWIG SLEPT past noon, till he rolled over onto his arm and the pain woke him. Once he'd washed, then brewed a cup of coffee, he tried to call Karen.

Nobody answered the phone at her sister's in Cortez. When Anna's answering machine kicked in with a perky message, he growled and hung up.

He fried up some eggs, did his chores down at Webster's barn, then came back and called again. *Still* nobody. Damn it, where were they?

He tried on and off all day. He yearned to drive down

there and fetch his wife home, but he'd started to realize: much as he missed her, this was better for Karen.

Though their neighbors looked in on her here at the ranch when he was gone, took her for drives or ran errands, still he knew Karen was lonesome. At her big sister's, she'd have constant company while he was away, somebody to talk to and to see she ate her meals. When he wasn't around to cook for her, Natwig knew she ate like a chickadee.

The last thing he wanted was to go back to the mountains so soon—he felt as though he could sleep for a week. But the smart thing would be to get his butt back there and finish the job. Bag the female and her litter.

Then, one more quick trip to Wyoming and he'd call the whole mess quits—to hell with Larson and his faceless clients. Add up the bonus bounty on the female with kittens, plus the male he'd taken yesterday, plus the female from the Uncompahgre, and he'd be ninety thousand to the good. That was enough—it would have to do. He'd figure some way to finish paying their debts, but it couldn't be this way.

All this sneaking and lying was wrecking his marriage. *Just hang on another week, babe, then we'll put this behind us.*

Natwig called again at supper time, and stood there in a daze while the phone rang. Maybe something had happened? A wreck or a house fire. Or Karen had fallen out of her wheelchair and— He jumped half a foot when somebody picked up at the other end.

"Hello?" said his sister-in-law, Anna.

"Um, Anna…" The words he'd prepared had flown out the window. "Lemme speak to Karen. It's Joe."

"The wanderer, yes, I got that. But Karen is taking a nap right now. We just got back from her rehab appointment and she's whipped. I'm not going to wake her."

"I never asked you to." He blew out a gusty sigh. Maybe, much as he yearned to hear his wife's voice, this was for the best. He was done lying to her, but he sure didn't mean to explain. Not in depth.

This way he didn't have to tell her he was headed straight back to the mountains. Or try to find an explanation when she asked him why.

"Any message?" Anna said dryly.

"Yeah. Umm, would you tell her I read her note, and…" *She's crazy if she thinks I don't want her, need her. She's everything I care about.* "And I've got to head out again. I'm glad she's with you, in good company, 'cause I've got to go…do something."

"Surprise, surprise."

"Now don't you start in on me, Anna. I'm doing what I've gotta do."

"And that, precisely, is?"

None of your business! "You just tell her that…" He wrinkled his brows in thought. "That…she ought not to worry. That whatever's going on, it has nothing to do with me and her. I've just got to…see it through. Then it'll be over and done with and we can put it behind us." *We can get back to what matters. Me loving her.*

But that was too private to put in a message. "Would you please tell her that?"

"Ohh, I surely *will*." Anna slammed the phone down.

Natwig stared at his handset for a minute. "What'd I say?" He shrugged and hung up. Karen's sister had her moods.

As the party wound down, Adam offered to saddle Tess's horse. He watched with narrowed eyes as one emotion chased another across her expressive face—

worry, reluctance, and a longing to match his own. *What gives here?* he wondered, as he steeled himself for her refusal.

If she told him that she meant to spend the night and ride back in the morning, then he'd sleep by the burned-out fire. He was too tired to pry it out of her tonight, but whatever was bothering her, he meant to know it and soon.

Maybe she read the determination in his eyes. "Thanks," she said briefly, then continued her farewells to Sean and his other guests.

Some time after midnight, they set out by the light of the waning moon. The first stretch of trail was too narrow to ride abreast, so Adam let Tess take the lead. After skipping a night's sleep he was hammered. Still, watching her slender hips rock and sway in the saddle, he felt his blood surging. His jeans started to pinch.

Much more of this and he'd cripple himself. *Think about something else quick,* he told himself, averting his gaze. Like lynx. And lynx killers. Right, so what had he learned tonight?

Delighted when the subject of cats had arisen, he'd nudged it toward lynx, then fanned the flames. With the result that he'd learned Bob Wilcox was a loudmouthed fool, at least when he had a woman to hear him talk tough.

But Adam would eat his hat if that one was his man. Sure, Wilcox might blow a cat away if they met face to face, but it would be an act of impulse. Adam couldn't see him having the forethought to acquire the radio-tracking gear, nor the patience and persistence to use it from January through July.

Nor would Wilcox have the sense to keep his mouth

shut while he risked prison time, violating the Endangered Species Act again and again. If he'd bagged twenty-one lynx, he'd have bragged.

No, I'm looking for someone clever here. The killer was a subtle, systematic person. Somebody with the self-discipline to keep a low profile, in public and in the wild. The poacher had taken a lynx practically in Adam's backyard without him catching even a glimpse of the guy!

He'll be someone who knows animals. Who can hunt—and hit—his prey time after time. Which again ruled out Wilcox. In the shooting match tonight, Tess had won first place, Adam had learned. Wilcox had hit two pine cones in twelve attempts.

He's somebody who's either passionate about his cause, figuring he's shooting on the side of the angels. Or he's doing it strictly for money. A hired hitman.

Mulling it over with Gabe this afternoon, Adam had guessed that Sean Kershaw might be their man. He liked the kid and hoped he was wrong. But Sean was bright enough. Young enough to be passionate about cowboying. Quixotic enough to sign up for a lost cause and risk his future defending it. And at nineteen, fine-boned Sean had been Adam's best bet to wear a boy's boot size.

Checking out footgear tonight, Adam had found that Wilcox's feet matched his mouth—size thirteens, at least. The rest of the men varied from roughly nines to twelves. And Sean? The kid's feet were as large as his own. So there went that theory.

Tess swung halfway around to call teasingly, "Still back there?"

Oh, cher! *With my tongue hanging out.* "Count on it." His eyes caressed her graceful silhouette, then he frowned. The only one whose boots he'd failed to check was…

No, he was crazy even to let that cross his mind. *Forget it.* The obvious conclusion was that once he'd eliminated the men at the cookout, he was looking for an outsider. Somebody he'd yet to meet. A killer who, according to Watson, had departed by pickup from the trailhead past Two Bear Peak.

Unless somebody had shot the lynx, then handed the carcass over to somebody *else* at the trailhead?

Too complicated, he scoffed, then urged his mare to a trot as the path widened. Riding up alongside Tess, he leaned over to kiss her on the ear.

Her horse swerved aside to some signal of knee or rein, increasing the gap between them.

"Ah," he said softly. "My mistake." Something *had* changed. Riding stirrup to stirrup, they stared at each other. He should have waited till they reached her cabin, with its lamp. With moonlight and leaf shadow flowing across her face, all he could tell was that Tess wasn't smiling.

"I guess I'm just starting to realize," she said huskily, after a minute, "that I don't really know you."

"Ah." If that's all this was… He shrugged the tension from his shoulders. "You know what's important." He'd told her what mattered with his hands and his lips. When she lay with her head on his chest, hadn't she heard his heart beat? *Are you blind, girl? You don't see the way I look at you?*

"Adam, I *don't* know. For instance, are you married? I don't sleep with married men. At least…not knowingly."

His spirits bounced toward the sky, though he was careful not to grin. "No wives, Tess. And no sweethearts. I'm footloose and fancy-free." *At least, I was till I met you.* He edged his mare over till their calves brushed. "What else d'you need to know?"

"Where do you come from?"

"N'Orleans, I told you that."

"Yes, but most recently?"

Damn. If he didn't want to break his cover, he'd have to lie. "For this last year, I've been wrangling for an outfit out of Jackson Hole." No way could she verify that from here.

And later on? he asked himself wryly.

Later he'd either make amends for the lies he'd been forced to tell—or they'd no longer matter.

"And where will you go after this?" she challenged. "The McGraws won't need help in the winter."

Where else would he go but back to his job? Back to the Big Easy. Though riding these moon-washed mountains, Adam could hardly picture it. That would be him there, back in a car, cruising those hot humid streets?

And if he couldn't imagine himself, how could he picture Tess in his world? A child of nature, she'd hate the concrete, the noise, the tawdriness, the dirt... The bleeding, crying meanness of a cop's life. His spirits came tumbling back to earth—dropped into a pit he hadn't foreseen. *Even if I wanted her, it would never work.*

"Will you stick around Trueheart—or go?" she prodded his silence.

"Umm... Haven't quite decided yet."

She turned away. Her hair swung like a dark curtain between them. "I see..."

CHAPTER SEVENTEEN

SHE'D GONE FOR the easy questions and flinched from the tough ones, Tess scolded herself as they crossed her home meadow and the pack mare nickered a greeting.

The easy questions had been hard enough to ask—and Adam's answers even harder to hear. *Haven't quite decided yet.* Translated from male-speak, that meant *I'm leaving come the fall, babe.*

Yet she had no earthly right to complain. Hadn't *she* walked away from lovers who'd grown too eager, too clinging? Given the kind of life she meant to lead, that always had seemed the kind thing to do, as well as the wise.

Adam was the first man to make her question her dream. Was being a rootless field biologist worth the price of living single? Was loving on the fly, instead of for keeps really the way she wanted to go?

But though she might consider veering from her course for him, apparently Adam had no such intention. And it served her right. Now it was her turn to cry.

Still the pain she'd felt at his reply had startled her. Had distracted her from the tough things she'd intended to ask, like *Why do you need a hand gun? Who do you contact with that phone? Was that your hat with the lynx hatband? Do you use it to train Watson to track down cats?*

"Asleep in the saddle?" Adam teased.

Surprised to find him standing beside her, Tess murmured, "Um, no, I—" But before she could dismount, he slipped her left boot from its stirrup. Stood, frowning down at it.

She swallowed around the lump in her throat. Just the feel of his fingers around her ankle… Oh, this wasn't good! Adam had such power to move her, and yet she didn't know him. Didn't know who he was, or what he wanted.

Though he was making his desire of the moment plain enough. He let go of her boot and reached up to grip her waist.

"You don't need to—"

"Yeah, I do." He lifted her down, brought her in till their bodies brushed, holding her so their faces were on a level. "Oh, Tess…"

Her lips parted to protest, but when he slanted his mouth across hers, resistance melted to a dizzying kiss. The stars spun in the sky. With a helpless groan, she wrapped her arms around his neck, swung her legs up to lock them behind his lean waist.

"Oh, *sweet*…" His hands slid down her hips to cup her bottom and pull her in against the rock-hard bulge in his jeans.

Crazy, crazy, crazy, she shouldn't *do* this!

How could she resist? She was desperate to feel his naked skin against her own…his urgent heat inside her…his muscled weight bearing her deliciously down to a place where worries couldn't follow. Where nothing mattered but—

Watson barked. Pawed at Adam's leg.

"What the blue blazes?" He dragged his mouth aside to

glare at the dog. "Think you could mind your own business?"

Apparently not. The bloodhound barked again, then did a wriggling dance and ran off a few feet—whirled around with an impatient *"Woof!"*

"He's trying to tell you some—oh!" Beyond Adam's shoulder, Tess saw the distant shape of his mare, dragging her reins as she headed for home. "Your mare, Adam! She's taking off."

"Damn and—" Adam set her on her feet. Kissed her nose. "Hold that thought. I'll be right— *Hey,* Blackie, come back here!" He sprinted after the fleeing animal, with Watson bustling importantly beside him.

"Whew…" With a breathless laugh, Tess ran a hand through her tangled hair, then turned to Cannonball. The gelding had drifted only a few feet to crop virtuously at the grass. "Good boy." She unsaddled him and led him down to his picket. Clipped the lead on his halter, then removed his bridle. Rubbed his ugly head where he liked it—on his forehead, then around the ears. "Good fella. At least *you* know your manners."

At the edge of the trees, Adam had captured his truant. He mounted and started back.

Tess smiled to herself. Whatever else he might be, the man was a cowboy. None of them would walk twenty feet if they could ride. Her smile faded. *What else are you, Adam?*

She still didn't know. Still hadn't asked the hardest question, and yet she'd go to bed with him as if it didn't matter?

She gripped her elbows as a shiver racked up her spine. It *did* matter. Geronimo had mattered. What had she been *thinking* to—

She hadn't been thinking.

But if she let Adam drive what was important right out of her mind, she'd remember it tomorrow. And regret this bitterly. Love without respect, without shared values, was...

Something she'd never done before. And she didn't want to start now, Tess realized, looking up as he arrived.

"Sorry 'bout that." Adam smiled down at her. "Now, where were we?"

As he started to swing down, she stepped close and put a hand on his knee. "Adam."

Something in her voice stopped him cold, a vibrato that sounded as if it hurt her throat. He paused, eyes narrowing. "Yes?"

"Do you..." She hesitated so long it seemed she'd forgotten what she meant to ask.

"Do I what?" He dropped his hand over hers and found her fingers limp and icy, where just minutes before they'd clung to him, fever-hot.

"Do you ever go...hunting? You and Watson?"

"What?" She'd seen him? Up on the peaks, with his binoculars, hunting for the poacher? Or did she mean— "As in, for animals?"

Her breath sucked in sharply. She bit her lip and nodded.

What was this, a political correctness test? He'd met women who posed such questions, wanting to know whether a man smoked or hunted or voted Republican before they'd date him. But Tess and he were surely past such nonsense. "Like for elk?"

She swallowed with an effort, nodded again. "Or other...game?"

He shook his head. "I told you I was shot last spring. Well, knowing how it feels, I'm not inclined to aim a gun at any living creature, man or beast." Two of the Ski-Mask Killers had died by his hand; the third probably wished he had. Though he'd had no alternative, still he prayed to God he'd never have to shoot anybody, ever again.

"Yet you have a…" She stared down at the ground. "A rifle."

He laughed softly in bewilderment. "So do you, hot-shot. That was some shootin' tonight. But why are we talkin' about this? I can think of happier things." *To do to you. To do to me.*

"I…" She shrugged. "I don't know. Just tired, I guess."

Ah, so that's how the wind blew. Hot, now cold. A nerve fluttered in his jaw. "A few minutes ago you—"

"Yes, but I've changed my mind," she said quickly and pulled her fingers out from under his. "It's very late."

"Not so late I couldn't change it back again," he said, his voice harsh with frustration. With one kiss! *You're as hot for me, as I am for you.*

"I…" A cool breeze blew a skein of hair across her parted lips. Holding his gaze, she brushed it aside. "Even so."

At least she didn't deny it, his power to move her. But he needed much more than mere acquiescence. He wanted all she had to give—or nothing. "So…" he echoed grimly. "Then I'd best be on my way."

He didn't let himself look back till he'd reached the shadows under the trees.

Tiny under the wide bowl of the night, she stood where he'd left her, looking after him.

ADAM WOKE at dawn. He lay there blinking at the rafters while the night came back to him. Tess. What had changed between them—and why? *Something I did or said?*

Or failed to do?

With a groan, he rolled out of bed. A cold wash, then coffee, then he'd try to figure it out. How to put things right again.

Because no way was he walking away from this—from her—Adam realized, while he winced and sputtered beneath the bucket that served for his primitive shower.

Maybe she just needs some space, he told himself as he waited for the grounds to settle in his boiled coffee. Space and time. "God knows, I've felt that way before," he assured Watson, dumping dry food into his bowl. Edgy and confused at the start of a new relationship. Uncertain whether to go forward or retreat.

But *relationship* was too bland and clinical a term for what he'd felt last night, holding her. What he felt just as strongly this morning. Deep inside his own mind, the words welled up like crystal water from a spring. *If I ever mean to love again, here she is. This is The One.*

He put down his mug and glared at the dog. "Dammit!"

Watson wagged his tail agreeably, then sat to scratch a flea.

While he cooked and ate his breakfast, Adam planned out his day. No way could he go to Tess before he'd checked the cattle. And while he was checking them, he should move the herd to new grazing.

And then the lynx collar Gabe had given him yesterday…when would he put that to use?

Since the device wasn't constructed to switch on and off at will, thoughtful Gabe had also supplied a lead-foil pouch. Only when the collar was removed from this shield could anyone with tracking gear receive its signals. Adam intended to search at dawn and twilight, when his target—and the lynx his target was seeking—were most likely to be active.

"We'll start that late this afternoon," he informed the bloodhound. He meant to put the collar on Watson, then follow him at a distance. The signal would imitate a moving cat, but when the hunter homed in on his decoy, he'd find Adam waiting.

"We'll cover the trail from south of here to Tess's cabin," he decided. Once darkness fell, if he'd had no luck by then, he'd call the hunt quits. Start again at dawn.

And how would he spend the interlude between dusk and dawn? Well, that depended on his mystifying, exasperating, irresistibly hot and cold Tess.

"So…" The sooner he started his day, the sooner he'd reach its end. He strode impatiently around the cabin, dumping his dirty plate in the dishpan, stowing the supplies he'd bought in Durango. He tucked the collar in its pouch up on the same beam where he'd hidden the map—not because he expected anyone to be looking for it. But, only a fool left evidence lying around that could blow his cover.

Adam reached for his hat, then realized he'd left the charged replacement batteries that Gabe had given him for his phone on the table. He took them over to the bookcase, pulled out the concealing books—and hissed in surprise.

"What the—?" He sank down on the bunk and stared, then withdrew a few more volumes just to be certain. He'd left his Browning lying with its muzzle pointed toward the wall, and the top of the gun facing out, butt to the right, so that in an emergency, a right-handed man could turn over in bed, slap a few books to the floor and grip the weapon without a fumble.

Now the automatic lay reversed, with its butt to the *left!*

Somebody had made him.

But who?

SHE'D PROMISED Liza she'd protect Zelda and her kittens, come what may, and Tess intended to keep her word. Though she'd barely closed her eyes all night for thinking of Adam, she dragged herself out of bed at dawn and reached the new-growth meadow near Zelda's den just as the sun cleared the eastern peaks.

Twenty yards downhill a flutter of white caught her eye, and Tess reined in. Another flicker—feathers sailing off on the cool morning breeze, then a flash of tawny movement. The lynx crouched in the long grass, plucking a dead ptarmigan. She ripped out a mouthful of feathers, sneezed and flung them aside.

A kitten shot out of the grass to rear and bat at the drifting plumage. A second spotted baby leaped from hiding to pounce on its sibling—the two clenched and rolled on the ground to the sound of falsetto snarls. A third danced on tiptoes alongside the fray.

All her night's misery dropped away in a second. Tess laughed silently—reached back for the camera she kept in her saddlebag.

But Cannonball seized that instant to dip his head and scratch his cheek against his knee; the rings on his bit clinked ever so slightly.

Tess swung around in time to see her photo op vanish. Carrying her prize, Zelda trotted toward the forest with her babies scuttling at her heels. "Thanks," Tess told the gelding wryly.

Still, she'd witnessed a couple of encouraging "firsts," she reflected, as she took out her thawed chicken and followed slowly toward the den. Zelda had widened her repertoire of prey, taking a wild bird. And her kittens were now tagging along when she hunted, which was how they'd learn to feed themselves.

There were even a few anecdotes Tess had run across in her research, suggesting that female lynx hunted cooperatively with their half-grown kittens, strung out in a line to flush their prey. These were still too young for that, but... "Imagine," she murmured—a pride of lynx on the prowl! There probably weren't a dozen people in the world who'd been lucky enough to see such a sight.

How anyone could dream of ending such marvels...erasing them from these mountains... Her smile faded. Adam...

He was as beautiful as a lynx, with a look just as wild and wary in his eyes. Something in her simply couldn't believe that her loves could collide like this. She'd hardly slept, wondering if she was doing him an injustice, suspecting him of killing Geronimo, wishing that she'd been able to banish her worries and simply celebrate the moment...glory in his hands and his lips. The way he made her feel... Tess sighed heavily. *Can't keep wondering like this. I've got to ask him outright.*

She'd tried to do that last night, asking him if he and Watson ever hunted. And he'd denied it.

So why does he need a gun? A gun by his bed?

And the way he'd repeated her question had spooked her, too. *As in for animals?* he'd asked—as if there were some alternative!

"Shut *up!*" she cried aloud. Oh, this was what came of worrying late in the night! Of wanting something as much as she wanted Adam. She was letting her imagination run wild, off to darker and darker corners. It would be far better to simply demand the truth—then live with whatever he told her.

"And that's what I'll do," she decided, stopping to blow the "breakfast!" signal on her silent dog whistle.

She put the chicken in her usual spot near the den. Smiled at the swath of feathers that had drifted across the clearing. *"Bon appétit!"* she called softly toward the shadowy entrance to the burrow—where she could see a blur of movement. One of the kittens, no doubt, watching her with wild, innocent eyes.

THE SUN had climbed nearly to its zenith by the time Tess reached Adam's line camp.

Naturally, he wasn't there. "Wouldn't you know!" She slumped down on his stoop. She'd pushed her courage to the red line on its meter riding over, promising herself she'd simply demand to know if he'd shot a lynx.

Now she'd have to teeter on the painful point of her resolve till she could find him. "Blast!" No doubt he was out tending his cattle, as he should be.

"Am I completely nuts?" she wondered aloud. What if Adam was simply a cowboy, and a good one? All her suspicions and worries could be explained away, with a bit of effort.

But if she forced him to make that effort… How would Adam feel once he realized she hadn't trusted him? She'd found his gun and phone by accident; but still, what if he viewed that as snooping? Whatever bridge they'd been building between them, it was still fragile as a thread of spider silk.

Yet if she didn't satisfy her doubts, they'd linger. Poison any chance of future intimacy and trust. "No, this has *got* to be settled," she muttered, jumping to her feet. "However he takes it."

For better or worse.

So now what? Should she ride in search of him, or wait here, hoping he'd return for lunch?

Her every instinct demanded action. An end to this agonizing. All right then, she'd look for him. But in case they missed each other…

"Adam, I'm looking for you,"

she scribbled on the pad of yellow paper that rested on his table.

"It's roughly noon. If I miss you, could you stick around for a bit? I'll check back here in a couple of hours. Tess."

She started to add a postscript, telling him how she regretted last night, how she'd missed him in her bed—then she didn't.

She sighed and slapped the pencil down. What if he *wasn't* what he claimed to be? Intuition kept whispering to her that something wasn't right here. Something didn't ring true.

Yet her heart kept clamoring that it didn't matter, that whatever he might be, Adam was *hers*.

"All right, all right, all *right!*" Find him and settle it, once and for all. But first, her thirst reminded her that she'd emptied her water bottle on the way over from Zelda's den. Striding into his kitchen corner, Tess poured herself a glass from the jar of filtered water that stood on his counter. Tipping her head back, she closed her eyes and drank.

"Just find him and settle it," she repeated, as she opened her eyes.

And found herself staring at the rough fir beam overhead. At something white and long lying upon it. The map!

As she went to the table, Tess glanced over her shoulder. Placed precisely on the back side of the wide beam—the rearmost beam that spanned the cabin—the scroll was invisible from the front. She'd stood at the one point from which it could be seen. Looked up only by chance.

"You don't want to know this," she warned herself, as she carried a chair into position. Yet not knowing would be even worse. She'd only wonder what he had to hide.

Stepping up onto the chair, she could see the top of the beam. Alongside the paper cylinder lay a pouch of dull, gleaming material. Heavy when she lifted it.

She carried both discoveries to the table, glanced nervously at the door. If he came home for lunch? "Whatever," she muttered—and unrolled the map.

To find, as she'd remembered, a topographic depiction of the San Juan Mountains, with inked-in asterisks and notations. Leaning down till her nose nearly touched the paper, she peered at the printed note on the Uncompahgre Plateau. "Female, collar BC02F1, 6/24," she read aloud.

"No." It couldn't mean what it seemed to mean. This was worse than her worst imaginings—too awful to be true. And yet, where else had Liza said a DOW lynx had vanished?

Creede. She looked for, then found, a notation north of that town. "Male, collar YK99M3, 5/17."

Her eyes watered, the map's bright details wavered as she blinked. She found Mount Sumner, looked west from there to roughly the location of Geronimo's den. "Oh, Adam, oh, *damn* you!"

Collarless lynx, 7/7th

read the notation next to the asterisk.

G. figures #BC00M3 or #YK00M2, both of which slipped their collars.

The date she'd found the blood at Geronimo's cave. Adam had recorded his kill with two emotionless lines. "You heartless, lying *bastard!*" A tear fell to mark the site of murder. She wiped it savagely away and kept on reading.

In all, twenty-two lynx had been listed, their points of disappearance scattered all over the San Juan Mountains, each with a date beside it.

She blew out a shaky breath and lifted both hands to wipe her eyes. The map snapped back to a cylinder, but she'd seen enough. Too much.

Adam hadn't simply chanced on Geronimo and shot him on impulse, as she'd pictured it happening. Though that would have been awful enough. Quite unforgivable.

Yet he'd done—*was doing*—something much worse. Adam was stalking—and methodically killing—all the lynx in the DOW restoration program. Then recording his hits on this map.

"But why?" she murmured dazedly. Could he be embarked on his own misguided crusade to rid the high country of lynx? To preserve the grazing rights of cattlemen?

Yet there was something so cold, so clinical, about this record. Instead of a passionate crusade, it suggested a man working down a checklist, ticking off lynx after murdered lynx.

And he *wasn't* working alone, come to think of it. Geronimo's epitaph had mentioned a "G." "G. figures," she repeated. Someone who was advising Adam in his hunt? Possibly *paying* him to hunt?

If the rumors Liza had reported were true, then one of the interests that opposed the lynx program had hired a hitman. A professional killer.

Who else would come riding with a hound to track lynx? A cell phone to communicate with his distant employers? A hand gun that no cowboy would carry?

If she'd had any doubts—any hope—at all, Tess found the clenching proof in the metallic pouch that also had been tucked away on the beam. A radio tracking collar of a type familiar to every wildlife biologist. Given its neck diameter, he'd taken it off a lynx.

"You unspeakable…" Moving in a trance, Tess crumpled the note she'd written and jammed it in her pocket. She put the map back where she'd found it, also the pouch, then brought the chair back to the table. The collar—she groaned and looped an arm through it, then stalked out his door without a farewell glance. She'd take the collar with her, as evidence.

Because she could not ignore what he'd done. He'd have to be stopped. He'd have to pay.

She rode slowly at first, like a rider who climbs back in the saddle after a bad fall—ribs cracked, pride in the dust, heading homeward simply by instinct. Then, halfway there, a thought sliced through her misery: *what made her so sure that Adam was out tending cattle?*

If instead he was hunting lynx...Zelda and her babies...

"Over my dead *body!*" Leaning over Cannonball's withers, she lashed the ends of her reins across his rump. The gelding lunged into a run and thundered west.

CHAPTER EIGHTEEN

PART OF BEING a successful detective was thinking the unthinkable. All morning while he worked the cattle, Adam tried to duck his conclusions. But now they had to be faced.

Someone had searched his cabin.

A person with a guilty conscience, who somehow had realized that Adam might be a threat. That he might be more than a harmless line-camp cowboy.

All morning he'd tried to persuade himself that his prey had spotted him searching, then followed him back to his cabin and tossed it to be sure.

Much as that theory would have dented his professional pride, Adam would have been happy to buy it. But common sense suggested a simpler explanation: Tess. He'd let her get close—closer than close—and somehow she'd seen through his cover.

And that explains why she backed off last night. If she's shooting lynx and now she fears I'm investigating, no way would she want me around.

He'd been a fool not to suspect her from the start. Any way you looked at it, she fit the profile he'd been building.

As he'd noted last night, she wore a man's size-six boot, which meant the footprint by the bloodstained cave was almost surely hers.

She was a crack shot; if lynx were her chosen target, she'd hit them with ease.

She knew animals—probably understood them better than most men understood women. She'd know when and where and how to stalk her elusive quarry.

And that's just why she can't be my lynx killer, he told himself desperately as he rode back to his cabin. Tess loved animals. *Look at her with Watson, with her horses. Those beavers she studied...*

Or turn it around the other way, his coldly logical half argued. What if, more than any one species, Tess loved *a way of life*—cattle-ranching. The wild, fenceless, high country. A way of life that was threatened—or more accurately, was believed to be threatened—by lynx. And the environmental bureaucrats who were imposing their restoration program on the cattlemen and other local interests. What would she do to protect it?

He'd known from the start that her old man, Ben Tankersly, had financed the court battle to keep the lynx out of Colorado, Adam reminded himself.

Had he thought that meant nothing? Had he thought that Tess would walk away from her upbringing and her friends and all they believed? That she'd stand alone?

She should have been his prime suspect from the first day he'd met her—prowling these mountains with a rifle in hand! Then later, when she'd returned after that unexplained absence, with scratches on her back?

She'd told him they'd come from riding under a branch and he'd believed her. He'd closed his eyes to every fact that had stared him in the face. Tess hadn't needed to seduce him—one look in her big, beautiful eyes and he'd fooled himself!

"The ol' honey trap," he muttered. It had worked on

men since his namesake had taken one look at Eve's apples—and thrown the rules over the garden gate. "Sucker!" he snarled as he banged through the screen door and into his cabin, with Watson skulking anxiously at his heels.

Right. He stood convicted—a jerk and a sucker, through and through. And so now what?

"Get the facts, get the proof," he growled, wandering into his kitchen. That was what he was trained to do. What he'd come here to do for Gabe. Get the proof, then nail the bad guy.

Who happened to be Tess.

What was he thinking? This was federal law she'd broken! The penalty, serious hard time. A cage for his Tess, wild and free as a bird? "Dammit to *hell!*"

Swearing a blue streak, he grabbed the glass in the sink. Held it under the tap on his filtered water jug—and paused. Blinked, then put the glass down gingerly as if it were a ticking bomb.

"Didn't I put my—" He checked and there it was, the jelly jar he'd drunk from this morning, still soaking in the dishpan.

"Son of a bitch!" The brazen little— She'd come back?

To do what? Give his heart another kick?

His eyes scanned the cabin—noted the chair not pushed in quite square to the table, but slightly angled. She'd pulled it out and sat, or— As it hit him, he glanced at the beam overhead.

Tess was too short to reach his hiding place without standing on something. So she'd brought the chair over and— Rising on tiptoe, Adam stretched to full length. His fingers just grazed the pouch. As it toppled into his hands, he groaned. He didn't have to unzip it to know: she'd taken the collar!

WHEN SHE REACHED her usual stopping point on the old avalanche scar, Tess looked around. No sign of Adam or his mare. She blew out a long breath of relief, wiped her eyes, then sat for a minute watching Cannonball's ears.

They rotated hither and yon, locating a camp robber bird hopping from limb to limb along the edge of the forest…a rock squirrel, perched cheekily on a tree stump in the midst of Zelda's hunting domain. But the gelding's ears didn't prick to the rigid attention he'd have given the sound or scent of a nearby horse.

"Good," she murmured, and rode him on into the woods. If Adam was out hunting lynx, he wasn't nearby. Not yet. Finding a pocket clearing with sufficient graze, she staked the gelding out where he couldn't be easily seen.

Though—she bit her lower lip till she winced—if Adam came hunting in this direction, he'd come with Watson. And no way would the bloodhound miss Cannonball—or her.

"Tough," she muttered darkly. Adam wouldn't dare shoot an endangered species with a witness at hand. Especially not if that witness was ready to scratch his eyes out if he so much as reached for his gun!

She meant to guard Zelda's den till nightfall. It wasn't much of a plan, but miserably muddled as she was, it would have to do for today. By now, the lynx and her kittens should be holed up and safely sleeping. So she'd watch over their burrow till it was too dark for a hunter to aim or shoot.

"Then tomorrow?" she agonized, rummaging in her saddlebag for the protein bars she kept there.

She hadn't a clue. At the moment she was still staggering, punch-drunk with what she'd learned at Adam's cabin. Give her a day to come to terms with his betrayal, then perhaps she'd think of a solution. "Should have stolen his phone," she realized. She could have called Liza for help.

But what sort of help? She knew the Division of Wildlife had investigators to enforce environmental laws, as did the US Fish and Wildlife Service. But…*Adam.* Could she really set the law on him? Send him off to jail?

Well, what's the choice—let him go on killing lynx?

Tears welled to blind her. Swearing helplessly, Tess pawed through her bags. She found her water bottle by feel. And cursed again as she realized she'd forgotten to fill it at his cabin.

No matter, she groped for her emergency camper's water filter, which would clean a few pints if she got unbearably thirsty. "What else?"

She slung the strap of her camera around her neck. If the kittens didn't snooze all day long, perhaps she'd snap some pictures; any distraction from her heartache would be welcome.

Deep in the bag, her hand grazed the flexible hoop of the radio collar. Tess let out a little moan. Here was her only proof of Adam's crime. If she really intended to turn him in, she shouldn't risk losing it. Best to leave it in the bag, where she couldn't mislay it. She closed the leather flap and trudged off toward the den.

NATWIG HAD PARKED his pickup and trailer at the Two Bear trailhead at dawn, then spent the morning sweeping the valleys below for a radio signal.

He'd heard not a peep in his earphones.

By noon he'd drifted down to the lower elevations, a few miles west of the ridge where he'd taken the tom. Since he knew that a male lynx's larger range often overlapped a few females' hunting grounds—especially females that he'd bred—Natwig reasoned that the queen with kittens might be located close by.

Going on that theory, he was riding a narrow stream that stair-stepped down through forested slopes, looking for prints along its banks. He stopped every so often to scan the woods with his tracking gear.

He proceeded warily, nerves stretched taut, ears alert for the sounds of an approaching horseman. This lower elevation was mixed trees and grazing land, which meant somewhere near at hand a cowboy would be riding his herd, on the lookout for trouble.

Trouble was something Natwig would just about welcome. His bitten hand ached. The wounds on his bandaged arms itched. He might be running a fever. All he wanted was to finish this friggin' job and get home to Karen.

Seventy thousand dollars, he reminded himself, as he reined in to rotate in the saddle, focusing his tracking rod on the surrounding forested slopes. *Quit your bitchin' and concentrate on that.*

When a faint *beep!* sounded in his earphones, he almost dropped the wand. Using the compass he wore on his wrist, he took a bearing. Coming from northeast of where he sat. "Don't go to earth. Please, *please,* stay up where I can find you!"

Miles away, but clear as a beacon, the signal continued. *Oh, critter, comin' to get you!* Clucking to his horse,
he turned away from the trail and up through the woods.

ADAM ACHED for a confrontation. Forget proper procedure, or reading Tess her rights. And just let her dare to
pretend innocence! Or ignorance! *Not a chance, sweetheart.*

Let him once lay his hands on her and he'd shake her
till he shook the truth from those lovely, lying lips. *What
was real, what was false? Was loving me part of some
plan to confuse and distract me—or a detour you didn't
mean to make? Tell me!*

And then?

His mind couldn't move beyond the image of him
holding her so close she'd never break free.

He could barely believe that she wasn't home when he
needed to yell at her. Cursing as he stalked through her
cabin, Adam didn't bother to conceal his search as he looked
for evidence to prove what he already knew to be true.
Where was her radio tracking gear? The signal collars she'd
have smashed when she removed them from the dead lynx?

"There'll be a cell phone some place," he assured the
bloodhound, who crouched on her rag rug and rolled his
eyes. "She's got an accomplice. Somebody she hands the
bodies off to, I'm thinking. The guy you tracked to the
Two Bear trailhead. Which means she's got to have some
way to call him."

And who the hell is he? Somebody punchable, Adam
prayed. He damn sure needed to punch *somebody*.

Rummaging through the clothes in her shabby pine bureau, he found a bowl of dried honeysuckle blossoms, a
cache of blue feathers. A photo of two laughing young

women, one a blonde, one a redhead, but they both had Tess's winged, sexy eyebrows. No hidden collars, no electronic gear.

The second drawer produced a harmonica, a racy romance novel, a black thong bikini that stopped him cold. *"Dammit!"*

Adam slammed that drawer and tried the last, and there, below her neatly folded jeans, lay an inch-thick stack of papers on— "Lynx!"

His heart sank down to his boots; he dropped down on her bed. Here it was. Proof he couldn't deny. Tess had researched lynx on the Internet, pulling facts and photos off dozens of Web sites, including the Division of Wildlife's. The huntress had studied her quarry.

"Try and explain this away!" he growled—then glanced up and around. Where was she, anyway? It had to be past three in the afternoon.

"She's run for it?" he surmised to the dog. Didn't matter. Let her run anywhere in the world, she'd find him breathing down her neck.

"Can't have run," he answered himself. The pack mare was still staked out in her meadow. Tess had bamboozled him from first to last, but still, this much about her he'd willingly swear in any court of law: She wouldn't leave a horse tied, where it would run out of feed.

The ache in his heart eased ever so slightly. *Come on, baby, let's have it out.* He set the lynx papers aside, stood and turned a perplexed circle in the center of her cabin. There was no place left to search. Not inside.

"Ah." Of course! The first time he'd dropped over, Watson had pulled a fit.

Her old kerosene-powered box freezer still chugged

away in the lean-to. Adam opened its lid—to peer down at a flock of frozen chickens. "Lynx bait! You tried to tell me, didn't you?"

The bloodhound modestly wagged his tail, then wandered out of the shed—to stare nearsightedly across the empty meadow.

"You miss her, too," Adam muttered. "Coupla damn fools, handin' our hearts to a devil woman."

And she wasn't even there to collect them.

"To hell with this waiting, pal. The sooner we find her, the sooner we can tell her she's busted." Banging back into the cabin, Adam selected a T-shirt from a basket that held her dirty laundry. He offered it to the bloodhound, who snuffled eagerly. "*Find* her, Watson. *Find Tess!*"

SHE'D CHOSEN a bush some twenty yards south of the den to serve for a blind. Tess lay in the leaf duff below it, with her chin propped on her crossed forearms. Her gaze rested on the sunlit burrow, but her mind trudged a dark trail of misery and confusion. *Oh, Adam, Adam*…could she stop him somehow, without hurting him?

But then why should she care if he were arrested? Sent to prison? If he'd killed twenty-two lynx, then he wasn't the man she'd thought he was. Wasn't a man she could ever love.

Tell that to her aching heart.

If she didn't stop thinking about him, she'd go mad! She made herself count leaves instead, on the bush that sheltered her. Lost count around thirty-seven and found herself wondering, W*hat if it's all a dreadful mistake?* Adam was blameless. He'd found the radio collar on the mountainside; some lynx had wriggled out of it.

Yeah, right, and how do you explain his map? she jeered at herself. *He marks the death sites of lynx as a hobby? And how did he know where Geronimo died?*

With no answer for that, she resumed counting. After forty-two leaves she found herself thinking, *And that story about being wounded in a grocery store holdup? What a lovesick sap I was to believe that one! What if this is what he does for a living? Shoots things? Adam's a hitman and somebody hired him—the ski people, or the timber interests—to eliminate the lynx problem.*

She shoved her mind brutally back to her leaf-counting, but found herself remembering: Adam's gentleness when he patched up her scratches. The way he'd kissed her eyelids as she fell asleep. *This has got to be some kind of dreadful mistake. Just got to be.* She would go to him tonight, accuse him to his face, then see what he said…

The day crawled on, minute by minute, leaf by leaf, one misery after another. When a movement finally caught her eye, Tess seized it with a gasp of gratitude. A kitten crept out of Zelda's den, stared round-eyed at its enormous, fascinating world—then pounced on something in the grass. A second spotted baby ventured forth, to sit with a thump, yawning hugely. Next, Zelda appeared from the shadows; she leaped up onto the fallen tree.

While her kittens gamboled below her, she groomed her coat like any house cat. Tess stealthily lifted her camera, focused, then snapped off a shot. Then a whole slapstick series, as all three kittens swatted frantically at a passing butterfly, colliding with each other, then squabbling when they lost it.

Finally the lynx settled in a patch of sunlight, and called her babies to nurse with an imperious, birdlike chirp.

Oversize paws kneaded her creamy stomach; heads butted her hungrily. When Zelda leaned down to lick a squirming back, her black lips seemed to smile.

Tess found her eyes blurring. She held the camera aside to wipe them. Oh, if she was forced to trade her happiness for a cause, she could have chosen worse than this one!

But as she brought the viewfinder back to her eye, Zelda screamed.

"Wha—?" Tess dropped her camera.

Leaping straight up in the air, the cat landed in a heap. She spun to bite desperately at her flank, while her kittens backed away in confusion.

The lynx raised her head, tried a wobbling step—and collapsed.

As if she'd been shot, yet Tess had heard nothing! *Adam!* Could he be here, using a hitman's silencer? She scrambled backward out of her bush, stood—and gasped.

From the thick undergrowth ahead on her right, a man advanced. Someone she'd never seen before. His attention was riveted on the fallen lynx and her babies, two of which scuttled back into their den. The third stood by its mother. Arching its back, it hissed at the oncoming monster.

Tess had had nightmares before where she couldn't scream… Seemed to be wading through water when she needed to run—that's what this felt like. *Stop,* she cried inwardly as she flew across the clearing. *Oh, don't!*

With his back turned, the killer didn't see her stumbling charge. He lowered his rifle, taking aim at Zelda's tiny defender.

"Nooo!" Tess shrieked, as she launched herself in a flying tackle.

A sound like a banshee—an oncoming shadow seen from the corner of his eye! *Mountain lion* was Natwig's sole thought, as he spun and fired into the shape.

It hit him chest-high and he toppled backward, almost on top of the lynx—to find himself clutching a woman. *"Geez!"*

His dart had hit her just above the collarbone. She plucked at it feebly, her gaze fixed on his face. *"Don'..."* she mumbled, her eyes already losing focus. "I-I-I-I-I saw...you." She yanked the dart out, frowned at it, then shook her head groggily. "Breakin' law."

"Oh, *geez*, lady!" Natwig rolled and laid her down on the ground. Oh, God, what had he done? The tranquilizer was made for cats—what would it do to a woman? "Talk to me! Stay with me! Don't—" But her lashes drooped as he patted her cheek. "Oh, shit!" He slapped her face—her head rolled to one side. Out cold!

Or dying?

And he knew her from somewhere. Little Miss Jabber-Mouth, from the spring near the tomcat's ridge. "Hell and damnation!" He felt for the pulse in her throat—but all he could feel was his own panicked blood roaring through his fingertips.

And she'd seen him! Must have seen his face, good and clear. "Aw, no. Please..."

Crouched against its mother, the kitten snarled, a ridiculously savage sound.

"Shut the hell up!" Natwig roared back.

The kitten shot off to its burrow.

Natwig stared up between the treetops at a merciless blue sky. *What do I do?*

Either she was dying...or she'd wake to wreck his life.

CHAPTER NINETEEN

HALFWAY to his own cabin, Adam realized his mistake. Commanded to find Tess, the bloodhound was pursuing her most recent path. Apparently that would lead them back to Sumner line camp, which Tess had searched this morning. At an excruciating, sniff-every-blade-of-grass dog's pace. Why hurry when you're having such fun?

"Okay, *okay,* I got this part. Come *on.*" Adam spurred on ahead, yelling over his shoulder, "Watson, *come!* Cancel that! Come on, boy!"

By the time the hound caught up with him at the cabin, he'd packed his gun, his cell phone, food and water and a coat in his saddlebags. He'd tucked his rifle into its scabbard. Something told him they might not be back this way for a while. *Whither thou goest, Tess…*so would he follow.

"Not your fault. You had the right idea," he consoled the bloodhound, while he lapped the bowl of water Adam brought him. "Now eat—"

The dog inhaled the chunk of canned ham and nearly took a finger with it.

"—this," Adam finished wryly.

Licking his chops, Watson looked up hopefully for more.

"And now—" Adam held out Tess's T-shirt. "*Find.* Find Tess. *Find her.*"

The dog whined in pleasure, put his nose to the cabin floor and snuffled into the kitchen, then back again. He padded out the door, sucking dirt. *So slow!* Adam could feel a nerve ticking in his cheek. Something told him that time was running out… Something precious trickling away…yet here he was stuck, following a four-legged vacuum cleaner at a snail's pace!

BY THE TIME they reached a clearing in the woods, some eight miles southwest of his cabin, the day was fading fast.

"She stopped here awhile," Adam interpreted the dog's discovery. "At least, she left her horse here." Long enough for it to crop the grass and leave a pungent pile. "What have you got there?"

The dog had fixed on an oblong patch of ground, where he whined and pawed at the earth.

"What's so special? Huh, boy?" Adam dropped on his boot heels to see.

The vegetation had been flattened in a roughly rectangular pattern. When the dog growled, Adam felt the hair rise on his nape. *A body-shaped impression!* "She lay here, boy?" Was that what disturbed Watson? "Or she fell." Fell and lay still?

He lurched to his feet. "*Find* her!" he demanded hoarsely. *"Find Tess!"*

But this time the dog seemed confused. He snuffled south, deeper into the forest, then let out one of those peculiar bellows that seemed to mean *"lynx!"*

"Forget the damned cats!" Adam hurried after him with the T-shirt. "This is who we want! *Find Tess. Find her!*"

The bloodhound turned around and came back to the clearing. He whined as he rooted around the same place.

"Find her." Adam wanted to shake the mutt till his ears flapped. He forced himself to raging stillness, staring down at the spot where he was sure she'd lain. *Something's wrong.* He didn't know how he knew, but he knew. "Find her, pal, you can do it. She got back on Cannonball—and then what? Where?"

As if he'd come to some decision, Watson blew out a gusty snort—and headed north.

With the sun sinking fast, they tracked her in a nearly straight line. Tess must be headed for home, Adam guessed with a sigh of relief. Any time now, her track should turn off to the east.

It didn't.

On and on the dog snuffled, a quarter mile past her logical turning point... Half a mile. Just as the sun touched the peaks to the west in a bloody blaze of glory, Adam realized. Extend this line another two miles and it would hit the saddleback pass to the east of Two Bear!

Reining in, he yanked the binoculars from his bag and peered upward through the dusk, searching for the dip in the mountain's massive shoulder that would mark the pass.

Every boulder and bush threw a lengthening blue shadow, big as a horse. A wave of purple washed in from the east, sweeping the last ruddy light before it. Adam blinked his stinging eyes—then cried out in triumph as he zeroed in on a purposeful movement.

Purposeful—but not human. Three elk picked their way across an alpine meadow, then froze as if they could hear Adam's curse. Their heads swung sharply to the east—they melted away into a hollow.

What had spooked them? Adam skated his lens in the direction they'd looked. He found something shifting again, plunging awkwardly upward—a horse and rider!

No...two riders! "*Son* of a—" So Tess had joined her accomplice. He'd barely spotted them in time. Another fifty yards and they'd vanish beyond the pass. Adam's mare fidgeted and he lost the image.

Hastily he dismounted, searched for the figures again—caught them just as they gained the skyline.

A man rode in front—a wide-shouldered silhouette, wearing a Stetson. Half-turned in the saddle, he— Adam sucked in his breath. *The first rider led the second one's horse!*

The second, smaller rider had to be Tess, but what was this? She was hurt? She rode slumped so far forward, her head hung down, bobbing alongside Cannonball's shoulder. Her dark hair swung and swayed halfway to the ground.

"*Son of a bitch!*" Adam cried as he realized. She couldn't be conscious, riding like that! The bastard had tied her in the saddle! Adam cursed aloud. Two miles above him, she might as well be on the moon!

Her horse topped the ridge—seemed to hang there for a heartbeat—then vanished.

Eyes watering, swearing helplessly, Adam hammered a fist on his saddle. "*Whoa!* Stay still!" He grabbed the reins of his side-stepping mare, touched the rifle in its scabbard. *If I'd dropped her horse before he topped the ridge?* That would have stopped them, sure as shooting the wheels out on a car.

But at that range, he might easily have shot Tess instead and anyway, now it was too late. "*I'll kill him!*"

First he had to catch him. Shaking with adrenaline, Adam computed the brutal math a second time, but his conclusion was inescapable. Two rugged miles straight uphill to the top of the pass...then beyond it, an easy mile downhill to the trailhead. That's where the bastard would be taking her.

Adam could flog Blackie straight up the mountainside. But he'd break her heart and her wind, and for what? He wouldn't reach Tess in time.

Given that sort of lead, they'd reach the creep's waiting pickup half an hour before Adam made the pass.

By the time he arrived at the trailhead itself, they'd be long gone.

Bound for where?

"GOT YOUR MESSAGE," Gabe said tersely when Adam answered his cell phone. "Can you hear me? What's wrong? Where are you?"

"In my truck, headed down toward Trueheart." Bucketing through the night, a roostertail of dust rising behind him. Watson had been thrown to the floorboards so many times, he'd given up and crouched there, with his chin propped on the seat. The whites of his eyes gleamed in the dark. "Now listen up. The poacher's got Tess."

Weaving the truck one-handed between potholes and around the snakily descending curves, Adam explained.

"But if you don't think she's part of this, how did she get involved?" Gabe demanded.

"Damned if I know. All I can figure is she found the collar you gave me, and carried it away for some reason. And its signal brought the guy down on her, instead of on me." Adam's fingers clenched the wheel till they ached. *My fault. If I'd trusted her. Warned her.* At the very least, he should never have let her into his life while he was working undercover.

Too late for that now. She was in all the way. The thought of Tess being hurt made him want to howl at the sky. He blew out a shaking breath. *Steady.* Losing his cool wouldn't help her.

"So what should I do?" Gabe asked, the voice of calm. "Call the cops? The sheriff over Trueheart way is a good guy. I could—"

"No, not yet. He'd have nothing to go on." Nowhere to look.

Besides, if the perp learned the law was seeking him— wanted him for kidnapping—silencing his prisoner, then hiding her body, might seem his only option.

A good and rational reason to play this close to the vest, but beneath it, raw instinct drove him: *Tess is my woman, so it's my place to save her.*

"This is what I want from you. The collar you gave me, it signals to a satellite, as well as to a radio direction-finder?"

"Right. But the way the system works, each lynx collar in the program broadcasts its location up to the satellite once a week. Then once a week, the satellite downloads seven days' collected data to DOW head-quarters, pinpointing where each animal was last spotted."

Adam banged his head against his backrest in frustration. "Okay, that's your usual program. But if you wanted to find one particular lynx, and wanted to find her—it— this minute, not a week from now, could you do that? Is there any other program you could run?"

"I-I'm not sure, Adam. There might be. I'd have to ask our techie, Lou-the-guru. He handles all our computer and electronic biz."

"Right. You drag Lou out of bed, and if there's any way in the world to tell me where that collar is *right now,* that's what I need. And I need it yesterday."

"If it's gettable, you got it. I'm on my way. But, Adam…"

"Yeah." Adam slammed the truck around a hairpin curve. Its back wheels skidded on the gravel—then caught and carved the turn. "I know."

"If the guy who grabbed her *is* our poacher, and he found the collar, he knows what to do with it. He'll smash it, the same way he broke the others."

"If he finds it," Adam agreed grimly. And why wouldn't he, since he'd homed in on its signal?

Except the hunter had expected to find a radio collar on a cat, not possessed by a woman.

The bastard must have been stunned speechless when he came face to face with Tess. Tess, who might be a bantam-weight, but she'd never be a pushover. If in the confusion and struggle that surely followed, the creep had panicked, forgotten the collar…

"It's a longshot, but it's all we've got to go on," Adam continued. All that stood between him and a raving, tree-punching meltdown. The thought of Tess tied, in danger… "I reckon she'd have been carrying it in her saddlebag. If he didn't search her gear right away…" If the bastard took her saddle and tack along, when he drove her away from the trailhead…

If, if, if! If there's an angel in charge of "ifs"…

"Even if he finds it somewhere along the way, if he destroys it later on, it'll send out a—" Adam swallowed around the stone in his throat. "—a death signal, right?"

"Right," Gabe agreed somberly. "It will."

"So say he finds it halfway home, then wrecks it? Pinpointing that location would still narrow my area of search."

"I hear you."

"The logging road that comes down from the Two Bear trailhead, the road he'll have taken, ends up southwest of the mountains. It forks when it reaches the valley, one way heading north, the other southeast. If I knew even which fork to search along…"

"That would help," Gabe agreed. "Okay, so Lou and I will go pound the computers at headquarters. And you?"

"I'm headed down to Trueheart, then west to reach the base of that road." Roughly two hundred miles, by the time he'd circled the southern half of the mountain range. Damnable Western distances! Back in New Orleans he'd have been there—anywhere—by now. "So what time is it?" Even if he'd worn a watch, he couldn't have spared a hand to consult it.

"Umm, almost three."

"Right. So call me in an hour, Gabe—with some good news."

"Do my best, cuz, and meanwhile…drive to get there, okay?"

The devil himself couldn't stop me!

Not ten minutes later, the devil blew out one of his tires.

DRIVING DREAMILY through the dark, the comforting smells of horse and leather nearby… Tess's eyelashes fluttered as she tried to focus. *Where…? When…?* Driving back to Suntop from a rodeo, or maybe a branding? Lara and Risa would be riding up front with their father. She hated to be left out, treated like the baby of the family, but driving always made her sooooo…

SOMEBODY LIFTING her gently, carrying her in strong arms… "Are…" Tess yawned hugely. "Are we…there yet?"

"Huh!" The arms holding her jerked, then a gruff voice said, "Not just yet. Go back to sleep."

Not her daddy, then who? Her nose brushed his sleeve; she smelled sweaty man and smiled. Joe Wiggly, their ranch manager, he was the sweetest man… This must be the time she'd climbed that cliff in Blindman's Canyon, trying to peek in an eagle's nest. She fell and hit her head and Lara had run to get Joe. He'd carried her home before him on his saddle…

Metal creaked, then "Get back there!" the man growled. "Go on! *Skat!* Move!"

Tess frowned. Not Joe, then who?

She sailed dizzily through the dark, came to a landing on something hard. Something soft and warm and smelling of wool was tucked around her.

Tess wrinkled her nose. "*Eww.* Somebody oughta… change that catbox." She snuggled the blanket up to her chin. "Joe retired a long time ago," she recalled. "Rafe Montana's ranch manager…now."

"What ranch does he manage?" demanded the voice.

Tess rubbed her eyes. "Who…are you? Where's…" Time swooped like a bat's wing over her head; faces and places reeled past. She let out a squeak of alarm.

A hand patted her shoulder. "Never mind. Go back to sleep." Steps on concrete, then he growled, "*Scat, dammit! G'wan! Move!*"

Something soft and big brushed past her, growling in the dark.

"Where's Adam?" Tess said distinctly. "I want…"

A door closed in the distance.

"I want you!" she whispered. *Always, forever… Your lips, your arms, your babies, I want it all. I want…us.* Smiling, she drifted off to sleep.

"YOU HAVE REACHED my voicemail box. Please leave a message after the tone."

"Larson, it's Natwig. If you can hear this, then pick up the damn phone!" Waiting, praying, Natwig closed his eyes and rested his forehead against the glass wall of the phone booth. Glass so cool, his face so hot; he had a fever, for sure.

When the silence continued, he gave a weary grunt. "Okay, when you get this, we've got trouble. Big trouble. I've got t'talk to you. But don't call me at home. *Do not.* I'm not there, I'm on the road.

"I'll…" He tore a hand up through his hair. "It's nigh on dawn. Reckon you won't be checking your messages for a while, so… Shit!"

He flogged his brains for a space. "I'm gonna drive on into town. We've got to talk, figure out…something. I'll keep tryin' to reach you, so when I call, pick up your friggin' phone!" He slammed the receiver down and staggered back to his truck.

And all the while a voice in the back of his mind kept chanting, *Please, please, aw, please*… Even though he knew he'd crossed some line…wandered off into a wilderness where maybe even God didn't pick up His messages.

SOMETHING TICKLED her nose…her lips… Adam, teasing her with a lock of her own hair? Tess smiled, opened her eyes—and looked up past a spray of arching white whiskers, into fierce golden eyes. A furry feline upside-down face, only inches above her own. *"Eeep!"*

Pupils expanded to black in surprise—the face withdrew.

Tess rolled to one elbow, to see a lynx padding away toward a gate in a chain-link fence. "Zelda? *Zelda!*"

The lynx flattened her tufted ears in displeasure and slapped at the gate with a paw. She commenced stalking to and fro before it, the picture of surly outrage.

"Oh, it *is* you, isn't it?" Tess shoved herself up to sit, then leaned back against more mesh—a galvanized wall of it. She glanced up to find a ceiling of chain links, roughly eight feet above the concrete floor. She turned toward the rear of the cage.

Hunched down as if to pounce, a much larger lynx glared at her from the recesses of a doghouse built at the rear of their jail. A low, sing-song growl filled the air. The hair rose along the lynx's shaggy back.

"Geronimo?" Tess whispered. Oh, it *was*, she'd know that white snip on his chest anywhere! Geronimo, alive, healthy—and looking spitting mad to be sharing his cage with a couple of mere females! "Oh, sweetie, you're alive!"

His snarl climbed half an octave. The look in his eyes suggested *she* wouldn't be, if she didn't stop bothering him!

"Sooorry." Tess turned humbly away. Predators hated to be stared at, she reminded herself. Often they took it as a sign of aggression, requiring an angry response. "*So* sorry." Making no sudden moves, she drew her blanket up over her bent knees and gripped its top hem. It wouldn't serve for much of a shield if he lost his temper, but still, she could pull it over her head.

When he didn't attack, she dared to look carefully back toward Zelda. The female still paced, head down, ears pinned. Coming to a frustrated halt each time she reached a side wall, she'd rock to and fro on her forepaws, then spin and pace again. "Where're your babies, sweet-heart?"

Tess glanced around. They were penned in what looked like a dog run, roughly eight feet wide by twenty deep, inside—she focused beyond the confines of their cage. "We're in a barn?" In the dim, dusty light she could make out bare rafters and beams above. Unfinished plank walls streaked with cracks of pale daylight.

Another dog run was built adjoining theirs. Peering through the shared wall, Tess saw a second doghouse. Something shaggy and brindled lay curled up in its door-way—a third lynx? "Where the heck *are* we? Or am I still dreaming?"

She winced as Geronimo gave a growl straight out of a nightmare. *"Grouch!"* she whispered. Craning her neck, Tess studied the pile of fur in the other pen, but it didn't resolve itself into three huddled kittens. She could discern one tasseled ear poking out above a paw, which cupped the critter's nose against the chilly air. Yes, an-other lynx, and definitely an adult.

She glanced back at the anguished queen pacing the front of her cage. "Oh, Zelda, he didn't bring your babies?" No wonder she was so upset! Not only must she be worried sick, but her breasts would be painful by now, for want of nursing.

"Okay, that does it. We're outta here." Tess started to stand—then sat down hastily when Geronimo snarled.

CHAPTER TWENTY

"But why didn't you just leave her, if she was knocked out?" fretted Larson. For the first time in their acquaintance, the man had lost his icy smugness. He sounded rattled.

"How could I do that? Leave her with night comin' on, for maybe a cougar or bear to find?" Natwig slumped against the phone booth and stared out at the early morning Durango traffic. "And I didn't know she'd just sleep, then wake up. If she'd been allergic to animal tranqs, or they hit her different than they do—"

"All right, all right, the damage is done. Do you at least know who she is?"

"No, I…"

"She wasn't carrying ID?"

Natwig rubbed his aching head. "I don't know." He glanced across the parking lot to his pickup, still with trailer attached. He'd unsaddled her horse at the trailhead, then shooed him off home. Nobody would ever accuse *him* of rustling. "I've got her saddle and saddlebags, but I haven't—"

"It hardly matters, I suppose. You'll still have to deal with her."

"*I* will! You mean 'we,' don't you? It's *your* business I'm—"

"And *your* mistake! Nobody told you to assault a woman."

"Assault! Now you listen here!"

"No, *you* listen. This is nothing to do with me and my clients. *Nothing.* And may I remind you that cell phones can be monitored? We've said too much already. Go handle your own problem, and don't contact me again till you're in the clear. *Completely in the clear.* Is that understood?"

"It damn sure—!" But he was yelling at empty air. Natwig stared openmouthed at the handset—then hung it up so hard, it shattered.

Slamming out of the booth, he stood panting, hands fisted, glaring sightlessly at the passing cars. He didn't even know where Larson was—where he worked or lived—so he could go punch the bastard's lights out! Though they always met in Durango, he could have been phoning Colorado Springs or…anywhere.

"All you deserve," he muttered drearily. His grandma had been right. He'd supped with the devil, and he hadn't brought a long spoon.

But what spoon would have been long enough for this mess?

He trudged toward his pickup, then swerved to the tailgate of his trailer. Might as well check her saddlebags, see if she carried a wallet.

"FOUND a tire yet?" Gabe asked, when Adam answered his phone.

They'd last spoken at sunrise. Adam and Watson had been jogging down the mountain, in search of a spare tire.

He'd blown out his second tire miles before he reached paved road. Since the spare was already in use, he'd pressed on regardless, driving on rubber shreds, then the rim itself in a shower of sparks, till he'd had to stop for fear of damaging his axle.

"Yep," he said now. "I finally waved down a truck. The guy loaned me his spare." The cowboy had driven Adam ten miles back to his pickup, then helped him change the flat. In these parts, the Code of the West still stood for something.

"So I'm just leaving Trueheart now. But what news have you got? Did you find your techie?" To Adam's frustration, Lou-the-guru had apparently spent the night in somebody else's bed. Gabe had spent the past few hours chasing down old girlfriends and ex-wives all over Denver.

"Found him, and he's been pounding the keyboard. We've got something for you. Three somethings, but it's not all—"

"Give," Adam said heavily. Good or bad, he'd take any news at all.

"Lou did have a subprogram he could run, and it gave us three hits. Three locations where the collar stopped moving for a while."

"Let me have 'em." Adam reached for the road map on the dash. He spread it out over Watson, who snoozed, curled up in the passenger seat.

"'Fraid you've got a choice to make," Gabe said grimly. "First stopping point after they left the Two Bear trailhead was around 3:30 a.m. A site on the north fork of that logging trail that comes down from the mountains. I can give you rough coordinates. Anyway, the collar stayed there for about fifteen minutes."

"And then?"

"Then it proceeded *back* down that same fork to the

junction, and this time chose the south fork—then headed
for Durango. Stopped once for about three minutes, then
continued on southeast. Finally came to a halt for about
ten minutes on the western outskirts of Durango, and
then…"

Adam swallowed, and said harshly. "Lay it on me."

"Kill signal. He must have found the collar and
smashed it."

Adam stepped on the brakes, swerved to the shoulder,
then sat for a moment, forehead pressed to the steering
wheel between his clenched hands. *Oh, God.* No more
help. He either had enough to save her now—or he didn't.

He drew a shaking breath, then brought the phone
back to his ear. "Give me the coordinates." Once he had
them, he sat in silence, frowning at the map.

"If I catch the early shuttle, I could reach Durango in,
say, two hours," Gabe volunteered.

"I'm closer than that." But he had to choose. Either
continue the direction he was heading—or turn around
the way he'd come, to dash southeast for Durango.

And how much time did he have? The guy who'd
grabbed Tess must be coming up to his own hard choice.

If he hadn't made it already.

No, she's still out there. If Tess was no longer in his
world, somehow, some way, he'd know it. The sun would
go dim, or his heart would stop, or… Adam shook his
head to clear it. "He drove up the north fork, up into the
back of beyond. Then he turned around and came back
again." *And he didn't dump her body or I'd know it.*

And so?

"Maybe he got lost and had to backtrack," Gabe suggested.

"Except this guy has to be a local," Adam said slowly,

thinking it through. "Somebody who knows these mountains like the back of his hand, plus he's driven that trail before. So, no, he didn't get lost."

Adam massaged his brow. "Taking it from the other end, at his second halt, he stopped for three minutes. That sounds like either a pit stop—except that he'd stopped only twenty minutes before. Or a stop at a phone booth, to call somebody."

"Unless he has a cell phone," Gabe reminded him.

Adam snorted. "I haven't met a cowboy up here yet who carries one. We're talking a guy with a pickup and horse trailer, hunting lynx through the high country. I'm betting he's a traditionalist. Still uses a land line when he needs to communicate."

"Okay." Gabe sounded doubtful.

"So he stopped, made his phone call. He wanted to ask somebody for help. But three minutes to park, dig up change, dial, then explain his predicament and get some advice?"

"Not long enough. He didn't reach whoever he was calling!" Gabe guessed, his voice quickening.

"Right. But he's panicked. Tess isn't part of his plan. He *needs* to talk, needs help. So when he couldn't complete his call, he kept on driving toward Durango. Which is where he was phoning in the first place, I'll bet."

"And Tess?"

"Wouldn't be easy to conceal her in his pickup. So he must have been carrying her in the second stall of his horse trailer—had her tied up." His teeth clenched so tight his jaw spasmed; Adam had to pause for a minute. "But think about it," he continued finally. "Would you want to take a kidnap victim into a good-size city, if you had a choice? If she got loose, or screamed…"

"And the rear of a horse trailer is usually open above the gates. Somebody could even glance inside."

"So he *didn't* take her with him. He used that first fifteen-minute stop to stash her someplace. His home, a ranch, an outbuilding… Most likely an outbuilding without a phone, since he stopped again only twenty minutes down the road to call." Adam started the truck and swung out onto the highway. He trod down on the gas and held it there as the speedometer climbed.

"I take it you're headed up the north fork," Gabe concluded. "So reckon I'll check the site in Durango. Shall I call you once I get there?"

"Nope. Next time, let me call you." Two hours from now—God willing—Adam would be stalking a man with the worst of intentions. A phone ringing in the midst of that would be the last thing he'd need.

THE TRANQUILIZER had muddled her thinking more than she realized. Nearly an hour had passed, before it dawned on Tess why, in spite of her predicament, she felt like singing.

Some time in the night, her subconscious had worked it out. If that nameless sandy-haired man was capturing lynx—DOW lynx, as well as her own—then Adam was not.

He didn't do it—oh, thank You, God!—he didn't do it! Adam hadn't killed Geronimo or snatched poor Zelda.

Clearly she was missing lots of pieces to this puzzle—like who Sandy Hair was. Or why Adam should possess a map that showed missing lynx locations.

But the two best and most essential pieces of her mystery had fallen into place. Whatever Adam was, he was not a hitman.

And her lynx had not been killed.

Now all she had to do was break them all out of here, then find Adam.

Returning to Adam seemed as natural and necessary as a joggled compass needle swinging back to north. Because something else seemed to have been settled while she slept. *I want him in my life, and in my arms.*

How she could reconcile that with her plans for a foot-loose career, Tess hadn't a clue.

Whether Adam wanted *her* for more than a summer, she just didn't know. But next time she saw him, she sure meant to find out!

After she'd kissed him silly.

But before she could get on with the rest of her life, she had to escape this cage. Standing at the locked gate, Tess hammered at a nut on one of the hundreds of galvanized bolts that held the kennel together. *"Darn!"* She paused to shake out her bruised fingers. She'd shaped a crude tool from the wire handle of the bucket that Sandy had left, apparently for her convenience. "At this rate, we'll be here a year!"

She cringed inwardly with the thought. It was easy to be brave as long as she stayed too busy to think. But every so often her panic broke through. Sooner or later the man would return—and then what?

She'd witnessed him breaking the law and been fool enough to say so. Just because he hadn't killed her outright didn't mean he wasn't busily arranging some discreet way to do the deed.

Seizing this moment of worried silence, Zelda prowled along the opposite wall of the pen to nose the gate, then glanced warily up at Tess.

"Yeah, I know. You must think I'm a pretty dumb

human. Here I've got two thumbs, and I still can't open a door. But in case you haven't noticed, there's this minor detail called a padlock."

They both jumped as the barn door rattled.

"Oh, *damn!*" Tess muttered. The door creaked again, and Zelda retreated as far as Geronimo would permit. Tess hid her homemade tool in the back of her waistband. If Sandy thought she'd let him "disappear" *her* without a fight...

Wood screeched. Something popped with a loud metallic *whang!* The massive wooden gate swung inward on a widening blade of sunlight.

As Tess clenched her fingers through the mesh, her heart took wing. *Whoever it was out there, he didn't have a key!* Which meant— "Adam?" she whispered wistfully. He must know by now that she'd gone missing. Though how he could ever find her, she couldn't imagine. Still, some instinct insisted Adam was looking, just as she'd have been looking for him.

A short, square silhouette glided through the widening gap. An orange cat tiptoed past it—to freeze midstride, staring with round eyes at the cage.

"Who the—?" The shape traveled farther into the dusk, where it proved to be a woman seated in a wheelchair. A half-grown calico cat lounged across her lap. A tabby cat peered around the edge of the door—then withdrew. "What are you *doing* in there?"

Tess felt her face flush with embarrassment. To be found caged like a critter... "I'm doing my damnedest to get *out*. You wouldn't happen have a key to this padlock?"

"But... But..."

Zelda padded to the front of the cage. Fixing her gaze on her half-pint cousin, she gave a menacing rumble.

As the orange cat leaped backward, it seemed to inflate. It landed puffed up to twice its normal size. With back arched in a perfect U and ears flat to its skull, it spat a mouthful of cat curses.

At the rear of the cage, Geronimo lunged to his feet and snarled.

"Yikes!" Tess made herself small in a front corner of the pen.

The calico slipped down from the chair and streaked for the exit, while, advancing broadside in mincing steps, the orange cat swore again.

"I don't know *what* he's saying, but shut him *up,* before these guys go crazy!" Tess begged.

"Pumpkin, *scoot!*" The woman wheeled closer and nudged him with a foot. The cat retreated, growling—to peek out from behind her.

Moving her chair right up to the cage, the woman peered through the mesh. "Omigod, they're…*beautiful!* Those funny ears…they're lynx?"

"Umm," Tess agreed, crossing her arms and propping one shoulder against the gatepost. "The one back there with an attitude problem is Geronimo. Zelda's just upset because she's a nursing mom and she's been taken away from her kittens. I'm Tess—and who are you?"

"Karen Natwig." She looked to be about ten years older than Tess. A slight woman with ash-blond hair. Lines of tension or pain edged the wide, beautiful eyes that stayed fixed upon the cats. "This isn't what I thought I'd find."

She laughed painfully and tugged on the thick braid that hung down over her shoulder. "I came over here this morning meaning to sort things out, once and for all, but I never *dreamed*…" She glanced up at Tess. "What have you and my husband been *doing?*"

Tess stared in openmouthed amazement. "You think *I'm* doing something—" She searched her mind for a more tactful word than *kinky.* "—anything, with your husband? Would he by any chance be a big husky guy with sandy-colored hair?"

"You—" Karen laughed again on a note of bewildered hope. "You don't even know his name?"

"He didn't exactly introduce himself before he nailed me with a tranquilizer dart," Tess said grimly—then softened her tone as Karen gasped. "Not that he set *out* to shoot me, you understand. I caught him darting my lynx, so I jumped him. Next thing I knew—" She gave a rueful shrug. "I woke up here."

Karen pinned her with a fierce blue gaze. "Look, you better give it to me straight and true. You *haven't* been meeting Joe here in the barn? Or every month or so up in Wyoming?"

"On a stack of Bibles I haven't," Tess swore earnestly. "I never met your husband in my life, before we bumped into each other yesterday, up near Two Bear Peak. And *believe* me, that was no pleasure."

Tess watched as the strain eased in Karen's face, happiness slowly dawning in a flush of pink. "Besides," she added. "I don't need to chase your husband. I'm crazy in love with somebody else. And if your guy's been sneaking around, my guess is he's been hunting lynx, not women.

"So if that's straight enough for you…" She nodded at the small crowbar, which rested on the seat alongside Karen's legs. "If you don't have a key to this lock, how about loaning me that crowbar?"

Karen touched the padlock. "*Joe* locked you in here?"

"Well, I didn't lock myself!"

Karen frowned. She glanced down at her crowbar, then up again with a new resolve. "Look, I reckon... maybe we should back up and take this from the top."

Tess held on to her temper with an effort. "Fine by me, but why don't we start by letting me out of here? I think with that crowbar..."

Karen pushed herself backward a foot. "I...I'm sorry, Tess, but if Joe locked you in here, he must have had his reasons. I reckon I'll need to hear his side of the story, before I undo what he's done." She looked up with a wry, winsome smile. "Not that I don't mean to rip out the man's gizzard and feed it to my cats, the next chance I get. But...he's my husband."

Stamping her feet and yelling would clearly get her nowhere. Karen might be trapped in a wheelchair, but she looked tough as a diamond. "In that case," Tess growled, "you might want to start by asking your Joe what he's done with the twenty or so lynx that have disappeared from the San Juan Mountains these past few months. A whole bunch of people have been wondering." *Like the Division of Wildlife!*

"Wyoming!" Karen murmured to herself.

"What?"

"He's driven up north five times since January, with the lamest kind of excuses. That's why I thought— That and because, since I've been stuck in this chair, Joe hasn't wanted to—" She paused, sighed, shook her head. "But I did keep wondering, if he was seeing some woman, why he'd take his horse trailer along each time."

"He's been deporting Colorado lynx—to Wyoming?"

"It's starting to look that way." Karen's smile was both rueful and luminous. "You see, years and years ago, I made Joe promise he'd never hurt a cat. I'm pretty partial to cats. I guess, whatever no good he's been up to, he's been trying to keep that promise."

"O-o-okay. But why would Joe be picking on lynx?"

Karen turned up her palms. "He's a professional hunting guide. Somebody's got to be paying him. There's no other reason he'd do it. And we're…after my accident…" Her gesture included her legs and her chair. "We're pretty deep in hospital bills. It'll be something to do with that, for sure. There's no other reason I can imagine that he'd risk his outfitter's license to mess with an endangered species."

"I see…" Tess's head was starting to ache. "You're sure you can't let me out?"

"I… No, I— Please don't ask. But I swear, Tess, I *promise,* just as soon as I find Joe, we'll straighten this out. My sister brought me home late last night and I haven't seen him yet. But he can't have gone far."

"Probably not," Tess agreed bitterly. "We'll be running out of cat chow any time now." She dredged a sigh up from her toes. "Okay, if you won't, you won't. But in that case, would you do one thing for me?"

Unbuckling her belt, she threaded it through the mesh. "If you love your guy, then you ought to understand. There's somebody who might be worrying about me. Could you call that number printed there on the back, and tell Adam that I'm alive and well? That I hope to see him soon?"

Ducking her head in shame, Karen gave a troubled nod. "Of *course* I will. It'll take me a while to get these big wheels up the hill to our place, but just as soon as I get there…"

TESS STOOD with her fingers clenched through the mesh, watching the slice of sunlight narrow behind Karen's chair, till the closing door pinched it off. "Am I a fool or what?" she muttered to Zelda. "I should have screamed the place down!"

But that had been a stand-by-your-man kind of woman. Pulling a fit would have simply hardened her resistance. If Tess forced Karen to choose sides, it wouldn't be hers.

"The question is, how far will she back up her guy?" Tess reached for her wire tool. "If he's terrified we'll turn him in, stuffing us in a bag and throwing us in the river may seem like the best idea he's had all week." If Karen Natwig went along…

Tess leaned down for the steel food bowl she'd been using for a hammer. Positioning her improvised punch against the corner of a nut, she gave it a whack. The nut didn't budge. She scowled and hit it again.

Half an hour and four bolts later, Tess was resting her aching fingers when the door creaked. Quickly she tucked the tool in her waistband. *Adam?* Call it wishful thinking, but she had the strangest conviction that he was near. Missing her as much as she missed him. Now she half expected him to come bursting into the barn.

Someone taller and burlier than Adam entered with ominous deliberation. Face in shadow, Joe Natwig pushed the door shut behind him—then turned.

Tess smothered a squeak. Uh-oh. His face wasn't in shadow—he wore a black ski mask.

And carried a dart rifle. Double uh-oh! Somehow, some way, she should have made Karen release her.

CHAPTER TWENTY-ONE

AS HE LOOMED closer and closer, Tess thrust out her chin. *I won't scream and beg. I won't!* "Would you please unlock this?" She nodded haughtily at the gate.

Miracle of miracles, he took out a key and did so! But as she reached for the latch, a hand the size of a hambone gripped the gate. "Who took the lock off, out there?" He jerked his head toward the barn door.

Oh, rats, she'd forgotten that!

And if Natwig didn't know, that meant Karen hadn't found him yet. Tess folded her arms to contain her trembling. Would threatening him with his wife's wrath be a good idea—or a rotten one? Behind his mask, his blue eyes were dilated and desperate, ringed entirely with bloodshot white. Did she want to nudge this bruiser any closer to the edge?

Pushing a cornered lynx or a terrified horse was generally a bad idea. Prodding a rattlesnake was downright stupid. *Let Karen be my ace in the hole,* she decided. At least, for the moment.

"Who?" he growled, shoving the gate inward a few inches.

Tess shrugged and backed up. "Haven't a clue. I was sleeping. You sure you remembered to lock it?"

"Of course, I—" Natwig stopped, blinked, scratched his head through the mask. "I-I-I…"

Ah ha! He didn't remember! While she'd been peacefully napping, driving down from the mountains, her captor had missed a night's sleep. And been sweating bullets, by the smell of him. He looked stressed-out, exhausted at the bleary stage of triple-guessing himself. Also wounded, Tess realized, noting the stained bandages on his left hand and both arms.

Served him right, but the question was, did all this even the odds—or simply make him more dangerous?

"Hell with it. Here. Drink this." He thrust a paper bag through the gap in the gate, then pulled it shut.

Tess drew out a bottle. "Whisky!" She wrinkled her nose. "No, thank you, I'm not much of a drinker. And on an empty stomach—"

"I'm not *asking* you, I'm telling! If you want to get out of here, drink up." Natwig raised his rifle. "Or would you like me to dart you instead?"

"Umm." She had a bruise the size of a saucer from his last dart. "Why do you—"

"Quit yer arguing! Sit down and drink!" he roared.

At the rear of the pen, Geronimo snarled and vanished into the doghouse. Zelda bristled.

"Sure, fine, whatever you…" Her knees were shaking so bad, she might as well sit. Leaning back against the mesh, she uncapped the fifth, took a doubtful sip. Coughed and clutched her burning throat. "Yow! *Oh!*"

Her captor leaned moodily against the gate. "I can either knock you on the head and bury you someplace up in the hills…"

Tess took a hasty gulp. "That seems sort of…extreme. Maybe we should discuss—"

"Or I can fix it so nobody'll believe a word you'll say," he went on heavily. "Drink."

A warm glow crept out from her quaking middle. Tess tipped the bottle up—and plugged it with the tip of her tongue as she mimed a swallow. "How…will you fix it?" she inquired. Give *her* a vote, and she'd go for option two!

"You, me and your pals are drivin' up to Wyoming. I'll dump them in the mountains, same as I did the others. You, I'm gonna dump on the way, in some backwoods ma-and-pa motel. By then you'll be smashed and—hey! Keep drinking."

Tess took a sip—coughed and pounded her breastbone. "B-but—"

"It's the best I can do," Natwig plowed gloomily on. "I'll take your clothes, your shoes, all the covers and towels. Then I'll pour more booze all over you and the bed. When I get a ways down the road, I'll phone the sheriff. Tell him some crazy lady in the next room at the motel was screamin' and ravin' about seein' lynx all night long. Sounds like she had the D.T.s and maybe he'd better check her out."

Tess stared at him, appalled. That wasn't half-bad!

"By the time you sober up and limp back home, wherever the hell that is, I'll have dumped all the evidence. Where's your proof of anything, even if you could make the cops believe you after that? Or tell them who—" Natwig cocked his head at her bottle. "Hey. Hold that up where I can see it." He snorted. "Stop faking and *drink,* dammit!"

"Okay, okay. Sorry." Tess gulped, gasped, rubbed her watering eyes. Drank some more.

"Then after that, I'm done with this mess. It just ain't

worth it." Natwig braced his forehead against a splayed hand and glowered down at her. "So…I've got just one question for you. Back on the mountain…how well did you see my face?"

Well, du-uh! Trick question? Tess had a wild impulse to giggle. "It hap…pened so fast," she said gravely, "you were all a blur."

Come to think of it, he was blurring now.

"Good," he said gruffly. "Keep drinkin'."

Tess took another sip. "Now *I've* got a question. What did you do with Zelda's kittens?"

Natwig sighed and actually hung his head. "I had my hands full, between you and the queen. So I left 'em. They're too young to wander. They'll stick close to the burrow."

"Oh, *great,* wonnerful—so they wait for their mama…till they starve?"

He shrugged, ducked away from her accusing gaze. "Lynx don't belong in Colorado anyway. Not anymore. It's all a government scheme to run us out of the high country. They're makin' it where a man can't earn a living."

"Oh, *hogwash!* Lynx and cattle are perfectly compat…combat…" Tess screwed up her nose, then shrugged and said grandly, "No problem at all—cats and cattle. Same for hunters, long as you don't hunt *them.* Really. I should know. I'm a wildlife biolg'st. Almost got my… Well…nearly almost."

She heaved a sigh and drank. "No…t'be perfectly honest, this rate, I'm *never* gonna finish my disserta…"

Her voice trailed away as her eyes caught a movement beyond Natwig's bulk. Her mouth rounded to an O.

Adam. *Oh, Adam!* Sliding through a gap in the barn door!

With an incredulous laugh, Tess scrambled to her

feet—then realized: Natwig stood between them with his dart gun in hand!

Distract him. Fetching up against the gate, she waved the bottle under his nose. "You know, this actually is…*very* good…stuff. Have a drink? You need it more than I do."

He snorted. "You're some kinda pistol, Miss Jabber-Mouth, but no, thanks. Gotta keep a clear head for drivin'."

"Aww, *come* on, Joe," she coaxed. "Just a *little* bitty—" She met his widening eyes—and it hit her. They hadn't been introduced. *"Oops."*

He straightened, shook his head like a bull with a deerfly. "Who… How..?"

"Umm, we really need to discuss this." Tess waved the bottle again. "But first, you'd better have a—"

"*Hellfire and damnation, woman!* How do you know my *name?*" Natwig roared.

The devil! Adam thumbed the safety on his Browning. *Sweetheart, get out of my way!* This guy was about to blow, but he couldn't take him down with Tess standing directly in line! He angled to one side in hopes of a clear shot—

And a phone rang—the one clipped to his belt.

That tore it.

Can't be Gabe, he noted absently as he lunged farther to his left and raised his gun. As always in moments like this, time had slowed to a river of honey. Adam had at least a year between heartbeats to watch his target spin, his odd-looking rifle swinging up and around—

"Oh, *nooo!*" Tess screamed, dropping the bottle she held. It seemed to float toward the floor.

No way would he risk a shot, with the love of his life standing— Adam dived under the rising muzzle.

A puff of air passed his cheek, the blasted phone rang again.

He smacked headfirst into the man's solid gut— *"Oof!"*—Time turned to a spinning merry-go-round. A whirl of flying fists and savage grunts. Dust rising, as they punched and grappled and rolled.

By the fifth ring of his phone, he'd dumped the masked guy onto his stomach and yanked one beefy arm up to his shoulder blades. Adam pressed his gun to the back of his skull. "That's…*enough,*" he gasped. "Be still! You're…under arrest. You…have the right to…"

Reciting on automatic, he read the guy his rights, wondering all the while what was Colorado's policy on a citizen's arrest. Or maybe a retroactive deputization would be the thing here? Whatever.

Done with that formality, Adam glanced aside, panting.

Tess stood, her fingers clenched through the cage, staring at him with stricken owl eyes. "Who…*are*…you?"

"Detective Adam Dubois, New Orleans Police."

The laughter burst out of her, even as a tear dripped down her cheek. "Aren't you a…lil' bit out of your juris…juristic—*bah!* Your home *range,* detec—" She hiccuped, laughing helplessly. "—Adam?"

"Nope. Not the way I see it." Soon as he could get to her, he meant to kiss those tears off her spiky lashes. "I reckon I've about figured it out. Wherever you are, Tess, that's my jurisdiction."

ALL THE STUFFING had been knocked from his prisoner. He gave no resistance as Adam patted him down, hauled him to his feet, then locked him in the dog kennel. He sank down on the concrete, yanked off his mask, then huddled into himself, staring at nothing. Oblivious to the lynx that lashed their stubby tails and growled in the back of the cage.

"And *now*," Adam said huskily, turning to where Tess leaned against the fence. He scooped her off her feet, kissed the tip of her nose, then headed for the door. What he was feeling, he wasn't in a mood to share with an audience.

"I can walk," she insisted, though her body belied that declaration, the way it curled into his.

"Yeah, but after last night, I feel so much safer with my hands on you." Out in the sunlight, he paused. *"Oh, Tess!" God, if I'd lost you...*

Time slowed again as their mouths met...clung...caressed. Tess purred in pleasure; he groaned with relief. As he deepened their kiss, Adam leaned back against the sun-heated barn. All the rage and fear and adrenaline were still roaring through his veins—he could have taken her then and there. Proved to himself and the whole damned world that she was his. *Nobody* was snatching her away.

"Be damned if I ever set you down again!" he vowed, shoving himself away from the boards to start for his truck, which he'd parked past the burned-out house down by the road.

"Lugging me around might get a bit old," she teased, limp as a cat in his arms. She drew a fingertip down his stubbled cheek. "But Adam, 'fore I start showin' you how much I...I've missed you, there's just one thing."

"Anything!" he swore. The moon, the stars, a diamond ring if he had his way. And he intended to have his way.

"I haven't a clue…how you fit into all this. Legalwise, I mean. Sure seems you're operatin' as…more than a cowboy here. But if I get any say, and I hope I do… I don' want charges pressed against that man back there—Natwig."

"What!" Adam stopped short to scowl down at her.

"You heard me." Tess rubbed the nape of his neck. "He didn't hurt me. And he didn't hurt the lynx—just trucked 'em around some. And I think there's a…lot more to this story that we need to find out."

"Are you crazy?" Adam hoisted her tighter against his ribs, as if he could squeeze all this nonsense out of her. "You want me to go easy on a guy who kidnapped you, drugged you—" He nodded down at the open throat of her shirt, where a livid bruise surrounded the dart puncture. "And who—even if he didn't kill any lynx—interfered with a federally and state-protected endangered species, a couple of dozen times?"

"That's 'bout the size of it," Tess agreed serenely. She rubbed his nape some more.

Trying to soothe him the way she'd have soothed Watson, Adam realized. Well, he was too aroused to be soothed. "Sweetie, a tender heart is one thing, but there's such a thing as the law. Justice. You seem to have been drinking mighty early in the day. Once you sober up—"

"Oh!" Her eyes sparked dangerously. "For the record, Adam Dubois, I was plied! I didn't choose to drink. But smashed or sober, I'll see it *precisely* the same way—and I still won't press charges." She kicked her size-six boots hanging over his forearm. "You'd better set me down."

"Not a chance," he growled, striding on toward his truck, where Watson was smearing the windshield with his wet nose.

She made a small sputtering sound of feminine outrage, yanked a curl of his hair—then settled again in his arms.

And that was the bottom line, Adam realized with intense satisfaction. Maybe they'd fight like cats and dogs from time to time—given their temperaments, he could count on it. Still at some basic level, they remained in harmony. Make-up sex was bound to be phenomenal.

"B'sides," Tess added reflectively, "if you bring the law into this…well, I've got my own secrets to hide. If my father ever finds out I've been aiding and abetting lynx—and right on his own summer range!—he'll disinherit me, for sure. Wouldn't you rather date an heiress to Suntop, than otherwise?"

"I don't give a damn about Suntop," he assured her. "And my plans for you go well past dating."

"They do?" Her voice came out in a squeak. She made a mortified face, then added suspiciously, "what d'you mean by *that?*"

He gave her a wicked grin. "Wait and see."

"I…" Her indignation faded to amusement, then something much better. "All right," she agreed.

"But about Suntop." Adam frowned, leaned back against the fender of the truck, ignoring Watson's whines from within. "You mean it? Your father would disinherit you if he found out?" He didn't give a damn for her ranch. He loved the cowboy way in small doses—but a lifetime of pinkeye ointment? He'd rather chase bad guys than calves.

But as for Tess, how could he cut her off from her family and heritage?

"You better believe I mean it! Why d'you think I've been sneaking around all summer, feeding lynx on the sly?"

"And that's why the frozen chickens?" Adam shook his head, marveling. She might drive him crazy from time to time, but he'd never be bored. "You have a *heap* of explaining to do, once we crawl out of the sack."

"Like you don't?" Tess retorted—but he sipped the words off her lips, till she laughed and kissed him back.

Her breath was coming faster when they finally broke for air. "Adam, if you'd just *think* about it—find some way to balance your law with some mercy," she beseeched. "First off, we've got to get Zelda back to her kittens. If you'd just wait till we've done that... And meantime, you could let Natwig go. His place is right up this hill. I'm just about certain he won't run anywhere."

Reluctantly Adam set her on her feet. "Now you've gone too far."

"You think?" Tess smoothed a hand over his chest, then leaned against him, her gaze fixed on something up the road. "Well...here comes somebody who's bound t'think otherwise."

Hands on her waist, Adam turned to look where she nodded.

At the top of the rise, a small figure in a wheelchair trundled along. And what the heck was that orange creature, padding down the road at her side?

"You pick on that woman's husband," Tess warned with soft laughter, "and I promise, she'll feed your gizzard to her cats!"

CHAPTER TWENTY-TWO

"Mrs. Dubois?" A weight settled on the edge of the bed. A big, warm hand curled around the nape of her neck. Work-roughened fingertips massaged in a slow, sexy rhythm. "Mrs. Sweet Dubois?" Two weeks into their marriage, Adam hadn't yet tired of calling her that.

Tess hadn't tired of hearing him say it. "Mmm," she purred drowsily, rolling over beneath the blanket to find the cabin flooded with moonlight. "You're back! Didn't expect you before—"

His kiss swallowed the rest of that thought. Their tongues danced in the darkness. Fireworks blossomed behind her lashes…in her stomach… His fingers laced through her hair, caressed her head.

With a rueful groan, Adam toppled over to haul her into his arms. "Was gonna shower, but…"

"You smell good just like this." Tess nuzzled her nose into the pulsing hollow at the base of his throat. "*So* good." She yawned, snuggled closer, insinuated a thigh between his. Smiled when his legs clamped to hold her there. "So tell me…how'd it go?"

Adam had gone down to Durango to help arrest the man who'd been paying Joe Natwig to kill lynx. At least, that was what the creep had thought he was paying for. "Did you catch him?"

In the end, her refusal to press charges, plus Adam and Gabe's growing compassion as they learned the Natwigs' circumstances, along with Karen's flat refusal to let them jail her feverish husband—all those motives had combined to effect a merciful compromise.

Natwig had been granted immunity, provided he helped the Division of Wildlife investigators follow the chain of criminals all the way to the top—then testify against them.

"We got the bag man. A lawyer name of Larson. Caught the pay-off on tape, too, with Natwig wearin' a wire." Adam kissed the top of her head. "Hey, you're asleep. I'll have to tell you this all over again, come tomorrow."

"Am not. Could I do *this* if I were dreaming?" Tess unbuttoned the top button of his shirt, then fumbled for the next.

"A woman of your many talents? I expect so—*ow!*" Adam protested as she tweaked a curl on his chest. Laughing, he caught her arms to hold her off.

"Tell!" Tess insisted—then shivered when he licked the underside of her wrist. One of her erogenous zones that he'd been so zealously charting.

"Well…he was a nasty one. We recorded him pussy-footing all 'round the question of what Natwig had done with you. Dying to know, but not wanting to ask, you understand. It was all I could do, hearing that, not to bang out of the police van and wipe the road with him then and there, the smug bastard. *God,* Tess, when I think—" Adam pressed his mouth to her other wrist as he shuddered.

"But you got him," Tess soothed, kissing his knuckles.

"Oh, yeah," he agreed huskily. "Got him dead to

rights. And he knew it. Blustered and fumed till we played his words back to him—then he caved and started whimpering. Offered to tell us everything he knew, if we'd only let him walk.

"But we said thanks, we figured we could back-track his client's money from his bank account with-out assistance. We didn't need to give him an inch. So he told us anyway, to show us how eager he was to co-operate. Implicated the guy who hired him, and that man's boss."

His hands relaxed on her wrists; his thumbs caressed her in slow seductive circles that set her hips to rocking. She reached for his third button, undid it. "So…did you figure who these people were? Their quarrel with lynx?"

For a second, she held her breath. Her father had fought the lynx restoration in the courts. And cantanker-ous Ben Tankersly might have taken the law into his own hands when the lawsuits failed.

"Yeah. Turns out it was ski money."

"Ahh…" she breathed a sigh of relief.

"A big syndicate that had been all set to build a new resort northeast of here. When lynx were granted en-dangered species status, all work on their development permits was frozen. They figured the fastest way to get it moving again was make the lynx go away. No endan-gered species—no need to protect their habitat. What's a few cats, when you hope to make millions?"

"A few very special cats." Zelda had taken her kittens hunting last night. Tess had seen them returning at dawn, dappled shadows gliding through a mountain mist. One more thread in Nature's gorgeous tapestry restored. Lynx back in Colorado.

"So what happens next?" she wondered, as Adam

drew her hands up to his shoulders. Smiling, she took the hint and wrapped her arms around his neck. Arching her back, she molded herself against him.

"I'll give you one guess. That ain't the sun that's risin' down there." Adam rolled onto his back, pulling her with him. Holding her close with one arm around her waist, he tugged at the blanket tangled between them.

Laughing, Tess caught the hem and held it in place. "*Wait* a minute! First, tell me what happens to the Natwigs. Are you going to make Joe give back all that bounty money?"

"What money?" Adam looked as innocent as a man can manage when he's doing his best to strip his naked wife of her covers.

"Ah," Tess said with satisfaction. "Like that, huh?"

"Well, it's not DOW money, so what do we care? And the ski syndicate won't be any too anxious to claim it, since it's proof of the crime. Besides which, Natwig's already passed it on to a hospital and a pack of doctors. Try asking those guys for a refund."

"So they won't have to repay it. That's wonderful!" Tess and Liza both had a growing affection for Karen Natwig. In fact, the three of them were working on plans for that isolated barn, with its nice spacious runs.

"But they're still in debt," she murmured, refusing to release the blanket when Adam yanked at it.

He fell back on the pillow with a groan. "You'd really rather talk than…"

"Why, Detective Dubois," she drawled, batting her lashes, "didn't they teach you, back there in N'Orleans, that talking's the best kind of foreplay?"

"Not so's I recall. But back home, *cher*, they do believe in striking a bargain. Lower that blanket a foot, and I'll tell you whatever you want to know."

"O-o-okay." She squirmed higher on his body to prop herself above him on one elbow. Letting the blanket fall to her waist, she smiled when his body jolted beneath her. His eyes darkened to pools of smoldering pitch. "So how—" Her breath caught as his hands cupped her. "H-how…do we help the Natwigs? They still…umm… owe so much."

"Ah, that?" Adam gave her a slow, sinful smile. "Gabe's taking care of that." His thumbs found her budding nipples and traced tiny, exquisite patterns. Her hips helplessly echoed the motion; the bedframe creaked softly. "Gabe figures that, even counting your and Liza's contributions, his program's down about sixteen cats. He wants 'em back."

He paused as she trembled against him. His smile deepened. His thumbs resumed their swirling magic. "Since Natwig knows where he dumped 'em in Wyoming, and he seems to know more about catching lynx than anybody else in these mountains, why not put him to work?

"Gabe plans to tell those ski developers that if they want the court to go easy on them, the best thing they could do is show some up-front contrition. Like making a substantial donation to the Division of Wildlife. Which should pay for a lynx trapper to recover those animals.

"Natwig's going to be kept pretty busy, all this fall and next spring, herding cats. Apparently Gabe's have an embedded ear chip. So they can be sorted out from any Wyoming lynx that Natwig takes by mistake."

"Oh…" It was wonderful. Better than she could have hoped. But her own heartbeats were drowning out his words.

"So what else d'you want to know?" Adam teased, as his fingertips danced on her breasts. Like a moth to a flame, her mouth drooped toward his. Her hair brushed his face.

"I…" But she was past thinking. Beyond words. Desperately ready. Crazy in love.

"Ah?" His smile declared him the winner. "Then…since you believe in uncaging the wild things, Mrs. Dubois…want to reach down and pull that zipper?"

NATWIG had stayed late in Durango, talking things out with Gabe Monahan. Planning when he'd start hunting lynx and where.

Then on the road home, he'd pulled into a high overlook and simply sat for an hour, staring out at the sky. With Larson's arrest, it was over. He'd missed jail by the skin of his teeth.

And it looked like he'd come out of the scrape better than he'd any right to. Better than he'd dared to hope. As if Somebody beyond all those stars had been listening to his prayers, after all. With the lynx bounty Gabe meant to pay him—not so much as Larson's dirty cash, but still, it was enough—he'd have them in the clear by next spring.

And Karen still loved him. She'd found it in her big heart to forgive him every lie, all his sneaking around. Even his darting the cats. Natwig sighed heavily. *So then why am I not happy?*

Just numb, he supposed, fingering the steering wheel. He'd been sick in bed for a week, with Karen nursing *him,* for Pete's sake. Maybe he wasn't quite back up to snuff?

Or maybe it was too many people giving him a second chance that made him uneasy. He'd meant to dig his way out of their troubles on his own. He'd never been one to ask for help. Accepting it always went against his grain. And now to be helped without his even asking…just because nice people could see he and his wife were in need?

Not his way. He knew he ought to be grateful, but still…

Gabe had made it clear this wasn't charity. He'd be working his butt off for the next six months, undoing what he'd done. And if he couldn't recover all the original lynx, he'd have to journey up to Alaska next spring to catch some replacements.

Natwig sighed again. Alaska! He'd always dreamed of exploring that last raw wilderness. If Karen could have gone along to see it, too…

Maybe that was the root of his blues. For all his efforts, no matter how misguided, he hadn't been able to change the one thing that mattered. She was still trapped in that chair. He could roam the wide world, but if she wasn't free to ride with him…

He sighed, turned the key in the ignition, then looked up—and his jaw dropped.

A star burned across the black, tracing a smoky line from the Summer Triangle clear to the horizon.

"Whew!" he whispered—then remembered to wish. *Please. I'll never ask for anything more.*

He waited a while longer, but the show was over. Just that one. He steered the truck out on the vacant highway and drove for home.

By the time he unlocked his back door, it was well past midnight. Seeing a light on in the living room, he frowned. Karen's tabby padded in to strop his shins, then the chairlegs, as he strode on past. He paused in the doorway. "You should've been in bed hours ago!"

And how had Karen managed to switch from her chair to the couch? It didn't have a frame to grasp, the way their bed did.

She rubbed her droopy lashes and smiled. "Couldn't sleep for thinking about you. How it was going."

"It went fine," he said gruffly. Sinking down beside her, he moved the calico cat out of the way, then wrapped his arm carefully around her. So tiny, so fragile, *so* damn brave. He kissed her temple. "Have a good evenin'?"

"Mmm." She nodded, leaning against him and rubbing his chest. "Liza—the vet that came that day to tranquilize the lynx for their trip back to the mountains—she called. We chatted for quite a while."

"Huh?" He shot her a worried look, but Karen was playing with his shirt buttons, smiling to herself. "What about?"

"Well, Liza's involved with some of these rescue leagues for big cats around the country. And she's learned about this fur farm in South Dakota that's going out of business. They have three breeder lynx and two kittens, all in pitiful condition. She says she can raise donations from various cat-lovers, a sort of grant for each animal. If I could nurse them back to health, build them up over this winter, she can pay me for my time."

Karen looked up at him, her eyes sparkling. "Then, come the spring, the younger ones can be loosed up in the high country. Hopefully they'll adapt well. Liza says Tess will loan her cabin to whoever wants to mind them, while they're learning to hunt.

"And then the older ones, who're maybe too old to learn new ways? Well, with our location in the foothills,

Liza thinks I could run a halfway house for half-wild lynx. They could be allowed to run free as they please, but they could drop in there when they need a square meal and a warm nest. Any kittens they produce would likely be born outdoors, so they should be able to take to the wild."

"Gabe wasn't entirely pleased with a couple of amateurs horning in on his territory, as I recall," Natwig reminded her. "And now you women mean to do it again?"

Karen tipped up her chin. "As long as there are lynx in need, why not? It's a big country. Plenty of room for all."

But Natwig didn't care. Three cats or three hundred. Anything that brought such a glow to her face was fine by him. "Then do it. I'll help any way I can."

"What you can do is kneel right down there." Karen pointed at the rug in front of her.

He cocked his head at her, then obeyed. "Do you want me to propose all over again?" He'd do it in a heartbeat.

"I would like that, very much, but not just now." Karen leaned forward, face alight with mischief, to rest her small hands on his shoulders. "Now…close your eyes."

Puzzled and smiling, he did as she asked.

Clothes rustled. The pressure on his shoulders increased. His breath caught. *Oh, God,* was he dreaming?

Her hand moved to cup his cheek and catch the first tears as they trickled through his lashes. "So…what do you think?" she coaxed.

When he found the courage to look, there she was. Standing on her own two feet. Blazing with joy.

"I th-think—" But with his heart jammed in his throat and the tears overflowing, Natwig couldn't find a word to match his feelings. He flung his arms around her hips and buried his face in her warmth.

Miracle. That was the word he wanted.

THE LIGHT was fading to rosy pearl beyond the window screen. Still at last, they lay spooned together, Tess's cheek pillowed on Adam's hard, hot bicep. He stroked her damp stomach with one idle fingertip.

"I keep looking over by your stove, expecting to see Watson snoring away," Tess murmured drowsily. "I'm gonna miss the big goof."

"Yeah." Adam stroked her lips…her chin. He traced the contours of her throat, her breasts, her ribs, to dreamily circle her navel. "Never thought I'd say it, but me, too. But Gabe's friend wanted him back, so…" His finger retraced its sensual path.

"Which reminds me. He said to tell you that Tracy says the same breeder where she found Watson has got another litter. Same parents, so they'd be his full brothers and sisters. Tracy says we can reserve the pick of the litter, if we want him. Word is, he's got Watson's bionic nose, his ears, and his sense of humor."

"I'd…" Love to have Watson's brother! But she couldn't imagine a big dog being happy in New Orleans, where they'd be headed, come the fall. Adam had to report back for duty in a month. Tess sighed. "Maybe we'd better think about that?"

All that concrete and heat and noise. People crowded together. It was going to take some getting used to. But if having Adam in her life meant living in his world, she'd make the best of it and count her blessings. Maybe she'd switch her specialty from beavers to nutria. Once she got into it, the bayou fauna was bound to be fascinating.

"Why the sigh?" Adam leaned over to kiss her ear.

"Mmm." She reached behind to stroke the back of his head. "Just…sleepy."

"Can't imagine why," he teased. "These past two weeks…"

Nodding, Tess laughed softly. "Silly me. I used to think beds were for sleeping." His fingers feathered down her breasts and she shivered with desire. These past two weeks, the word *enough* had dropped right out of her vocabulary.

"By the by," Adam drawled. "I met this long, tall, drop-dead gorgeous redhead at the general store in Trueheart on my way into town."

"You mean— You met Risa? My big sister?"

"Uh-huh." He nuzzled his face through her hair. "She says to tell you we're forgiven for running off to a Justice of the Peace. Said she didn't blame you one bit, after what happened at *her* wedding."

Tess groaned. "But was she smiling when she said that?"

"Kinda…twinkling. Why, what happened?"

"Well, the short gruesome story is I thought I was saving her from a fate worse than death—and I wrecked her wedding. But I was only twelve."

"Ah. Guess that explains her evil smirk when she said to tell you that if we think we've gotten away with anything, then think again. Your dad's planning a wedding reception for us and he's invited the whole county."

"Oh, *rats!* What she means is Dad's brought one of his old flames, Belle Lowrey, up from Texas to plan us a party. Everything I hoped to avoid. We're in for mariachi bands, elephants and ice sculptures—the works, Dallas-style."

Growling in despair, Tess rolled over to face him. "I'm sorry!"

"Hey, you marry a woman, you marry her crazy family." Adam kissed her nose, her exasperated smile. "Even if it's elephants and I have to ride one, I count myself lucky. The luckiest man in the world." He backed off to give her a considering grin. "But maybe I should invite a few of my ol' buddies from N'Orleans, to round things out?"

"Cops and cowboys? Well, why not? The more the merrier. They'll love Dad's gun collection."

"And it'll give me a chance to say so long," Adam reflected.

It was Tess's turn to rear back where she could properly inspect his whimsical expression. "So long to what?"

"Oh, maybe I didn't tell you?" Adam said, looking too smug for words. "Figured I'd better wait to see if things panned out. But now that they have…"

His eyes tracked down over her face, then lower. His hand followed, doing delicious, wicked things. " By the way, did I tell you yet tonight that you're the most beautiful woman I ev—"

"You're doing it on *purpose*—torturing me!" She flew at him, digging her fingers into his ribs.

He yelped, grabbed for her wrists, trapped them in one hand, then tickled her back. They wrestled at last to a panting standstill, Adam's muscled weight pinning her to the mattress, both of them shaking with laughter.

"Tell me!" she insisted, wriggling helplessly.

"Umm, maybe we could discuss this later?" His voice had gone all husky with desire, his body taut with it.

"In your dreams, Dubois! *Tell* me."

"Okay, okay, then to make it *very* short, when I went

down to Durango last week, to set up this bust? Gabe told
me there was an opening over at the U.S. Fish and Wildlife Service for an experienced law enforcement agent.
He put in a word for me, I dropped by for an interview,
and what d'you know? I found out yesterday that they
want me. I've got to report up to Idaho in four weeks, a
case of black bear poaching. So my one question for you
is—"

"No more homicide detecting?" she murmured in a
daze, hardly daring to believe it.

"Not in the city, anyway. But it's still investigating,
which is all I care about. But does this work for you? Are
there any beavers in Idaho?"

"Ohh, maybe two or three—hundred thousand." Tess
shook her head, marveling. "You'd really do this for
me?" She could get a job up there for sure, either state
or federal, once she'd finished her degree.

"Better get used to it. Whither you wander, Tess? Look
for me right behind."

"B-but…you'd really be happy, doing this?"

"Working outdoors? Chasing bad guys when I'm not
chasing you? Being more of my own boss than I'd ever
be back in the city? Sounds like a bit of heaven to me."

And to me! Oh, there'd be problems to figure out. No
doubt one of them would always be coming or going. But
they'd be working outdoors, under the big Western sky.
She could study nature; he could serve and protect it. This
way their marriage wouldn't be an end to all her plans,
but an expansion of them. An enrichment beyond her
wildest imagining. What could be better than doing what
she loved, while loving Adam?

"But you know what else would be heaven?" he asked
in a smoky whisper.

Widening her eyes in teasing question, Tess slowly shook her head. Her lips barely brushed his smile.

"Then put your arms 'round my neck…and let me show you."

AUTHOR'S AFTERWORD

The only thing I like better than a double-happy ending is a triple-happy ending!

When I started writing *More Than a Cowboy* in the spring of 2003, the basic facts of the story were true. Since 1999, the Colorado Division of Wildlife had released 129 lynx in the mountains of southwest Colorado. After four years of waiting and praying and hoping, not one single lynx kitten had been born. At least 46 of the lynx had died, and another 20 or so were missing. (Their collars were no longer signaling, for reasons unknown.)

The many critics of the program were insisting in louder and louder voices that the cats' failure to reproduce proved it: Lynx were no longer able to survive in modern Colorado.

The program's staunch supporters countered that the problem was simply a lack of lynx—the cats were too few on the ground to find each other.

Well, I'm delighted to report that a number of feline romances occurred in the spring of 2003, and the courtships were successful. As I finish this book in the late fall of 2003, fourteen healthy native-born lynx kittens prowl the mountains of Colorado with their five devoted mothers. Congratulations to the proud parents and to the determined men and women of the Colorado DOW, who midwived a miracle!

Peggy Nicholson

P.S. If you'd like to learn more about lynx in Colorado—or see some wonderful photos of lynx—check out the following Web site:

http://wildlife.state.co.us

Once the DOW Web site opens, look at the sidebar to the left on your screen. Click on "species conservation." When the menu pops up, choose lynx. Once you're inside the lynx sub-site, be sure to check out the photo gallery!

HARLEQUIN *Super*ROMANCE®

Twins

The Right Woman
by Linda Warren
(Harlequin Superromance #1221)

Sarah Welch didn't know she had a twin until five years ago, when a string of events led her through the seedy underbelly of Dallas to the family she didn't know she had. Sarah's spent those years trying to forget about the man she helped put behind bars—and trying to forget Daniel Garrett, the cop who saved her life. But when she begins to accept her past, she also begins to accept Daniel as a part of it. And as a part of her future…

The exciting sequel to THE WRONG WOMAN (Harlequin Superromance #1125, April 2003)

Available August 2004 wherever Harlequin books are sold.

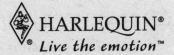

HARLEQUIN®
Live the emotion™

www.eHarlequin.com   HSRLWTRW

Men of the True North—
Wilde and Free

The Wilde Men

Homecoming Wife
(Superromance #1212)
On-sale July 2004

Ten years ago Nate Wilde's wife, Angela, left and never came back.
Nate is now quite happy to spend his days on the rugged trails of
Whistler, British Columbia. When Angela returns to the resort
town, the same old attraction flares to life between them. Will
Nate be able to convince his wife to stay for good this time?

Family Matters
(Superromance #1224)
On-sale September 2004

Marc was the most reckless Wilde of the bunch. But when an
accident forces him to reevaluate his life, he has trouble accepting
his fate and even more trouble accepting help from Fiona Gordon.
Marc is accustomed to knowing what he wants and going after it.
But getting Fiona may be his most difficult challenge yet.

A Mom for Christmas
(Superromance #1236)
On-sale November 2004

Aidan Wilde is a member of the Whistler Mountain ski patrol, but
he has never forgiven himself for being unable to save his wife's
life. Six years after her death, Aidan and his young daughter still
live under the shadow of suspicion. Travel photographer Nicola
Bond comes to Whistler on an assignment and falls for Aidan. But
she can never live up to his wife's memory…

Available wherever Harlequin books are sold.

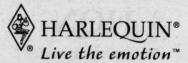

HARLEQUIN®
Live the emotion™

www.eHarlequin.com   HSRWM